Charles Thurber

Our Charlie

a memorial

Charles Thurber

Our Charlie
a memorial

ISBN/EAN: 9783337093105

Printed in Europe, USA, Canada, Australia, Japan

Cover: Foto ©Andreas Hilbeck / pixelio.de

More available books at **www.hansebooks.com**

Our Charlie:

A MEMORIAL.

By HIS FATHER.

CAMBRIDGE:
PRINTED AT THE RIVERSIDE PRESS.
1867.

Dedicated

TO

Mrs. CAROLINE ESTEY THURBER,

THE MOTHER OF "OUR CHARLIE,"

BY HER

AFFECTIONATE HUSBAND.

PREFACE.

——◆——

THIS volume owes its origin to the death of my only beloved son CHARLES THURBER, Junior. He died August 5, 1861, at the age of five years and seven months. The frontispiece presents a faithful likeness of him.

He was a boy of unusual promise and sweetness of disposition. His biography is very brief, and I have tried that what I say of him shall not be mere panegyric and the creation of parental partiality.

I have given the title of " Our Charlie " to the book, that it might be a memorial of my boy, and because from him as from the seed the work germinated.

The death of children seems, *primâ facie*, unnatural. On mature reflection, it seems eminently natural. The analogy pervades all nature. In so far as the unnaturalness of death consists in taking the

living away in the progress of development and usefulness, it pervades all ages.

We can find reasons more or less satisfactory why
God should take away the living, but none that seem
to serve as a law by which He acts. His sovereign
will seems to be the only law. This ought to satisfy
us. We may be sure that it is a perfectly wise,
just, and benevolent rule of action.

The stories in the first part of the book are all
facts. Of most of them I have personal knowledge,
—many of them I have heard related by parties
interested; some of them I have read in the papers,
and one, " The Artist and his Ideals," is founded on
an old story.

I have taken no liberties with the main facts, but
have dressed them up in my own language and supplied what seemed to be the natural links in the
chain of events.

I have gone to fact, rather than fiction, because,
although truth may be illustrated as well and sometimes better by the latter than by the former, I
think the afflicted find illustrations from the former
far more impressive than from the latter.

In the latter part of the book will be found the reflections to which the sad event has directed my mind. I think they have been beneficial to me, and that I have found in them many sources of comfort and profit. Perhaps some of my readers may find their own hearts in sympathy with them and find comfort and profit also. The speculations, not to call them views, of spiritual things may not commend themselves to all my readers, but I cannot avoid thinking them somewhat natural and not wholly erroneous.

The anecdotes and incidents of Charlie might have been placed by themselves, but I preferred to place them in the order in which they suggested themselves to my mind.

The book is not published. It is printed for private distribution. It is not for sale. It is not to take its place with the literature of the day. It is a memorial of my beloved son. It is to show others my sources of consolation in the midst of affliction. It is to be given to relatives and friends and such others as I may happen to know from time to time who have passed through the deep waters and may be supposed to be in sympathy with the subject.

I should tremble to publish this volume. I do not tremble to put it into the hands of the afflicted. If, as an intellectual effort, it is rejected, as the outgush of a wounded heart, I am sure it will be respected.

CHARLES THURBER.

Brooklyn, N. Y., June, 1863.

PREFACE TO THE SECOND EDITION.

THE present edition of " Our Charlie " is published by and for the Sabbath - school connected with the Pierrepont Street Baptist Church of Brooklyn, of which school my dear boy was a member. Whatever profits may accrue from its sale belong wholly and exclusively to the school.

It will not be on general sale, but may be had on application to T. T. Sheffield, Esq., of Brooklyn.

It is not because I think the first edition a success in a literary point of view that it is succeeded by a second. Few commendations have been bestowed upon it except by the afflicted, many of whom have assured me that they have sympathized in its thoughts and have been profited and comforted by them. By far the greater number of those to whom I have given it, have never intimated that it was acceptable to them even as a gift. The reader therefore can see that neither vanity nor ambition could have prompted me to consent to a second edition.

The warm and hearty thanks of the afflicted who have read the book and assured me that it has been a source of comfort and profit to them, and the earnestly expressed wish of very many of this class of readers that I would publish a second edition, and a desire to contribute, if I could, to the pecuniary interest of the Sabbath-school, are the sole reasons why I have given my assent to its being published.

I think I have found consolation in my sorrow in the thought that the blow was given me by a loving Father.

Perhaps the thoughts and suggestions contained in these pages may aid the reader in obtaining like consolation.

God help the mourner, and prevent His loving chastisements from being sent in vain.

C. T.

Brooklyn. N. Y., 1867.

CONTENTS.

CONTENTS.

OUR CHARLIE.

PART FIRST.

OUR CHARLIE.

PART FIRST.

WHERE is the home, where is the sweet retreat,
  Where some fond bosom has not ceased to beat?
Where their gay feasts are not less rich and rare,
Because the feasters see some vacant chair?
Where their fond bosoms do not feel a smart
At the sad absence of a loving heart?
Such homes must be, if they are ever seen,
Like angels' visits, — few and far between.

" All men must die " has never been denied
Since Adam lived and the first martyr died;
Yet the word " mystery " drops from every tongue,
Whene'er our loved ones droop and perish young;
And though earth's babes scarce entering on their
      years
Fill more than half of earth's funereal biers,
When fond affection is compelled to part
With some sweet nursling idoled in its heart,
It sits down sad with many a tear and sigh,
And says, How strange our little ones should die!

When Love bends o'er its little cherub boy,
All lit with hope and brimming o'er with joy,
And, breathless, watches every day and hour
Each new-born gush of loveliness and power,
And daily sees, as fond Affection can,
The first young kindlings of the coming man,
And deems these proofs as plain as aught can give.
That the dear idol of its heart will live;
And as these proofs before its fancy play,
And each grows stronger each succeeding day,
Though thousands fall as young and bright and fair,
'Tis manhood's signet has its impress there.
But lo! he droops, and Love, that could not save,
Bends o'er and wets the little hero's grave,
And shrieks aloud with sorrow's shrillest cry, —
Strange that a boy as sweet as ours should die.

Strange that a bud that has the magic power,
While yet a bud, to deck its native bower,
Should, ere one petal shows us half its charms,
Fade like a vision in Affection's arms,
And full of perfume, waste its rosy breath
In the damp, fetid charnel-house of death.

Strange that a being of mysterious birth, ·
Sent on its mission to this checkered earth,
Whose fresh young spirit in its earliest spring

Shows 'tis a godlike and mysterious thing,
Before it plies its wondrous powers and arts,
Except in sporting or enchanting hearts,
Should, like a dew-drop 'neath a scorching sky,
Melt and mount upward to its home on high.

Some years ago, one cold December day,
A little stranger came along our way,
And, of all places on this good round earth,
Begged for admission to our home and hearth,
And, quick as lightning through yon azure darts,
We took him in and shrined him in our hearts.
He was a stranger whom we'd never seen,
But yet we gladly took the stranger in;
The mild blue eyes that shot their beams about,
Showed the sweet spirit that was looking out;
The spacious head and high arched brow bespoke
The dread machinery of a soul new woke.
O! day by day we watched with purest joy
The young revealings of that little boy.
Affection tender as an angel's filled
His little heart and every other thrilled;
His gentle spirit, if it flashed, was brought
Mild as a lamb's at one calm hint from thought;
And though e'en prouder than a lord or earl,
At being a boy instead of being a girl,
Yet not the purest and most charming miss

E'er gave a sweeter or a heartier kiss.
His manly manners, manly looks and airs,
And business ways of aping man's affairs;
His wise remarks, precocious thoughts and views,
And reasonings often such as sages use; —
All these things told us, with a prophet tongue,
That so much promise could not perish young.

O manly boy! yet tender, sweet, and mild,
The hero almost, yet the trusting child;
The little traveller gathering up the lore
Of his own land and many a foreign shore;
The little linguist, who, without alloy,
Could gibber French like any Gallic boy;
Who talked of Paris, Florence, London, Rome,
Familiar almost as of home, sweet home!
And with his blocks made coliseums stand,
And reared St. Peter's with his cunning hand;
And talked of strolls through London parks so green,
Where rode the princes, princesses, and queen;
And how, in Paris, our *pro tempore* home,
He went with Helen and his nurse to roam
Through parks and gardens, the most charming ones,
Brimful of children with their white-capped *bonnes;*
And how at Florence he was wont to rove
That gay Cascine that a nymph might love,
And thread the walks of Boboli's *parterre,*

Or Pitti Palace midst the wonders there;
And how at Rome, at old imperial Rome,
He walked St. Peter's 'neath its lofty dome,
Saw coliseums with their huge high walls,
Old ruined temples, columns, arches, halls;
And where he oft drank gladness to the fill,
'Midst walks and flowers upon the Pincian Hill,
Where the élite from earth's remotest bounds
Walk in gay groups all o'er the fairy grounds;
And often saw, upon its flowery slope,
The gaudy Cardinals and the poor old Pope;
And how, at Naples, roving day by day,
He saw the beauties of that charming bay;
Or walked Pompeii's ancient streets exhumed,
Which twenty centuries almost had entombed;
Or saw Vesuvius, black with lava strown,
Throw sulphurous smoke up from its swelling cone;
Or saw, when night wrapped all in gloom below,
Her spacious sea of red hot lava glow.

O blessed boy, who all these gems had shrined
Within the memory for his opening mind:
The little flowerets clipped by childhood's knife,
To strew the pathway of his future life.

O! as we watched his first expanding thought,
Out of the lore of rich experience wrought,

And saw his mind, far, far beyond his years,
By his own skill forge almost man's ideas,
And how his heart breathed sweeter every hour,
As fields and gardens with each new-blown flower!
O! then we thought, indeed we seemed to know,
That Charlie had a mission here below;
And from the way that mission had begun,
We fondly thought 'twould be no common one.

When five short years, and seven fleet months beside,
Had rolled away, the little fellow died;
Died, while the buds of intellectual power
Were forming, swelling, opening, every hour;
Died, while his heart, e'en in a world like this,
Was gathering honey for a feast of bliss;
Died when, poor boy, he daily seemed to give
New proofs and promise he would surely live.

Then we bent down above his little bier,
And wet his grave with sorrow's gushing tear,
And said, alas! with many a tear and sigh,
O! 'tis a mystery such a boy should die!

When Spring steps forth, and with inspiring breath,
Bursts the sere pall of Nature's wintry death,
And herb and tree start gayly up, and fling
Their sweetest offerings in the lap of Spring:

The leafless orchards with their naked brows
First string their leaflets on their Gothic boughs,
Then in the train gay Flora brings her gems,
With lavish kindness for the countless stems, —
Go to that orchard clad in beauty now,
And count the blossoms on the smallest bough.
When Winter shaking all her clouds of snow
In fleecy showers upon chill earth below,
Though every flake should on the branches light,
That fruit-tree could not be more gay and white.
O! one as well might rove by yonder sea,
And count the sands as blossoms on that tree.
But go when Autumn, with her yellow foot,
Calls from that bloom the ruddy ripened fruit,
One moment's effort will suffice to show
How many apples on the branches grow,
And 'twill appear that most of all that bloom
Went to the silence of an early tomb.
But very few within that lovely bower
Reached, in life's course, the manhood of a flower.

How few the flowers of Flora's royal blood
Have reared their offspring farther than the bud!
Though full of beauty, full of sweet perfume,
They pass unopened to the fetid tomb.
Or if they burst and throw their beauties out,
And sweetly breathe upon the bowers about,

Earth, sea, and air, brimful of fiendish foes,
Crush more than half with their unfriendly blows,
And few there are, just like their masters, men,
That reach a floweret's threescore years and ten.

How grand the schemes ambitious mortals lay,
And yet how poor the several parts they play!
Like earth's cathedrals, we can find scarce one,
On which is carved the magic motto " Done."
That " dream of beauty," decking Milan's street,
Will reel and tumble ere 'tis quite complete;
And that huge pile, the magic of Cologne,
Will fall, ere Art has laid the topmost stone;
And human progress, while in mid career,
Will join the crash of this terraqueous sphere.

The studious sage, charged high with learning's lore,
And all inspired to go and gather more,
Spares no expense, no labor, pains, or toil,
And lights up research with the midnight oil.
And when the spade, thrust in the cumbrous mould,
Strikes on a vein of purest virgin gold,
And but a few poor worthless spades-full more
Must be removed to reach the virgin ore,
The insatiate archer, with malicious thrust,
Strikes down the sage to mix in vulgar dust,
The spade drops down, the chasm disappears,

Filled with the debris of succeeding years,
And "labor lost" is chiselled on the stones
That mark the pillow of his crumbling bones,
And ages more must send the sage again,
Who'll ope the chasm and work the virgin vein.

Invention, looking with a prescient eye,
Sees unformed magic all in embryo lie;
And though gaunt want stand frowning at the
    door,
And toil and hardship hedge the way before,
And lordly wealth, to princely fortune born,
Points its gemmed finger with disdain and scorn,
It toils and toils in want, neglect, and pain,
Encouraged, thwarted, yet resolved again,
Till just as it has bidden doubts "Good-night,"
And formed and grouped the magic agents right,
And there is now but just one day between
The imperfect model and complete machine,
And earth's applause almost begins to start,
And fill the inventor's long, long burdened heart,
The load of ills, 'neath which he's staggered so,
Deals its dark work and lays the victim low.
He reels, he falls, and as he gasps and dies,
With his last grasp unloosing from the prize,
The wise, wise world declares it and believes,
"How little, useful, genius e'er achieves."

Some lucky wight who saw the victim reel,
And the last blow that he designed to deal,
Just strikes that blow, the magic to evoke,
And genius' dream stands marshalled from the stroke.
The chance-made genius, more than hero now,
Wears the bright wreath meant for another's brow.

In fortune's race, though all contend and run,
O! by how few the glittering prize is won!
Rags flaunt and flutter o'er the rolling globe,
Ten thousand times to one e'en decent robe;
And if one, ever upon land or wave,
Gained all he hoped and all he wished to have,
He must have been, if not a mythic thing,
Some richer rich man than the Lydian king.
Hopes crushed in myriads perish at the root,
To one bright hope that blossoms into fruit.

In yonder wood, the scene of many a chase,
Young saplings start up of surpassing grace.
O! when they've grown up high and broad as these,
Those that come here will see unblemished trees,
And this green wood, now shapeless and defaced,
Will be a scene of faultless Gothic taste.
Alas! the world, when this old wood was young,
The siren song that we are singing, sung;
The saplings then were like the saplings now,

Without a blemish in a limb or bough.
But thousands, when but tender nurslings, died,
As many maimed or ruined at their side;
And these old trees that now the forest deck
Are all that really have survived the wreck,
And of all these that in this maze we see,
Not one old veteran is a perfect tree,
And tortuous shrubs in every tangled nook
Give to the graceful many an ugly crook;
As a fair boy, sweet, lovely, beauteous, mild,
Grows a rough man, unlovely, wicked, wild,
So these young plants, symmetric as can be,
Are dead or maimed, or such as these we see.

There's nothing here that has the skill or power
To make life certain for a single hour,
Nor has the potence to detain one breath,
That stands between it and the monster, death.
Though toward success the wisest project speeds,
It oftener stops or stumbles than succeeds;
And beauty's germs will, into being warmed,
Oft die or grow up ugly and deformed.

The matchless diamond in the womb of earth,
Must pass along through centuries to its birth,
Yet for each gem in all its charms arrayed,
Unnumbered perish by the hoe and spade;

And unknown thousands, to perfection brought,
Lie in the earth unvalued and unsought.
And, when earth dies, within her hills and moors,
There'll sleep unnumbered unformed Koh-i-noors.
Earth, meant to till, and be at length subdued,
Will melt at last, half sterile, rough, and rude.

'Twas meant that skill should train our fruits and
　　　　flowers,
To rival those that grow in heavenly bowers;
Yet skill, when striving to her latest blow,
Will ne'er plant gardens such as Heaven's below.
Progress on earth, however swiftly driven,
Will ne'er reach half way to the gates of heaven;
The prancing steeds that draw her chariot fret,
And lose much time in many a gay curvet;
And although upward is their general bent,
The path oft suffers an abrupt descent.
Exhumed creations, daily brought to view,
Show men have done what moderns cannot do;
And as in rocks, as plain as Saxon words,
We read of known and unknown beasts and birds,
So midst the debris of old time we sit,
And see "lost arts" all o'er the rubbish writ.

Invention never gives us something new,
Till we've some mission for the thing to do;

Want goes ahead, and wit behind it hies,
And brings the rear up with its fresh supplies.
In Eden's ground, a Fulton with his steam
Had found its mission useless as a dream;
And all earth's navies, were they all afloat,
Had been as useless as a schoolboy's boat,
Had Galileo, with capacious soul,
Ne'er made the needle show the unseen pole;
And the fierce Congos, with a hearty laugh,
Would hail the approach of Morse's telegraph;
Though it were stretched around earth's broad do-
    main,
Till it should enter Congo's fields again,
No friend would e'er send greeting to a friend,
Nor merchant have one short dispatch to send.

Hard, earnest labor is the price we pay
For every inch of Progress' upward way;
Rest but an instant, and the cortege stops, —
Her horses falter, and the chariot drops,
And not till man gives labor heart and brain,
Will Progress ever rise aloft again.

Peace reigns, and labor plies its merry blows,
And Progress upward like an eagle goes;
War marches forward with an angry frown,
Toil stops, and Progress drives its chariot down;

War spends its wrath and labor works amain,
And then the chariot mounts aloft again.
Ah, casualties, too great to number, play
In Progress' track, and block the upward way:
Half of man's powers at every fresh attack
Must lose much time in clearing off the track.
Old Ocean is not, of *all* things below,
The sole creation made to ebb and flow:
Earth's history has, down from its earliest age,
Mutation written upon every page.

When man grows perfect, Progress will arise,
And both together be in Paradise;
Because, when man has to perfection striven.
That place must be, where'er it is, a heaven:
But as perfection ne'er existed here,
Progress must stop e'en while in mid career.

Each moral plant, though nurtured here in love,
Will bear its blossoms and its fruits above;
We catch some glimpses oftentimes below
Of charms to come when they shall ope and blow,
And oft a foretaste of that fruit is given,
That we shall eat if we e'er mount to heaven;
But the full harvest of the fruits and flowers
Can ne'er, this side of Paradise, be ours.

Our olive plants, that in our homesteads grow,
And make them almost Edens here below,
Bear fruits enough to fill them full of love,
But the ripe fruit grows nowhere but above.

Earth's but the nursery from whose verdant grove
The plants spring up to set in fields above,
And life's the school where young immortals come,
And train their hearts for their unending home;
And if prepared before ourselves to go,
Could we detain them one short hour below?

God's plans are countless, yet they smoothly run,
And twine themselves in one harmonious one, —
Forever twining, never wholly twined,
'Tis perfect only in the omniscient mind.
The noblest life, the noblest ever spent,
Is but a thread for that grand purpose meant.
The hearty patriot sees the foeman stand,
And threat destruction to his native land;
His swelling bosom full to bursting nigh,
He girds his sword upon his manly thigh;
And while his spirit burning high inspires
His gathering hosts with kindred hopes and fires,
He leads them on with heart that will not quail,
Amidst the screaming of the leaden hail.
O! God will shield him, God will spare the brave,

Nor let young hope go bleeding to the grave !
'Tis but for freedom, but for human rights,
For all that's sacred that the hero fights.
On, warriors, on ; rush to the combat now,
And victory's wreaths shall deck the victor's brow ;
Raise high the standard, let the banners wave ;
O ! rush to victory or the martyr's grave.

The grave, — O, yes, the gallant hero reels,
And Lyon falls beneath his horse's heels, —
Falls while the banner to the breeze is flung,
Falls while the war-shout lingers on his tongue.
O ! how it made the patriot's life-blood chill,
When martyred Warren fell on Bunker Hill ;
And how each good heart throbbed the funeral knell,
When Winthrop bled and gallant Baker fell !
And thousands, thousands in our country's fight,
For Justice, Union, Liberty, and Right,
Fall ere the prize for which they fight is won,
Fall when their mission has but just begun,
Fall while the Nation, looking at the brave,
Feel they're the ones that Heaven has sent to save.

A little being of mysterious birth,
Pure as a dew-drop, comes to visit earth ;
With eager haste, the little foundling's pressed,
Among the down of fond Affection's breast,

And bonds of love too strong for aught to part
Twine in an instant every throbbing heart.
Ha! manhood's stamped, not indistinct and dim,
On every feature, lineament, and limb,
And through those eyes that timid look about,
The new-waked soul is slyly looking out,
And with a power and majesty unseen,
It sets in play the marvellous machine.
At first *mere* play, and then the mimic strife,
Made by mere fancy aping genuine life.
In each new feat, new skill and potence lurk,
The pleasant transit out of play to work.
Ah, little one, God surely has for you
Some lofty mission in this world to do;
He is too wise to send a sage below,
And smite before he strikes one earnest blow,
And far too good to crush a noble boy,
Just entering o'er the threshold of employ.
But Charlie dies; the little hero falls;
The One that sent him to the earth recalls.
Heaven has another ransomed one to bless,
And home, *our* home, one little cherub less;
And that high mission to our Charlie given
Is so divine, it must be done in heaven.

Were man omniscient, seeing near and far,
And found in Nature one discordant jar,

Well might he boldly, proudly, walk abroad,
And play stern critic of the works of God.

Till we can trace our little martyr's doom,
Forever onward, e'en beyond the tomb,
And find how much life's fleetness here below
Affects the future of his weal or woe,
'Twere worse than folly, worse than impious even,
To say, " 'Tis strange," of any act of Heaven.
The very thought implies a lack of trust,
And that we almost think kind Heaven unjust.

If, like chastising, as the Hebrew sung,
'Tis God's " strange work," this cutting down our
          young,
'Tis passing strange, this self-same feature lurks
In all God's actions and through all his works ;
And either God is wicked and unwise,
Or finite optics are our mortal eyes,
And of all demons he would be the worst,
Who dares to say the truthful is the first.

O ! when promoted to the school above,
Where the Great Teacher is the God of love,
All seeming jars that sound so harshly here
Will be all harmony in a ransomed ear ;
All seeming wrong, illumed by heavenly light,

Will prove the essence of the true and right;
Our little ones, snatched from a mother's care
In all their beauty, are more beauteous there,
And, although severed to their new employ,
Act loftier parts in that pure world of joy,
And though they seem an injury to sustain,
Death in life's morning brings a world of gain.

Come, faith, pure envoy, to this world below,
The heaven of rest to mortal eyes to show,
O! let the truth upon our hearts be graven,
That our lost Charlie is at home in heaven;
That God knows well what moment would be best,
To call his dear ones to be loved and blest.
And though the tear will oft unbidden start,
And sighs come bursting from the aching heart,
Let us thank God that when our dear ones die,
Relief comes gushing in a tear or sigh,
And that life's path, though ending soon or late,
Is long enough to reach the pearly gate,
And sundered ties, though seeming formed in vain,
Are sure hereafter to reknit again.

O! Charlie, Charlie! thy sweet image yet
Lives in our hearts too vivid to forget,
And ne'er will fade till life itself departs,
And thou, once more, art nestling in our hearts.

'Tis sweet to think, dear, darling little boy,
That thou'rt a cherub in that home of joy;
Yet, midst that sweetness, shoot the pangs of woe,
To think we're lingering without thee below;
And then we bid the gushing tear-drops sleep,
And end it all by sitting down to weep.

Dear little boy! when thou wast here below,
Thy heart with sweetness used to overflow,
And, like a rose, send its aroma round,
To every heart within its magic ground;
And it must be. that, planted up above,
Your spotless bosom must o'erflow with love.

DO SPIRITS VISIT EARTH?

Do little spirits in your upper sphere,
E'er come to earth and visit loved ones here?
We've sometimes thought a little fairy thing
Was hovering o'er us with its outspread wing,
And while it poised on sparkling wings above,
Dropped down some honey of o'erflowing love.
Then we felt pure, and then we harbored not
One impure feeling or unhallowed thought;
And had grim death at that sweet moment come,
He had been welcome to our pleasant home.

Was Charlie there ? We've asked the question oft,
And then our hearts in gladness rose aloft;
Earth then seemed nothing but the eyry given,
Where spirits stop to plume their wings for heaven.

O ! if pure spirits from heaven's realms depart,
'Tis on some errand to the pure in heart;
They ne'er hold converse in the realms below,
But with the pure or panting to be so.

When Charlie lived, it made him doubly blest,
To sit and nestle in a parent's breast;
He only knew those pillows were his own:
He read that truth, and read that truth alone.
God grant he loves them as he did before,
Now that he reads them to the very core;
Then will his loss, that filled our souls with pain,
Prove both our present and eternal gain,
And we shall have some thrills of heavenly joy,
From converse sometimes with our darling boy.

DEATH SELDOM COMES AT THE RIGHT TIME.

'Tis very hard when, with a tearful eye,
We have to stand and see our darlings die;
And harder yet to lay their little heads

'Neath the green velvet of their mouldering beds;
But bitterest woe when we, home's threshold, cross,
And in dread earnest feel the bitter loss;
The widowed heart, all smarting 'neath the rod,
Can't feel the wisdom of an all-wise God,
And half thinks somehow 'tis injustice done,
Both to home's circle and its little one.

Alas! alas! in every age and clime,
Death comes but seldom at the proper time;
Too soon to meet the trembling victim's views,
The monster comes with his unwelcome news.
If it seem strange God takes away our young,
Just as life's banner to the breeze is flung,
Or when, perhaps, the little hero's blows
Begin to play on Progress' stubborn foes,
Just armed, equipped, and fitted for the strife
Man always finds in the rough path of life;
If it seem strange, mysterious, or unjust,
That dust so early should return to dust, —
The same three words with equal truth apply
To all that die, and whensoe'er they die.

THE YOUNG STUDENT.

He was a boy, — I knew him well, whilom, —
A fair, young hope-bud in the bowers of home;

Among the group that filled the sweet *parterre*,
He was the sweetest of the blossoms there;
Mild as the blue of yonder cloudless sky,
The soul looked laughing from his beaming eye,
Or if sometimes, beneath the auburn lash,
The soul looked outward with an angry flash,
The storm soon hushed, the rainbow spanned the
        plain,
And the clear sky spread out its blue again.

His mind, capacious, vigorous, clear, and strong,
Saw truth and grasped it in the way along,
With his keen wit shot folly as it flew,
And caught at error where the rank weeds grew;
Then, with the game well basted and well done,
He gave his friends a generous feast of fun;
And all within his sphere of friendship found
Felt happier far when Warren was around.

At length, a youth, he hasted to explore
The pure, rich fields of Greek and Roman lore,
And pluck the fruits the goddess Learning yields,
On the broad acres of her charming fields.

At length, a student, he began to rove
Within his honored Alma Mater's grove,
And then, dear fellow, almost at the start,

The Saviour came, and touched his generous heart.
His soul was full, his bosom leaped with love,
And his glad spirit meekly looked above,
And then we thought of nothing else to add,
For all he wanted in the world he had;
Then life seemed nothing with its witching scenes,
Weighed as an end against it as a means,
And all earth's luxuries were but pauper food,
Compared with that which comes from doing good.

O! what high hopes were centred in that boy!
What buds of promise and what germs of joy!
All loved that met him, all admired that knew,
And all felt sure he'd some good work to do,
And all prophetic felt 'twas very plain,
That so much promise was not given in vain.

O! how devout the scholar used to rove,
In thought profound, his Alma Mater's grove;
And while he dug for Learning's classic ore,
He went to Calvary for its holier lore,
And mind and heart in sweetest harmony grew,
And linked in beauty all he felt and knew,
And truth and goodness lent the sword and shield
To their young champion, soon to take the field.
But lo! he died, — died like a new-lit star;
Died, while yet arming for the coming war;

Died, while hope's sun shone brightest in its sphere ;
Died, while all thought he had a mission here ;
Died, while encircled in the arms of love,
Promoted to a higher school above.

How strange ! love deemed it when the dear youth
    died ;
Love prayed in faith, but found the prayer denied ;
Skill tried its best from Science' healing store,
And friendship nursed, till it could do no more.
He died, and all said, with a tear and sigh,
How strange it seemed that such a youth should
    die !

THE STATESMAN AND CHRISTIAN.

THERE was a boy, and God had cast his lot,
Not in a prince's, but a peasant's cot ;
Not wealth or honor greeted him at birth,
But health and virtue, his ancestral worth ;
The world showed splendors wheresoe'er he turned,
With none for him untoiled for and unearned,
And life, to wealth a scene of mirth and play,
To him a rugged and an up-hill way ;
But, nothing daunted, the young tyro rose,
And at the rugged dealt Herculean blows,
And every effort in the hearty strife

Made the way smoother in the path of life,
And the same blows that made the rugged smooth,
Brought up bright gems of virtue and of truth,
And between blows made recreation even,
The school to aid him on to truth and heaven.

Grace, in life's morning, dropping from above,
Filled his young bosom with a Saviour's love,
And life, whatever fortune it might bring,
Seemed from that hour a consecrated thing.
He sought not honors, honors sought him now,
And piled the garlands on his noble brow,
And at length placed him, at his country's call,
In Freedom's highest legislative hall.
Then his State, panting for his skill and care,
Called him and set him in her highest chair;
Then uncorrupt, sound, honest, and discreet,
Gave him at length a high judicial seat,
Where innocence ne'er asked his aid in vain,
And guilt, once there, ne'er wished to go again.
And never, midst official toil and strife,
Did he forget the ills and woes of life:
Vice at his presence hid its hideous head,
And Want's gaunt children looked to him for bread,
And no sweet deed, howe'er unknown or dim,
Appeared too humble or too small for him.
Whatever act had potence to impart　-

One thrill of joy to sorrow's shivering heart;
Whatever deed had magic to implant
One germ of plenty in the home of want;
Whatever words, spoke kindly in the ear,
Could vice rebuke or modest virtue cheer, —
Those acts and words he fitted to each case,
And just adapted to the time and place.
'Twas on a mission to some sufferers near,
He was that morn to aid, instruct, and cheer,
He rose to go, and passing through the hall,
Swept by a gun that rested 'gainst the wall;
It fell, exploded, and the good man stood
In a red pool of his own precious blood.
" 'Tis come," said he, while all around were awed,
" 'Tis come; be still, and know that I am God!"

His country called, — his Henry had obeyed,
And led his hosts where her gay banners played,
And at the moment when his father fell,
Thought of sweet home, and fancied all was well.

Love bent and whispered in the father's ear,
Shall Henry come, to aid you and to cheer?
Shall he come home, and at your bedside stand,
To take the blessing and the parting hand?
Shall Henry come, to kneel once more beside
So kind a father and so wise a guide?

"No! as I look, I see on either hand
A bleeding father and a bleeding land;
Let him not come, but to the rescue fly,
His country needs him far, far more than I;
So like a soldier's is this death of mine,
God may accept it, gallant boy, for thine!"

And thus he died, just as experience' lore
Had filled his bosom full to running o'er,
And head and heart knit with a well-earned fame,
Backed by the magic of a spotless name,
Made him that moment where he proudly stood,
Most ripe for fame, most fit for doing good.
The world looked on, and, with a tearful eye,
Said, how mysterious such a man should die,
While at each turn in common life are found
Myriads who're only cumberers of the ground,
Whom had God's thunders long ago destroyed,
The world had been far better for the void!

THE WIDOW'S SON.

THERE was a boy, — a widowed mother's son, —
Her sweet heart-blossom, — 'twas her only one;
'Neath Love's soft wing he felt a mother's care,
And wished no Eden but the sweet one there.

'Twas no weak mother, with a doating pride,
Had that young boy to counsel and to guide;
Her heart all chastened by Affliction's rod,
And calmly leaning on the arm of God,
She felt that boy was, in her bosom, given,
To train for honor, usefulness, and heaven.
What need of aid that Christian mother felt,
The altar witnessed where she daily knelt;
What counsel asked she of her heavenly guide,
Her closet witnessed — no one else beside.
Her prayers were heard, and counsel from above
Came down to aid and consecrate her love;
And, while a boy, the Friend of childhood bent,
And the pure spirit of adoption sent.
O! what a future seemed for him to ope
To the fond heart and eager eye of hope;
His was a mind that seemed, in earliest youth,
To feast itself upon the richest truth;
His was a heart where virtue's germ was set,
And all the graces of the Christian met,
And when at length he went away to rove,
And thread the paths in Academus' grove,
Each little learner with ambition fired,
Looked up to him and wondered and admired,
And the dear centre of the love and joy
Of those young tyros was that youthful boy.
O! how they'd cluster round him in their sports,

Their mimic gatherings, and their mimic courts!
And the bright sky of that gay school was dim,
Without the presence and the smiles of him.
The green, high mountains that begirt his home,
The rough-tilled fields o'er which he loved to roam,
The babbling brooks that leaped adown the hill,
The mimic lakes the brooklets came to fill, —
All had a charm so potent, 'twould entice
The little rovers from the haunts of vice.

A mimic lake, scooped by the hand of art,
Lay in a grove encircled and apart;
Its glassy face, without a ripple, spread,
A crystal sheet above the pebbly bed,
And oft attracted thither to the wave,
The merry tyros used to come and lave.

The sky was clear, and Sol's solstitial ray
Streamed down to earth and made a pleasant day;
The merry youth went out with nimble feet,
Within the shadow of the green retreat,
And with his comrades, with their heyday cheered,
Plunged in the flood, and quickly disappeared;
Ah! disappeared, for when their sports were done,
Among the throng there was no widow's son.

On yonder couch behold him sleeping now,
That boy of promise with the noble brow,
That widow's son, brought up and trained with care,
Wrapped in a sleep that knows no waking there.
That mother — see her mildly drawing nigh —
Calm as her lost one, with a tearless eye,
Parts the bright locks upon his manly brow,
And plants a kiss upon the mimic snow,
And says, My son, gone, gone to thy reward;
Well, long ago, I gave thee to the Lord.

Alas! how strange, since death might take but one,
His dreaded bolt should strike the widow's son;
Strange it should be at such a victim hurled,
That it should wound the widow and the world.

THE ONLY SON.

There's a fair city on New England's Thames,
One of her sweetest architectural gems,
Where stately mansions, filled with beauty, lift,
And lovely dwellings, reared by toil and thrift,
And where home-bliss, in like profusion, comes
To stately mansions and to humble homes,
And few, how few, of all her thousands dwell
In want's chill cot or vice's gloomy cell,

And church and school impart their aid before
The little traveller reaches manhood's door,
And thus he enters on life's active field,
Armed *cap-a-pie* with helmet, spear, and shield;
Where spacious streets, smooth as Macadam's roads,
Conduct the traveller to her grand abodes,
And huge old trees, that form one Gothic arch,
Make marching through them one triumphant march;
Where Nature's features all in harmony chime,
The charming, fair, and rugged and sublime.
The smooth Shetucket, that in beauty glides,
And gayly mingles in the briny tides;
The foaming Yantic, whirling mill-wheels round,
Then leaping cataracts seaward at a bound;
The Thames, where Commerce her white sails un-
    furls,
And joins *her* interests with the outer world's, —
These make that city on the river Thames
One of the sweetest of New England's gems.

Well, in that city, so like Eden decked,
Two bosoms throb at sorrow's retrospect.
Once their glad hearts, and their beloved boy's,
Beat in a house full of domestic joys,
So blent together, sorrow, in one breast,
'Shot the same pang of anguish through the rest;
And thus that trio, as they daily roved

Along life's pathway, labored, lived, and loved.
Where is the spot beneath yon spreading dome
So much like heaven as a New England home?
Where fond affection knit with thrift and health,
Though gold it bring not, brings enough of wealth,
And crown and throne and glory's loftiest niche
Might make more wealthy, not a whit more rich.
O, yes, of bliss, the sweetest fruitage comes
From plants well trained in our New England homes.

They had one boy — it was their only one —
An only child as well as only son.
They loved that boy, yet 'twas their daily prayer
To make no idol of their darling there ;
They loved their Saviour with a love so true,
They wished their son to love and serve him too.
With them religion was a pleasant plant ;
Who can be cheerful, if the Christian can't ?
No sour, morose, or chilling look or air
Was ever mingled with parental care ;
By nature genial, God's redeeming grace,
Ne'er swept the sunbeams from the merry face ;
And so Religion, to that merry boy,
Came robed in beauty, innocence, and joy,
And seemed to him, e'en in a world like this,
A thing of love, a synonyme of bliss ;
And those fond parents saw with faith's clear eye,

That boy would be a Christian, by and by;
And, in old age, when earthly charms grew dim,
They fondly hoped that they might lean on him.
O! if there was beneath yon azure dome
One unspoiled Eden, 'twas that happy home;
They scarcely dreamed, or seemed to quite forget,
That their small circle might be smaller yet,
And laid their plans, as if their plans would stay
Throughout life's changes to its closing day.

'Tis ever thus, — till blessings take their flight,
We very seldom look upon them right;
We toil for wealth and then so firmly clasp,
We feel that nothing can unloose the grasp:
We pant for honor with unslaking thirst,
Grasp it, and see the empty bubble burst;
And though all things are fragile as the flowers,
We think, alas! 'twill not be so with ours;
And though earth's setting, every day, new stones
Above the ashes of our little ones,
Each parent thinks God will his darling save,
To plant the stones above his adult grave.

'Twas winter now, and Nature slept below
A funeral pall of chilly ice and snow;
The little rills that summer waked around,
Were fettered firmly as a prisoner bound;

The leafy trees and flowers, with balmy breath,
Slept still as if within the embrace of death ;
The Thames was screened with glittering crystal
    round,
Which spread far onward toward the treacherous
    sound ;
The frantic Yantic, down the rapids tossed,
Ran to the Thames unfettered by the frost ;
The gay Shetucket, down its native pass,
Moved 'neath a screen as smooth and clear as glass :
And to his eye, who midst the scenery roams,
All would seem gloom outside the genial homes.
But hark ! the bells, and lo ! the merry sleigh,
With merrier spirits, glides along the way,
And round the streets the gay and joyous shout
Shows plain as day that all the boys are out,
And each, a radius of the merry scene,
Flies toward Shetucket with its crystal screen ;
And there was Herbert and his merry mates,
All gliding gayly on their glittering skates ;
Swift as an arrow shoots across the sky,
The skaters dart, and seem almost to fly,
Now in platoons, and moving side by side,
They o'er the ice in graceful movements glide,
Then, like a rocket bursting in the sky,
They start, and off at different angles fly ;
Forward or backward, on one foot or two,

Bent like a crescent or inverted U,
They leap and fly, and lines and circles trace,
And do it all with faultless ease and grace;
The laugh, the shout, flushed cheek, and flashing eye,
Show health's the boon the merry skaters buy.
O, yes! there's pleasure, with no taint of vice,
This flying, sailing, o'er the crystal ice;
And we exclaim, as we behold the joy,—
"O! once again who would not be a boy?"

The brittle ice,—it bends, it breaks, and lo!
The little urchins in the waters go,
Then rise again, and many, in a trice,
Seize hold, and gayly leap upon the ice;
But one, still in, clings to the ice's brink,
Holds bravely on, resolving not to sink.
Cheer up, my boy, hold on a little more,
We'll bring thee succor, and 'twill all be o'er.

Men from the city hasten at the cry;
Men from the cars, for they were passing by.
The poor boy feels benumbed, and chilled with frost,
'Twill soon be over, and his grasp be lost,
And cries, "Good-by, boys; it is almost o'er;
Tell mother"—— What? Alas! he said no more;
The blue waves oped, and on the pebbly bed,
Death calmly pillowed little Herbert's head.

Alas! alas! who will the tidings bear
To that sweet home, and plant the anguish there?
Who'll tell the mother, who'll inform the sire,
That one chair's vacant at their winter fire?
Who'll plant the dagger that till life departs
Will ne'er cease rankling in their wounded hearts?

Can nothing come to modify the pain
When the dear idols of our hearts are slain?

When the kind mother, at the sick one's bed,
Spreads the down softly 'neath his weary head,
Turns his tired frame, his couch to rearrange,
To bring relief and comfort by the change,
Lists every sigh, hears every little groan,
And whispers comfort to the weary one,
And when pain racks and sorrow overflows,
Speaks some kind word to win him from his woes,
And when she can do nothing more than this,
Bends down above him and imprints a kiss,
'Tis sweet to think when all at length is past,
She tried to aid him to the very last.

But when the mother sees her darling boy
Go out for sport all brimming o'er with joy,
She feels e'en glad that where her boy resorts
He joins his fellows in their manly sports,

And pride perhaps her little hero can
Go out and in, self-guided like a man.
No anxious cares or sad forebodings swell
That mother's heart that all may not be well;
She never thinks, or deems the thought is vain,
Her darling boy may not come home again,
And waits as calm and undisturbed as though
He'd only stepped within a room below.

But the bell rings, and through the opening door
The tidings come, her darling is no more;
And tramping feet just on the threshold bring
Her poor dead boy, a cold and lifeless thing.

Calm as a statue stands the mother there,
The type of woe, the symbol of despair;
She cannot yet take in the tide of woe
Poured in her bosom by the fiendish foe.
The human heart has power to feel and bear
Life's common ills, that meet us everywhere;
But when woe sends her deadliest and her worst,
The stoutest cannot bear it all at first,
And so kind nature gives the human heart
Woe in instalments, when too keen the smart.
And as the eye, first opening in the gloom,
Expands ere seeing what is in the room,
So the heart, staggering at a sudden blow,

Feels not at first the full, full tide of woe;
The little wavelets first the rush begin,
Until at last the mighty flood comes in.

Dead ? he's but sleeping, — O ! how calm and still !
Ha ! ha ! that forehead, — O ! how pale and chill !
Dead ? God of mercy, — that my boy should die,
And no one near him, no kind watcher by,
Not even I, to bathe his aching head,
To smooth his pillow and arrange his bed,
To watch, and wait, and soothe, and aid, and cheer,
And let him feel a tender mother near,
And let him see, if the poor boy must die,
The tear of sorrow from a mother's eye,
And at the last, when all is done, do this :
Embrace my boy and give the parting kiss.
O ! then, methinks, I could have borne with joy
The loss, though bitter, of my darling boy.

" Tell mother "—what ? 'tis hard he could not tell.
Perhaps, I love you, or perhaps, farewell ;
Perhaps, I thank you for your love and care ;
Perhaps, I hope, or, God forbid, despair.
Whate'er it was, dear little fellow, I
Shall know it all and hear it by and by.

And thus that mother thinks it o'er and o'er,

And daily sees and feels it more and more,
Until at length the full, the boundless whole
Thrills every living fibre of the soul.
Then will that sorrow be her daily care
Till 'tis a burden she will love to bear;
And should you wipe it off from memory's leaf
'Twould be no solace, but a source of grief:
The merchant long a crushing burden bears
Till 'tis his life to battle with his cares;
Let him retire with fortune's highest prize,
And ten to one he's wretched or he dies.

Then let her weep, and let her ne'er forget,
Nor cease to feel till life's last sun shall set;
'Twill do her good to mourn her buried boy,
'Twill lighten sorrow and 'twill chasten joy;
And when death comes, faith will, with cloudless eye,
See the lost boy, and make it sweet to die.

When the grim Monster deals the deadly blow,
And lays the victim in life's heyday low,
When new ties daily fasten heart to heart,
Without one dream that they may have to part,
'Tis then that parting seems a bitterer thing,
And death's keen sting becomes a keener sting,
And bleeding sorrow with full many a sigh
Thinks 'tis so strange its little one should die.

NO STRANGER THAT THE YOUNG DIE THAN THE OLD.

Most of earth's graves are very little ones,
And short the stories chiselled on the stones,
And if 'tis strange when death inflicts the blow
That lays the tender and the youthful low,
Is it not strange when death's keen dart is sped,
And useful age lies numbered with the dead?

THE OLD SAGE.

I know a sage, almost a century old,
Whose name is with earth's noble names enrolled.
At fourscore years, when life has fewer joys,
His heart was young and buoyant as a boy's;
His mind, more full of life's and learning's lore,
Was ne'er so vigorous and so strong before;
A heartier champion or a doughtier knight
Ne'er toiled or fought for justice, truth, and right;
And eloquence — O! 'twas a feast to sit
And list the outbursts of his polished wit.
At seventy-five he saw, from all concealed,
The spot where fortune had a golden field;
And to the city, in whose curule chair
He was oft called to sit and act as mayor,

Threw off the veil, showed where the treasures were,
And begged her guardians get the gems for her;
But they, more wise, chose rather to refuse,
And said " fantastic " of the old man's views.
Well, said the sage, helped by a hand divine,
I'll take the field, and make the treasure mine.
The field was his, and with the riches there,
Within five years he was a millionnaire.
Now had he died at the full age of men,
At threescore years or threescore years and ten,
No one had thought 'twould heaven's pure plan de-
        range,
Or called his death mysterious, wrong, or strange;
Yet that old man has, since that moment, won
What very few through longest lives have done.

If it seem strange life's morning sun should set
While but just rising in the orient yet,
And the young pilgrim find his race is run
Before one act of earnest work is done,
'Tis just as strange that death should strike the blow
Before one does the whole he can below,
And stranger yet one lingers on the shore,
When so near nothing he can do no more,
And perhaps strangest, God not always gives
Power to act even while the creature lives.

THE AGED DIVINE.

THERE is a man who has, a giant, stood
Almost a century 'mong the wise and good,
Who, to old age, with all the fire of youth,
Was the wise teacher of the purest truth;
Men flocked to listen where his logic rung,
And caught the accents dropping from his tongue;
His thoughts ne'er varied in their shape and hue,
To stand in harmony with the current view;
He did his thinking, uttered what he thought,
And acted always in the way he taught;
Who's still erect as when a buoyant youth
Or stalwart man he hurled the bolts of truth,
But whose mind now, once vigorous, keen, and clear,
Too weak to grapple with a child's idea,
And that fine form in which whilom was shrined
The grand machinery of a noble mind,
Seems like a casket of the purest gold
Robbed of the jewels that it used to hold.

Strange, the mind's powers should hasten to decay,
And leave the body all in vigorous play;
Or body linger year by year behind,
In disobedience to its master-mind.
We think it strange that men so often should

Live till too helpless to do any good,
But far more strange that millions can be found
Who all through life are cumberers of the ground.

It seems mysterious that the noblest here
Oft drop while marching in their full career;
But history's leaves are filled with marvels o'er,
That untold thousands did not die before.

Had the same ball that maimed an Arnold slain,
Earth had not cursed him as a worse than Cain;
And had Burr died in boyhood's early bloom,
One villain less had found an earthly tomb.

GALLERY AT THE VATICAN.

WITHIN one gallery at imperial Rome,
Where Art, long buried, finds at last a home,
There is one bust that, as he's passing by,
Is pretty sure to catch the traveller's eye;
Its plump, fair face, and gentle, modest mien,
And genial air, so peaceful and serene,
All furnish proof without the least alloy,
'Twas of a lovely and enchanting boy,
One whom a mother might be proud to choose,
And whom 'twould break her heart of hearts to
    lose.

In that same gallery, farther on, is seen,
A marble demon, both in form and mien ;
The gross and vulgar in each feature twine,
The fierce and cruel live in every line ;
And then you feel no marvel in the case,
When you read Nero chiselled on the base.
But turn again, and a few steps retrace,
And gaze once more upon that cherub's face.
O ! what a contrast, so surpassing fair,
An angel here, a very demon there.
Who is that cherub? Look and read and know
That vile name Nero's chiselled down below.
Great Jove ! why was that little angel screened
From thy red bolts to grow a heartless fiend ?
The blackest wretch that ever cursed the world
Had never cursed it had the bolt been hurled ;
And Rome's heart-tears in rivers would have run
At the sad death of Agrippina's son,
And the sad mother shed affection's tear
While bending o'er her little Nero's bier.
But the boy lived, the imperial purple wore,
And Rome was deluged in her children's gore,
Until her blood, that monster mother's, run,
Pierced by the dagger of her fiendish son.

Strange that God lets a little cherub grow
Till 'tis a demon ripe for endless woe,

No less a marvel than to hurl the dart,
And pierce a heart pure as our Charlie's heart.

RESCUE OF THE IDIOT BOY.

I KNEW a man, a good old country 'squire,
An honest farmer and indulgent sire ;
Among his children patriarch-like he moved,
And all the circle felt the old man loved,
And 'mongst them all it was their chief employ
To care for one, his little idiot boy.
The father felt that, with a mind so dim,
That helpless boy must go for aid to him ;
And so he watched him when unwell and well,
And guessed the wants he had no power to tell,
And so unbroken was the vigil kept,
'Twas on his heart both when he waked and slept,
Until so yearning for his poor weak son,
Himself and boy became entirely one :
The woe or joy that thrilled his throbbing breast
Made the fond father's as unblest or blest,
And as he walked along life's rugged road,
Care pressed upon him with a double load ;
Yet the same blow that should, alas ! destroy
One half his cares, would crush one half his joy.

One summer day, with heat and toil oppressed,
He laid him down as was his wont to rest,
And, as he slept, his thoughts from habit run,
Without volition, on his helpless son.
He thought he saw him where he'd often seen,
Roving around and straying o'er the green;
And then he saw him at the river's brink,
Then plunging in, then struggling not to sink.
The old man waked, and, with excitement wild,
Rushed just in time to save his idiot child;
His heart was full, and the glad father wept
For joy, that God had watched him while he slept.

Then the world said, O! strangest of events!
Untoward chance, mysterious Providence!
Thus to detain a guiltless idiot boy,
Where there's for him not one sweet thrill of joy;
A deathless spirit to detain below,
And where it never could expand and grow,
And where its wants ne'er drink of plenty's bowl,
Save through the medium of another's soul.
And though that sire would feel full many a pain,
He ne'er should see nor aid that boy again,
Reason and time would heal the fleeting smart,
And bring relief to his o'erburdened heart;
And wisdom almost would have sought in vain
The slightest cause to sorrow or complain,

But could have found unnumbered reasons why
A drivelling idiot, lingering here, should die.

THE MISSIONARY.

The last command the Man of Sorrows gave
Was, preach my gospel where there's one to save;
Let the glad tidings that I bring be rung
In every land, by every tribe and tongue;
Let the good news be told in every ear,
Where there's a sinner in the world to hear:
Do this, and I, your Lord and God, will bless
And crown your labors with complete success.
The time will come, you'll reap the full reward
When all the nations know and fear the Lord,
When peace shall reign, and concord knit all lands,
Love fill all hearts, and friendship join all hands,
Earth's dreary deserts shall be filled with flowers,
And white-robed virtue rove among the bowers.
O glorious thought! the earnest Christian said,
Be mine the bliss the glorious news to spread.
I have a treasure shrined within my heart,
Which grows more precious as I spare a part;
A treasure which, as long as I shall live,
The more I give will leave me more to give;
A heavenly treasure, dropped in kindness, which

Will make the giver and receiver rich,
And which if spread will lift a world like this
Up to the realms of pure and fadeless bliss.
Where is the Christian that would hide the prize,
With this great truth all blazoned to his eyes?

Go preach my gospel wheresoe'er there's one
Whom sin has stained, or guilt or crime undone:
This great command for twenty centuries near
Has rolled its thunders into every ear,
And all men heard, where'er the summons went,
But few, how few, felt what the summons meant!
But now its import flashed on every one,
Clear as the lightnings through mid-ether run,
And one by one the Christian bosom felt,
And one by one began to warm and melt,
And one by one, as each began to see,
Cried out in triumph, " Here am I ; send me."
And many came, and many a one was sent,
And many a soldier to the combat went ;
Home, friends, possessions, comforts, country, all,
Compared with this, appeared surpassing small,
And hardship, suffering, pain, and death, to meet,
Seemed in the pathway of obedience sweet.
Then with the prayers and fond adieus of all,
He went, obedient to his Master's call,
Left home and friends, and social charms and joys,

And sweet refinements, pleasures, and employs,
And 'neath the banner of the cross unfurled,
Plunged in the midnight of a heathen world.

Not the gay steamer, that in calm or blow
Can through the waves with equal fleetness go,
Bears the poor herald toward an eastern sky,
Where he must go, to toil, and droop, and die;
Not the gay steamer, 'tis the snail-paced ship,
Where he embarks, in which he takes the trip.
Wealth has its gold, to purchase at its worth
The costly luxury of a steamer's berth,
But the poor herald of the cross must be,
For weary months, a sufferer on the sea,
And worn and weary, when he comes to land,
No friend will smile and give the welcome hand,
No well known face he'll see on that dark shore,
Nor one fair object he e'er saw before.

The trip was o'er, the white-winged ship, that day.
Rode out at anchor in that Eastern bay,
And the young herald, leaping on the strand,
Knelt and thanked God he saw the promised land.

A boat, a boat, behold the yellow rowers!
They're in the boat, already at the oars.
Aboard, aboard, and now they turn tne prow,

And row the herald up the river now.
For days and nights before the boat will reach
The lonely jungle, where he's sent to preach.
How strange the scene! the river, wood, and skies.
All, all seem strangers to his youthful eyes;
And home, sweet home, with all its loves and joys,
Its social pleasures and its sweet employs,
Loved forms and faces graven on his heart,
On memory's canvas every moment start.
Life, *all* of life, by mind and heart amassed,
Sleep in the graveyard of the buried past;
Friends, home, and country, all he'd loved before,
These all are objects he shall see no more;
And had his Master not beside him stood,
And fed his spirit with angelic food,
The lonely youth had sought the gallant ship,
And taken passage for a homeward trip;
But his kind Master still was hovering near,
And whispered comfort in the herald's ear.

And then he prayed, O Thou who bad'st me come
To this dark land that I must call my home,
Keep at my side, my close companion be.
I have no friend to whom to go but Thee;
Help, for I'm powerless, help, for I am dumb,
To speak the errand upon which I come;
But at Thy side, whatever may befall,

I'll toil for Thee. my God, my friend, my all.
He rose refreshed, and, brimming o'er with love,
Cried. " Toil is here, but rest and bliss above ;
This is my home, and 'neath my Master's eye
I'll toil and suffer, and, if need be, die."

The day was bright, the sky was blue and clear,
Beauty the eye, and music charmed the ear ;
And, as they rowed him up the sacred stream,
Life seemed a mystery, earth appeared a dream ;
And then he cried, glad-hearted that he'd come,
I thank Thee. Father, that I'm almost home.
But as he spoke God's tempest, fierce and strong,
Brought desolation in its path along,
Pagodas fell beneath its vengeful wrath,
And Indian homes lay scattered in its path,
And trees, like pipe-stems, shattered at a blow,
Flew through the air like arrows from a bow,
And, like a demon, made the bark a wreck,
With a dead herald lying on the deck.

Ah ! stranger things, it may not be denied,
Full oft occur than that our Charlie died ;
And the world said, while pointing to his bier,
God frowns on missions, it is written here,
While e'en the Christian scarce could understand
How God could thwart His own divine command.

Yes, stranger things, it cannot be denied,
Are happening here than that our Charlie died;
And then we think, and O! 'it soothes our woe,
What now we know not we shall sometime know;
What now seems dark will, in heaven's clearer light,
Seem all in harmony with unspotted right;
And every pang on earth that can annoy
Will end in heaven in one sweet thrill of joy.

THE YOUNG HERALD.

A CHOSEN vessel, — so they used to say
Of their young pastor every Sabbath-day;
A pious heart, a highly cultured mind,
And all the graces of the Christian twined,
With all the charms of polished rhetoric strung,
With grace of person, eloquence of tongue,
All these appeared in harmony to produce
A chosen vessel for the Master's use.
Alas! so young, yet, in his high employ,
He was a man, and not a whit a boy.
Deep-steeped in learning's, deep in heavenly, lore,
From truth's pure mine he dug the purest ore,
And, unalloyed by vanity and pride,
He was a safe, a most persuasive guide.
Crowds flocked to hear him, every Sabbath-day,

And ne'er unfed the hearers went away;
And willing converts to the Saviour flew,
At his entreaty, thick as drops of dew.
He sought not honors, sought not praise or fame,
For all unsought they clustered round his name;
And Christians called him, whatsoe'er their views,
A chosen vessel for the Master's use;
And if so young, so mighty he appears,
What will his might be in maturer years?
And his own sect looked to the youthful guide
With fondest hope and, it may be, with pride.

Schisms had oft wrought havoc with that flock,
That oft had served the wheels of truth to block;
But at his advent storm and tempest hushed,
And perfect union every discord crushed,
And all harmonious flock and shepherd strove,
To work together in the bonds of love.
God blessed the union, for He blessed the truth,
And blessed with man's the influence of the youth.
Not four full months had, in their lingering flight,
To pass before the new-sown fields were white;
The plough and sickle both together plied,
The sower and reaper labored side by side;
It was a scene o'er which the spirit bent,
And while faith prayed, the heavenly blessing sent.

'Twas summer now, and from the sweltering streets
The busy cits were seeking cool retreats;
Some down the bay, some up the river run,
Some down to Greenwood from the scorching sun,
Some to the mountain, some to merry spas,
Some farther northward in the dusty cars,
While some, too busied for a longer stay,
Sought the cool beach, to pass the current day,
Where the fresh sea-breeze its inspirings gave,
And weary limbs might in the waters lave.
And thus refreshed the crowded city seek
For life's stern duties for another week.
So the young servant of his Master, too,
Went, worn and tired, his vigor to renew,
Not to the mountain for its bracing air,
Not to the Spa, where pleasure's throngs repair,
Nor some sweet village in some rural clime,
Where he at ease could spend the summer-time;
He simply sailed across the narrow bay,
To pass a few hot summer hours away,
To walk the beach, by the cool breezes fanned,
Or watch the surges rushing on the sand,
Or plunge within and dash the waves aside,
And midst the surges in gay triumph ride.

The youthful pastor could the waters skim,
And 'midst the waves, with graceful movements,
    swim,

For from his boyhood he'd been wont to lave
Within the flood, and skim the yeasty wave.

And so he went along the beach's verge,
And boldly plunged within the angry surge,
And, with an easy and a graceful sweep,
Swam boldly out upon the briny deep;
With ease and grace he sailed as lightly there
As any bird that flits athwart the air;
He swam and floated, buoyant as a cork, —
It was all play, without a bit of work;
And danger felt there was no work for him
Where the young pastor gayly went to swim.
But, strange event, his mission was all o'er,
That chosen vessel never reached the shore;
The bonds that bound him to his home and flock,
The ties of friendship sundered by the shock,
The seeds that hope expected him to sow,
The yellow harvest from the seed to grow,
All were o'erwhelmed beneath the briny deep,
Where the young shepherd laid him down to sleep.
Such hopes to blast, such plans to disarrange,
The world beheld, and called it " passing strange."
Ah, yes! more ties, but not more sweet, are rent
Sometimes than those when our dear Charlie went.

THE HAPPY FAMILY.

If in this world there is a home, sweet home,
Where earth's chill winter never dares to come,
It is that home that never, never shares
The poor man's sufferings or the rich man's cares,
Where harvests spring up from its gay employ,
And thrift converts them into home-felt joy,
Where Agur's prayer from home's pure altar flies,
And the sweet boon comes dropping from the skies.
'Twas such a home, one of earth's happiest ones,
That held within two parents and two sons;
Love, virtue, vigor, competence, and health
Were to that homestead all its hoarded wealth,
And 'twas enough, with all these blessings given,
That home had many an element of heaven.
Their wants were few, but all they wished was theirs,
Without the rich man's panics, fears, and cares;
Banks, railroads, factories, prosperous or adverse,
Had no effect on person, place, or purse,
And Wall or State Street might be down or up,
Without affecting its o'erflowing cup;
The outside world might be all noise and din
And that sweet home be all at peace within.

There is no Eden in this world of ours,
But some blight's found among the lovely flowers,

The glorious sun, with all his golden rays,
Has many a spot upon his burnished face ;
And is it strange, that, in that fairy ground,
One drooping gem, one blasted bud, was found ?

They had two sons, — one was as bright a lad
As ever made a loving parent glad ;
The other blasted in life's early spring,
Was a poor idiot, — was a drivelling thing.
This was the bud that wasted with the blight,
This was the blot amidst the bower of light ;
But with a love unmingled with alloy,
The other three clung to that idiot boy.
And as a vacuum must be first supplied
By the freed air that's resting at its side,
So the poor idiot always, from the rest,
Got the first cupful of delight and best.
The blighted bud among the blooming flowers
Was, it is true, a blemish in the bowers,
But love all blazoned with a holier light
Shone midst the scene, and blotted out the blight.
And that home, maybe, felt more genuine joy
Because it held that helpless idiot boy.

The father died, and let the idiot be, —
And then men said, " God help the other three ! '
And the first grief-gush seemed all hope to sweep,

And leave that home no solace but to weep.
But mother's love, — there's nought so strong below,
Save what she'll suffer, what she'll dare to do.

Roused from the stupor that the blow had given,
She bowed submissive to the stroke of Heaven,
Then kissed her children both, her little ones,
And smiling sweetly on her little sons,
She said to him and took his tiny hand,
Who only could her meaning understand, —
Your father's dead, from whom there used to come
All that made ours a sweet and happy home;
Now there's no arm this side of the Divine
That we can lean on but on yours and mine,
And we, since Willie's is so weak and dim,
Must use our own for both ourselves and him.

And so they wrought, — she and her bright-eyed
        boy, —
And both felt happy in their new employ.
And home was happy, for the mother knew
If she would try, that God would help her too.
And little George kept longing for the day
When he could aid by work as well as play;
And little Willie's shallow cup of bliss
Was running o'er in such a home as this.
And they both felt although home's sun was set,

Bright sunlight streamed within their homestead yet.
But God now stepped within that home of joy,
And smote to dust that little bright-eyed boy;
The mother, awe-struck, said "Thy will be done,"
And sat down calmly by her idiot son.

Strange, said the world, that God should deal a blow
That spared the fool but laid the bright boy low;
That took the one that could her burdens share,
And left the one who'd be a constant care.
And human reason, wiser than Divine,
Would fain reverse it, every word and line;
And human kindness, had it had the rule,
Had spared the bright boy and recalled the fool.

Ah! human reason, hast thou power to look
And read man's future, as we read a book,
And trace, amidst their spiritual employs,
The boundless future of those little boys?
And weigh how much an early death or late
Gave shape and color to their changeless fate?
And how the death-blows, both the sire's and son's,
Swayed the long fate of those surviving ones?
When thou canst read this panorama through,
And see it plain as God and angels do,
And feel each pulse, and see each light and snade
Of future life, and why and how 'twas made,

Then if thou seest among what God has done
A seeming blemish, thou canst call it one,
Or aught inhuman dropping from above,
Then say that God is not a God of love.

Our hearts are bleeding that our boy was slain,
But, thanks to God, we never dared complain,
It may be, *will* be, if we e'er reach Heaven,
And thence look back to where this blow was given,
We'll feel and know whatever grief it cost,
'Twas just the blessing that we needed most,
And it may be the very thing was this
That sealed our title to unending bliss.

THE RICH AND POOR BOY.

'Twas in New York, where, mingled and combined,
Are all the grades of matter and of mind;
Where shivering want in scantiest raiment goes,
Chill as cold winter with its frosts and snows,
And muffled wealth, arranged with taste and care,
Goes warm as if in summer's genial air;
And every tint of social state between
Is daily mingling in the motley scene;
And in that city there is seen displayed
One panorama of each human grade.

One winter day, when through the swarming street,
The shivering crowds sped on with hurrying feet,
The cold, cold wind, in many an angry gust,
Swept on through Broadway in a cloud of dust,
And great and small, as the fierce whirlwind passed.
Turned round to 'scape the fury of the blast,
And muffling closer, shielding face and form
Against the fury of the wind and storm,
And all New York, the well and scanty clad,
Said of the day, — 'twas very, very bad.

Among the crowd two little boys were seen
Of equal age, to judge by size and mien:
One, warmly clad, went boldly on his way,
Nor seemed to feel that 'twas a blustering day.
His splendid dress betrayed a home of wealth,
His ruddy cheeks betokened perfect health;
His pleasant face and genial manners quite
Sufficed to prove him, although rich, polite;
And though within a home of luxury bred,
With not a want unanswered or unfed,
Wise heads had taught him, gentle spirits fired,
And generous hearts, his generous heart inspired,
And common sense had breathed within his soul,
And formed his powers in one harmonious whole.
The pride of wealth had never thrilled his mind:
His heart was generous, liberal, loving, kind.

And want and sorrow, and disease and pain,
Whene'er they asked him never asked in vain.
And that sweet boy, that loved to aid and give,
Was just the boy that one would wish to live, —
One of those sweet ones coming from above,
That all beholding watch, admire, and love.

The boy beside him was a child of want, —
A ragged, thieving, vicious mendicant.
Amidst old ruins, in a filthy den,
His home had been with vile and vicious men,
Who'd only taught him that the good and great
Were simply made for him to rob and hate : —
And all the wealth and splendor, round him strown,
Belonged to him no less than those that own ;
And 'twas his right, for blessings unpossessed,
To beg a portion, and to steal the rest.
And that poor boy, while yet so very young,
Lied, begged, swore, stole, nor dreamed of doing
        wrong,
For conscience ne'er upon his moral leaf
Had put one thought to check the little thief.

So while he walked beside that noble lad,
Who loved to see and make all others glad,
He, cold and shivering, 'midst the dusty storm,
And with a whine that rogues know how to form.

Begged for a trifle to procure a crumb
For his poor mother without bread at home.
And the boy gave the poor and shivering lad,
Glad he'd the power to make another glad; —
Yet that young villain, though he cried and whined,
Had no starved mother, who with hunger pined;
He took the shilling with a thankful look,
And then adroitly stole his pocket-book;
Then falling back he mixed among the train,
To find a chance to beg and rob again.

Just at that instant passing near the wall
Of an old building tottering to its fall,
A fiercer blast against the pile was sent,
And down the building into ruin went.
Beneath the weight the passers-by were crushed,
And all again was into silence hushed.
A few were killed, the most were mangled found,
But that young beggar came out safe and sound.
That generous boy who just had given relief,
And then been robbed by that unfeeling thief,
Was walking on, wreathed in a genial smile,
Out of the reach of that old crumbling pile,
When lo! a fragment like a leaden ball,
Shot far ahead out of the crumbling wall,
And that sweet boy, although so far before,
Was struck, and there lay weltering in his gore.

Strange, said the world, that God a blow should give,
That smote that boy, and let the villain live,
E'en when the thief was in the very path
Where the fierce wind-god swept along in wrath,
And that sweet boy had gone so far alas,
That he seemed safe beyond the falling mass.

How human wisdom in its pride will seize
And criticise such casualties as these,
And prove how much more natural to destroy
The little wretch, and spare the noble boy, —
And show by proofs as plain as noonday light,
Had God reversed it 'twould have been all right.
Like that young thief had that bright boy escaped,
With such a heart for virtue formed and shaped,
No tongue can tell of what surpassing worth
His life had been to this revolted earth,
And the best instincts of the heart had then
Cried, in a transport of delight, " Amen ! "
And had the thief been, like the good boy, crushed,
Those same good instincts had each murmur hushed,
The world had said that God had acted best,
And lofty reason kindly acquiesced ;
For that young rogue, while waxing worse and worse,
Would have been nothing but a social curse,
And to himself a constant source of woe, —
Been through all life his own most deadly foe.

When in our streets we've seen those wretched ones
Begging for bread and half-denuded bones,
And by feigned tears and simulated cries,
Make them pass current, their deceit and lies,
Then thought how Charlie, our dear, darling boy,
Had all he needed for his cup of joy, —
Had food, and clothes, and all that he required,
To be well fed and tidily attired,
And had a home, if not earth's very best,
With all but luxury furnished and possessed,
Where those that loved him clasped him to the breast,
And would have died to make their Charlie blest;
Yet Charlie died, with all these things to cheer,
While thousands live without one comfort here;
And our poor hearts will sometimes think and sigh,
Strange these should live and our dear Charlie die.

Was it a weakness with presumption fraught?
No matter what, our hearts will feel the thought,
And sometimes forced by such sad thoughts to melt.
Our hearts will whisper what they sadly felt,
Just as the world could not suppress its grief
When fell that good boy and survived the thief.

THE ARTIST AND HIS IDEAL.

THERE was an artist, had his humble home
Within the bosom of imperial Rome;
Midst her old ruins he had daily walked,
With Art's old masters he had daily talked,
Till, so in love with Nature's myriad charms,
He threw himself within her twining arms,
And, like a child, within her warm embrace,
Watched every change upon her lovely face.
He'd seen her mirrored midst the crumbling wrecks
And modern piles of earth's best architects;
He'd seen her springing from the shapeless block,
Riven from the quarries of the Parian rock;
He'd seen her gayly from dead canvas gush,
And live and breathe obedient to his brush,
And her own scenery of all tints and dyes,
In the mild azure of Italian skies,
And all the varying and bewitching miens
She takes to form her rich Italian scenes.
But still unsated with the luxury placed
Among the viands for his cultured taste,
There was one viand, one voluptuous dish,
That ne'er had sprung obedient to his wish:
He longed to see, and yet he knew not whence,
A perfect type of spotless innocence,

For he'd not seen the faultless picture yet,
Although he'd watched each form and face he met;
He'd seen the Pope, and tried in vain to trace
Its lineaments beneath those folds of lace,
He'd seen the Cardinals, clad in scarlet, rolled
Through Roman streets in chariots dressed in gold;
He'd seen the priests, old Rome's most common nouns,
In ugly hats and most ungraceful gowns,
And loathsome monks, in filthiest garments clad,
To show the world they're solemn, sour, and sad,
But 'mong them all, though sought with utmost care,
He did not find the gem he wanted there.
He'd seen the nuns in all their neat costumes,
Like lovely lilies in their snow-white blooms;
But howe'er fair, the picture was not fraught
With that sweet thing, the object that he sought;
The beau ideal that he wished to paint
Was not the child of penance and constraint;
The innocence that he was seeking there.
Must come from love and be as free as air,
Not merely known by badges and costumes,
But. like flowers, also by its rich perfumes;
And badge and costume, howe'er true, must be,
Like blossoms, outbursts of the parent tree.

He dreamed by night and he inquired by day,
Where is the jewel? Whither is the way?

He roved the halls of science and of art,
But did not find the vision of his heart;
He looked at Nature, — earth, and sea, and air, —
But did not find the bright creation there.

He roved beyond his usual rounds one day,
Among the tombs that skirt the Appian Way,
And then within the still Campagna roved,
But nowhere found the vision that he loved.
Then toward Frascati bent his steps, until
He reached the villa of the Alban Hill,
And ere scarce conscious, found that he had come
Up to the path that leads to Tusculum,
Whence Cato sprang, the censor of old Rome,
And Tulli wrote within his summer home.
He took the path and mounted up the hill,
Along where once was many a Roman ville,
Till, with an instinct that can never err,
He stood at Tusculum's ruined theatre;
And there he stopped and viewed the dappled west
Just at the hour red Phœbus sunk to rest:
The broad Campagna, by old arches spanned,
In endless lines, e'en though in ruins grand;
And farther on the ruins of old Rome,
And the huge grandeur of St. Peter's dome;
And farther west old Ostia's shimmering bay
In the dim twilight of departing day, —

'Twas lovely all, but the poor son of art
Found not the idol shrined within the heart.
He turned to go, but where he had to pass
An angel lay upon a tuft of grass:
A beauteous boy, surpassing sweet and fair,
Had lost his way, and thus lay sleeping there;
His little hands were crossed upon his breast,
A fresh-plucked flower was on his bosom pressed,
And unseen angels, bending o'er the child,
Were talking with him, and the cherub smiled.
Some little tear-drops on his sweet cheeks lay,
That he'd been shedding when he lost his way,
And tears and smiles in all their witchery wove,
Like shower and sunshine, made a thing to love;
And still he smiled, for still the angels talked,
And through the bowers of Paradise they walked;
And his lips moved, for round among the flowers
He walked and talked with angels in their bowers;
And fear and care bade not a ripple roll
Across the peaceful current of the soul, —
And like a being newly winged above,
Where each pulsation is a throb of love,
The sweet young spirit of that gentle boy
Was a pure gem of peace and love and joy;
So gazed the artist, for the beau ideal
Of his chaste fancy had become the real;
For innocence, he'd sought with sleepless care,

But never found, true to his dreams, was there;
And so he gazed, until the charming whole
Daguerreotyped his image on the soul;
And when again before his easel placed,
Out of his soul he drew the thing he traced,
Till on the canvas he beheld, with joy,
The mirrored image of that little boy,
The pure quintessence, not obscure and dim,
Of innocence's perfect synonyme.
"Eureka!" cried he, "for the victory's mine,"
And hung it up within his studio's shrine.

Long years had passed, and Innocence still hung
Within his home, extolled by every tongue,
And his own heart had daily feasts of joy,
Oft as he gazed upon that little boy;
But from the hour his magic pencil run
O'er the last line, and left the picture done,
His soul had yearned, with all an artist's pride,
To see Guilt's picture hanging at its side,
And he had roved by land and sea to find
The beau ideal cherished in his mind;
And though he'd found in many a face he'd seen
Some lineaments that mark the monster's mien,
And although some seemed demons black as night,
The blackest had some little gleams of light,
And 'twas, in fancy only, he had built
The loathsome fabric of unbroken guilt.

'Twas at a time when Nature's lovers stroll,
For feasts of reason and for flows of soul,
The artist left his studio and his care,
And walked abroad, it scarcely mattered where,
Till, having reached the Duke Colonna's lands,
He found himself where Paliano stands.
The dark old prison, the lion of the town,
Appeared to wear a more demoniac frown,
And guilt's dread children, from their gloomy cells,
Sent fiercely out their curses, shrieks, and yells,
And to fill full the harmony of their strains,
The clash of fetters and the clank of chains.
And soon he passed through the unbolted door,
The scenes within to study and explore;
From cell to cell he passed along, and leaned
'Gainst grated doors to see each prisoned fiend,
And his brain reeled as he beheld the trace
Of blackest guilt on every fiendish face;
Yet every one, howe'er of good bereft,
Had some slight trace of human nature left,
Some little marks that faintly seemed to tell,
'Twas not a demon, nor his prison a hell.

But there was one, whose cell was farther on,
From whom all human seemed forever gone;
The bloodshot eye, fierce brow, and matted hair,
Told but too plainly 'twas a demon there,

Not one pale beam or faintest tint of light
Shot through the darkness of his moral night,
But all was dark, and midnight round about
Had seemed to blot each trace of manhood out.

The artist viewed him with an earnest eye,
And scanned this demon of the darkest dye,
And shuddering cried, Whate'er the creature be,
'Tis just the monster that I've longed to see.

Few were the suns that ran their daily round,
Before the monster on the canvas frowned,
And then he saw, with all an artist's pride,
The fiend and cherub hanging side by side,
The perfect types, in contrast so immense,
Of blackest guilt and brightest innocence,
Where good and bad had left their typic trace,
To deck and mar the human form and face.

And then he'd daily look and study each,
And learn the lesson they were meant to teach.
Can such a cherub — no, he never can —
Become a creature like that monster man?
Or such a monster, when his race begun,
Have ever been that little cherub one?
And yet that monster was a boy whilom,
And he had parents and a pleasant home,

And those fond parents loved their cherub boy,
And that sweet home he filled with light and joy,
And love, blind love, predicted that his name
Would one day shine upon the scroll of fame.
He might have seemed in childhood's earliest spring
An innocent and very charming thing;
But had he then for his young portrait sat,
It could not sure have been a thing like that.

Mistaken artist, will it mar thy joy
To know that monster was that cherub boy?
And that the cherub, so angelic miened,
Became in manhood such a hideous fiend?
But so it is, — that boy, who first begun
So fair, so sweet, became that fiendish one.

God help our children, if the dear ones can
Become as loathsome as that hideous man,
And God help us, if culture or neglect
Can make them wrecks, as that sweet boy was
         wrecked.

We think of this, — and if it does not cheer,
It seems to dry up many and many a tear;
For though our Charlie surely never could
Have been aught else than sweet and kind and good,
Much less as hideous and deformed become

As that sweet boy that slept at Tusculum,
'Twas sweet to think that ere with cunning art
Guilt dropped a stain upon his spotless heart,
The Saviour came, and with a look of love,
Bore him in triumph to his home above,
Where not a stain can ever touch our boy,
And not a sorrow ever mar his joy.

O ! Charlie, Charlie, though our bosoms bleed,
We love to think that thou art blest indeed,
And that although we're sundered now in twain,
We soon shall meet our beauteous child again ;
Meet, not as now, to spend a few fleet years,
And part in sorrow, groans, and sighs, and tears,
But meet and sweetly mingle heart with heart,
Live, learn, and love, and never, never part ;
And then it sometimes gives us sweet relief
To think life here is so exceeding brief;
And hope's pulsations beat more full and strong,
To think hereafter life will be so long.

DEATH SELDOM COMES AT THE RIGHT TIME.

How seldom 'tis, in any age or clime,
Death claims his victims at the proper time.
Whate'er man is, whate'er he might have been,

Too soon or late Death thrusts his sickle in;
While on the road to honor and renown,
Death often comes and strikes the victim down,
Just freed from care, with boundless wealth in store,
The arrow flies, and it is his no more.
The warm-souled herald to the rescue flies,
When sorrow shrieks and trembling ignorance cries,
But in mid passage or but just ashore,
Expires or founders, and his mission's o'er;
The hale old man scarce reaching to decline,
Receives his summons when at ninety-nine,
And thinks 'tis hard, unfeeling, and severe,
God did not spare him to live out the year.

THE SAILOR.

I KNEW him well, a rover of the sea,
A braver tar you never saw than he,
At first a sailor, then in many a trip,
The gallant captain of a gallant ship;
Tears wet all faces when he went to roam,
And tears of joy whenever he came home.

A sparkling girl, who, in our social joys,
Was warmth and sunshine to the girls and boys,
Smiled on the sailor from the very start,

And sweetly gave him all he wished, — her heart;
And soon in gladness friends and kindred met
To see them tangled in the silken net;
And ne'er were seen a bridegroom and a bride
More full of joy than Ben and Zealide.

They lived and loved, united heart and heart,
Both when together and when far apart,
The bond of love from that domestic hearth
Oft stretched unbroken all around the earth.
Like olive plants their little prattlers sprung,
And sweetest perfumes o'er the homestead flung;
And each new cherub given them from above,
Gave added potence to the bond of love.

When the fierce wind-god swept along in wrath,
And carried death and havoc in his path,
How their hearts chilled to think that storm might be
Sweeping in anger o'er the troubled sea,
And he they loved, o'ertaken in his way,
Might be that moment in the deadly fray;
And how joy kindled in their bosoms when
Word came, "all safe," the vessel and the men!
And how sweet home run over with delight
At the glad tidings of "a sail in sight!"
And love grew lovelier when it looked to see
That manly form, and hear the word " 'Tis he."

Then came the presents, beauteous, rich, and rare,
Things to display and eat and drink and wear;
And more than these, those things that unpossessed,
Prevent e'en love from making households blest.

Three years had passed since, with his sails unfurled,
He had been cruising round and round the world;
And love was watching every hour at home
To see the lover and the father come.

At length it came, — the tidings came one day,
The gallant ship was coming up the Bay,
And o'er the Sound the steamer gliding hence
Bore the glad tidings on to Providence.

Home was astir, — all wore a merry air;
For in two days the rover would be there;
How oft they wished, and said it with a smile,
That Providence were on Manhattan Isle!
Then when the vessel into port had come,
The gallant captain would have been at home;
But ah! two days! — it seemed an age before
They should behold his pleasant face once more.

But time does fly, though snail-like to the mind,
That flies so swift it leaves old Time behind;
Hope will, so swiftly, towards the guerdon go,

It chides the hours and calls them very slow;
And when we sit at pleasure's sweet repast,
We chide old Time, and think he moves too fast.
Between the murderer and the fatal day
Days are but moments, but an inch of way;
But placed between the lover and his home,
It seems long ages in the time to come.
But time will move, — the captain, with his freight,
Leaped on the steamer, buoyant and elate;
And then he said, while looking round and round,
" Why was Long Island made so long a Sound?
Twelve, fourteen hours, it may be many more,
Ere I shall land on dear Rhode Island's shore;
Still 'tis no matter, — I'll my state-room keep,
And spend the moments in unconscious sleep,
Then, though *'tis* long ere those dear ones I see,
'Twill be a moment, only that, to me."

He slept and dreamed, — arrayed in all her charms,
His wife had rushed within his circling arms,
The children gabbled like so many geese,
And kissed and kissed him twenty times apiece,
And he and they kept wondering o'er and o'er
Why 'twas each other had not altered more;
Then came the presents, brilliant, rich, and rare,
Designed for each, and sought with nicest care;
And last the treasures after which he'd roved

And earned, to bless the little ones he loved.
" Enough," said he, " I've gained enough and more,
I'll stay henceforth with those I love on shore ;
Farewell old ocean, with thy restless main,
I ne'er shall battle with your waves again ;
Howl, howl, mad tempest, lash the waves and roar,
You'll no more harm me, high and dry ashore ;
Ye winds blow, blow, snap off the shrouds and spars,
Toss up the billows till they quench the stars, —
'Tis nought to me, I care not for your strife,
I'm with my children, living with my wife,
I've now enough for life's entire supply,
'Tis all I wish for till the day I die."

Fire ! fire ! He wakes, — the flames are flashing
        high,
And the red tempest lights the ebon sky ;
Groans, cries, and tears, from terror and affright,
Fill the grand chorus of that awful night ;
And ere the echo of that chorus died,
Ship, cargo, all lay silent 'neath the tide ;
Some, for a moment, struggled with the wave,
But baffled sunk to their unhonored grave.
The home-bound captain, with the wealth he'd won,
Slept midst the ashes of the Lexington.

But at his home, nor sleep nor dreams had they,
They all sat watching for the break of day;
Aurora first sent up her saffron streams,
Red Phœbus followed with his ruddy beams;
Hour after hour of broad and open day,
In quick succession came and went away,
Till the bright daylight into twilight grew,
And night threw o'er her dome of stars and blue,
When tidings came, first whispered faintly round,
The ship is lost and all on board are drowned.
Next came the news: the ship is tempest tossed,
Burned and disabled, but not wholly lost;
Now good, now bad, the flying rumors came, —
First, she was safe, then, perished in the flame,
Till the dread message proved, alas! too true, —
The ship was lost, and all were drowned but two.
But two? the names! O no! the deed is done,
But two are saved, but he, alas! not one;
But still hope flickered, and could not go out,
Till time passed on and brushed away the doubt.

Ah, human wisdom, how much more divine
Thou wouldst have done it, had the work been thine!
For three long years he'd suffered, toiled, and roved,
To bless the group that he so dearly loved,
And thou wouldst sure have wafted safe along
Him and his treasures to the little throng.

Yes, human reason sees with half an eye,
'Twas not the time for such an one to die.

Ah! noble reasoner, should the bolt have come,
While he was feeling the first thrill of home?
If not, tell when the arrow should have sped,
Wise seer, who canst not see an inch ahead.

THE INVENTOR.

A FEW years since, within a country ville,
There lived a youth of splendid taste and skill.
'Twas his delight, absorbed in thought profound,
To rove invention's yet untrodden ground;
He loved to pierce the pall of moral night,
And by his fiat bring out rays of light;
He loved to soar on thought's far-spreading wing,
And out of chaos, perfect order bring,
And of rude matter, at his plastic will,
Bring out creations of consummate skill;
He loved to watch the great world's ceaseless buzz,
And all the phases of the work it does,
Then, from the mysteries that in matter lurk,
Bring out the witcheries that can do the work;
He sometimes dreamed of that millennial day
When, matter working, men should only play.

His was a soul whose living cords were found
In harmony always with the charms of sound;
The soft piano, touched with well-trained art,
Thrilled every fibre of his tuneful heart,
And music's spirit floated on the breeze,
When his light finger touched the ivory keys;
But oft he thought, when playing Zion's lays,
Where social groups sang to their Maker's praise,
How sweet 'twould be if, like the organ's tones,
His own piano's could be lengthened ones,
Then like an organ in our social throngs
He could play sweetly Zion's sacred songs;
Can some device be conjured into view,
So that pianos can be organs too?
Some novel charm or new contrivance found,
So that each key shall give a lengthened sound?

He sought — he found; the youthful songster spoke,
And out of chaos all he wanted woke.
The world beholding in amazement stood,
And, smiling, called the new creation "good;"
Wealth flowed in streams, Pactolus-like, and brought
A golden harvest for the achievement wrought;
Fame, soon as Science had his praises said,
Wove laurelled wreaths for his unlaurelled head,
And Science, smiling, placed his humble name
Among earth's honored on the scroll of fame;

Till making rich the ones he loved at home,
He turned his steps in foreign climes to roam,
For fame stood beckoning on the Old World's shore,
And fortune, smiling, asked him to come o'er.
He went, saw, conquered. Lords and ladies smiled,
And lavished praise on fortune's foster-child,
Earls came to see him, dukes to hear him play,
And prince and princess their respects to pay,
And taste and learning hung with thrills of joy
Upon the music of that Yankee boy,
And England's queen, within her palace walls,
Bade him with music charm her royal halls.
Where'er he went, with unassuming air,
He was the observed of all observers there,
And public papers set the tidings down,
When the young charmer chanced to come to town;
And if gross flattery could have spoiled that one,
That youthful rover would have been undone.
Thus honored, praised and fêted and caressed,
With new wealth added to the wealth possessed,
Yet unseduced by flattery's siren smile,
And unenchained to England's queenly isle,
With thoughts of home still thrilling in his breast,
On wings of love he hastened to the west,
Where home stood brimming with bewitching charms,
Sweet smiles, warm hearts, kind cheers, and open
    arms,

Where, on the fortune God had deigned to give,
He and his loved ones could delighted live.

How sweet to think that merit can enjoy
The rich full harvest of its own employ;
That modest merit, when the deed is done,
Can wear the laurels it has fairly won;
That genius, poor, unfriended, and alone,
Can sometimes reap the harvest it has sown,
And genuine worth, by its own powers of mind,
Grow sometimes rich and still is good and kind.

So felt his country when her son, once more,
Planted his foot upon his native shore,
And all hearts wished him, with his well-earned
    wealth,
A long, long life of happiness and health.

He reached his home unspoiled by flattery's arts,
And there he met with open doors and hearts;
Hope bade him welcome to its feasts of joy,
And fortune smiled upon her favorite boy,
And reason kindly called it right and wise,
That he that earned it should enjoy the prize,
And common sense declared 'twas very plain
That one so worthy should enjoy the gain,
And common justice would indignant frown,

To cut so early conquering genius down,
E'en at the moment when his toils have ceased,
And he's scarce tasted of the well-earned feast.

Ah! human Reason, prophet, judge, and guide,
In one short week that son of genius died,
And that sweet home that just his welcome said,
Now rudely pushed him from its portals, dead;
And the rich prize for which he'd labored so,
Dropped into hands that ne'er had struck a blow,
And Reason frowned that Death should throw his dart,
At such a time, at such a noble heart,
And really rob him, though but just returned,
Of that rich prize that he'd so nobly earned.

But human Reason and that Christian youth
Held different views of justice, right, and truth;
For on his bed, when told that he must die,
He said, " All's well, sweet Paradise is nigh;
Home, home, sweet home, O! sing me now that song,
That on its harmony I may float along;
Home was my dream where'er I went to roam,
And now, O! now, I'm really going home;
Wealth, fare thee well, you've had no time to get
Your reign established in my bosom yet,
I've wealth above, untinctured with alloy,
That ne'er will fade nor fail to give me joy."

And so he died, and with faith-lighted eye,
He felt, he saw, 'twas just his time to die;
But human Reason still persists to find,
'Tis not in harmony with the good and kind.

THE RIGHT TIME TO DIE.

WHEN the Great Teacher meekly closed his eye,
And said, " 'Tis finished," 'twas his time to die.
His work accomplished and his mission o'er,
Why should he linger for a moment more?
Heaven's portals lifted for the King to come,
And his dear Father kindly asked him home.

When the ripe Christian, full of hope and love,
And whose heart-treasures are laid up above,
Resigned and calm lays down his aching head
In vain for rest upon his dying bed,
And yet whose spirit sweetly sinks to rest,
In downy ease upon a Saviour's breast,
Till quite forgetting he's with anguish riven,
His spirit revels midst the joys of heaven,
Breathes the fresh odors fanned from angel-wings,
Lists to the music heaven's assembly sings,
And lives in heaven with rapture all aglow,
E'en while the body writhes in pain below,

Go tell him, friendship, living, is a boon,
And that 'tis hard that he should die so soon;
He don't believe you, for 'tis all so plain,
That to die now, would be his dearest gain;
And when you tell him 'tis too soon to die,
If he make any, this is his reply:
Fly swifter round ye lagging wheels of time,
And waft me upward to a happier clime;
Avaunt, poor earth! you're poor beyond compare,
To that bright world just o'er the river there.

None seeing this and hearing this would, sure,
Say such a death is late or premature.

But there are cases that the world observes,
Where some few glimpses shock its moral nerves,
And when they seem love's harmony to derange,
As if omniscient, it exclaims, 'Tis strange!
When the young truant feels correction's lash,
The eyes of love with indignation flash;
Why should affection plant so keen a smart,
So inharmonious to the loving heart?
It grates harsh discord in affection's ear,
The sigh, the cry, the shriek of woe to hear;
But when that child, 'neath stern affection's rule,
Grows fond of books, of study, and of school,
And, what is more to fond affection's eyes,

Becomes more loving as he grows more wise,
O! then it feels, to judge aright an act,
One must weigh also each collateral fact,
See if, or not, its true vibrations blend
In faultless harmony onward to the end;
Thus to proud Reason, with no prescient skill,
He kindly whispers in its ear, " Be still!"

THE LITTLE MARTYR.

I know a man of cultured heart and mind,
In learning lofty and in taste refined;
His wife, accomplished, seems expressly sent
To be that husband's fitting complement,
And home is, therefore, but the magic spot,
Where love, peace, joy, are all in harmony wrought;
But still affliction has presumed to come,
And plant its anguish in that happy home.
So oft, so keen, the arrow that was thrown,
I scarcely dare to think about my own;
Four times the hearse had driven to that door,
Till one by one it robbed that home of four;
One little fellow running o'er with charms
Was dashed in pieces in his mother's arms, —
And now that hearse was at the door again,
To bear away the fifth young martyr slain.

He was a cripple, but with heart and mind
Of heaven's most noble and most lofty kind;
Though but a boy by sickness worn and wan,
He was, in spirit, every inch a man.

I heard the father tell the story, where
We'd met, one evening, at the place of prayer,
And then I wondered how, at such a blow,
He could have borne the crushing load of woe;
My poor boy's death seemed but a scene of joy,
Beside the death-pangs of that suffering boy.

The time had come when that young sufferer's
        life
Had but one resource — it was surgery's knife;
He'd suffered long, and yet the almost saint
Had never spoke one murmur or complaint;
He'd borne it all for many and many an hour,
With all a Christian's, all a martyr's, power;
And when the day for the new trial rose,
And a fresh pang must mingle with his woes,
The little hero's prayer-stayed spirit stood
Firm as a rock that stems old ocean's flood,
And heartless surgery scarce seemed calmer than
The pure calm spirit of that embryo man.

How stoic-like the surgeon's hand applied
The glittering knife to that young martyr's side!
And cut and hewed again, again, again,
Till the poor boy seemed almost cut in twain;
But not a groan, not one impatient word,
Was, midst his agony, for a moment heard.

At length 'twas done — the dreadful torture o'er,
And stern-eyed Science quickly left the door;
And there he lay, that little suffering child,
And toward his parents sweetly looked and smiled.
He dreamed of life and health and future joys,
When he could run and walk like other boys;
And hope, fond hope, with its bewitching spell,
Made him appear, just in the future, well:
He saw himself robust in mind and frame,
No longer sickly and no longer lame,
And then he thanked his heavenly friend once more,
That the dread ordeal he had passed was o'er.
Poor boy! he knew not agony like this,
Compared to that so soon to come, was bliss, —
That the dread ordeal, yet to come, would be
The keenest pang of bitterest agony.

In two days more, stern Science must again
Reope the wound and reproduce the pain, —
Nay, cause a torture so intense and keen,

A fiend might weep to see the dreadful scene;
Yet 'twas a boy that must that torture bear, —
A poor meek boy that lay all helpless there.
The moment came, and skill again had come,
At Science' bidding, to that weeping home,
And, with a touch soft as it could employ,
Dressed the dread wound of that poor suffering boy,
And shrieks and groans that ne'er were heard before
Now told the tortures the young sufferer bore.

'Twas done at last, and calm and peaceful rest
Soothed, for a moment, his o'eranguished breast;
And yet, God help him! — for the health he sees
Is reached — if reached — through tortures such as
      these.

The appointed time was almost at the door,
When the poor victim must be tortured more;
And when he thought of that dread scene again,
Of keenest torture and intensest pain,
He said, "Dear father, is there not a way,
To 'scape the anguish of that awful day?"
"My son, I fear not; the physicians know,
And say, in sorrow, that it must be so."

"But go and ask them, if they'll not, alas!
Permit this cup, this bitter cup, to pass."

He went and came, and going to his son,
Said, " My dear boy, 'tis so, it must be done.

" But you're my father, you've a right to say,
And 'tis the surgeon's duty to obey."

" O ! my dear son, 'twould fill my heart with joy,
Could I but suffer for my darling boy ;
All I can do is, try my best to save
The little life that God so kindly gave.
God gave you life, — 'tis yours to try to live,
Nor throw away what God has deigned to give ;
Nor you nor I can pierce these forms we wear,
And find disease and bring assistance there ;
'Tis just as dangerous and as far from right,
To work in darkness as neglect in light.
No, 'twould be wrong to issue my command,
And take you from the skilful surgeon's hand ;
I *cannot* then ; God gives the bitter cup,
And he will bless you, if you drink it up ;
Think how the Saviour suffered on the tree,
Not for his sins, but those of you and me."

The poor boy heard, and, overwhelmed with grief,
His whole frame quivering like an aspen leaf, —

" No friend to help me," said he, with a sigh.
Then I'll ask Jesus — He will hear my cry."

He closed his eyes, and clasped his hands, and there
His sweet lips moved as if in silent prayer;
His frame grew calm, he oped his eyes and smiled.
And said, " I've asked Him. He will help your child."

When, the next morn, the surgeons oped the door,
They found that Jesus had arrived before ;
And there He hovered o'er the sufferer's bed,
And calmed his heart and soothed his restless head,
And, in a moment, with a look, all kind,
He bore him up and left his wounds behind.

At such a scene proud Reason shrinks away.
And feels there's nothing it can safely say,
'Tis mystery, all, e'en to its piercing eye,
And if e'er fathomed, 'twill be by and by.
E'en scepticism the verdict would not give.
That such a sufferer should be left to live :
But Christian faith sees 'tis the purest love
That took that boy to realms of bliss above.

He had his mission, — 'twas a noble one,
And nobly, proudly was the mission done,
And many a soul may reach a home of joy

By seeing how faith sustained a little boy;
For faith ne'er helped a martyr here below
Bear up a bitterer, heavier load of woe;
And few who've come on this dim earth to dwell
Have lived and suffered and have died as well;
And 'twere the sheerest folly to maintain
That such a martyr lived and died in vain.

'Tis sweet, dear Charlie, to reflect that you
Had no such fiery furnace to go through,
But your pure spirit took its upward flight,
Sweet as the twilight fades away to-night, —
No shrieks or throes among the memories twine
Of that pure, calm, and peaceful death of thine.

THE TWO BROTHERS.

An honored pair, not many years whilom,
Lived, loved, and labored, in a happy home;
Their lives were sureties for their strength and health,
And wisdom taught them how to use their wealth.
They had two sons, — bright, active, healthy boys,
The warmth and sunshine of their home-felt joys;
And 'twas to them their pride and their delight,
To guide their minds and train their hearts aright.
And they were trained, and they were wisely taught,
Until from boyhood up to manhood brought;

When well prepared they went away to roam,
Each the young patriarch of a new-formed home;
And happier men were never seen than they
At their new homesteads on their wedding-day.

Life now began, with all its calms and storms,
With all its sweeter and its bitterer forms;
And which should rule, life's future good or ill,
Must be the product of their power and skill;
And so they knew, and so they felt, and so
To life's stern duties they resolved to go.

Long years had passed, and years of change to hosts,
But these two brothers still were at their posts;
Both had stood firm where myriads had been wrecked,
And both secured men's friendship and respect;
But one to wealth and one to want was heir,
Though both had toiled with equal skill and care;
Whene'er one struck, beneath the plastic blow
The streams of wealth were sure to burst and flow;
The other smote with just as strong a stroke,
But not a rill from the dry earth awoke,—
Whate'er one did was sure of golden gain,
Whate'er the other, seemed alas in vain!
Men thought them equal, both in power and skill,
With equal zeal their mission to fulfil,
But, with the contrast in their stations struck,

They called it luck, or called it lack of luck;
Although some said a faculty was what
A man must have to gain a happy lot;
But whate'er 'twas, one thing was very sure:
The one was rich, the other very poor.
Within the cottage where the poor man dwelt
Six little sons beside his altar knelt;
While in the mansion of the other, one
Was all he had, — a pure and noble son.
'Twas toil and thrift composed the poor man's stock,
To train and clothe and feed his little flock;
And scarce a day he did not feel perplexed,
From whence would come subsistence for the next;
And were it not he'd a kind brother near,
Who loved to send him many a boon, to cheer
Both cold and hunger, many a poor man's lot
Had been familiar in that humble cot.

The sweetest pleasure and the purest joy
That thrilled the bosom of the rich man's boy,
Was, when his cousins came with him to roam
O'er his green fields and in his spacious home,
And feast their souls on all around them stored,
And feast their bodies at his father's board.

Oh! 'twas a feast whene'er they went to play,
And rove the fields upon a Summer's day;

And the feast lasted not that day alone,
But blest the hours of many a following one;
For joy's vibrations, days and days, were felt,
In the thatched cottage where the poor man dwelt;
And when these ended, though they *never* ceased,
Anticipation spread another feast.
And in that home, with plenty unpossessed,
The past and future made the present blest.

They loved each other, all these cousin boys,
And love, the purest of their purest joys;
Their bond of love was never once untied
By pride or envy upon either side,
And the poor home 'scaped many a want and woe,
Thrilled by the rich one's generous overflow.
Still they oft suffered, for the rich know not
How oft there's suffering in the poor man's lot;
One half man's miseries would be overthrown.
Were their existence always seen and known;
The sensitive wish, not that their sighs and tears
Be seen and heard by others' eyes and ears,
And want would rather bear misfortune's blows
Than be forever harping on its woes.
True kindness does not reach its loftiest height,
When soothing suffering ready brought to light,
But when it soothes it, begging at its door;
And, like a Howard, goes and seeks for more.

So the rich brother would have given the poor
Whate'er of comfort riches could procure;
But life's stern duties, like huge mountains soared
'Twixt his kind heart and brother's scanty board.
So busy life, like Belial's heartless priests,
Oft keeps pure goodness from its daintiest feasts,
As without malice thoughtless Christians even
Keep, by example, myriads out of heaven.

'Twas at a time, when happy, light, and gay,
The boys had met to spend a holiday,
And they were roving in their usual rounds,
All o'er the rich man's pleasant rural grounds;
The heavens grew black, as with an ebon shroud,
And the whole sky seemed one unbroken cloud,
The lightnings flashed, the grumbling thunder roared,
And the full shower its dancing torrents poured.
The laughing cousins for the covert run,
Showers did not fright them, — they afforded fun:
They hied for shelter to a grove of green,
Where spreading branches formed a partial screen,
And there they sat, and from that leafy bower,
They watched the progress of that merry shower,
And oft looked up to see if heaven's clear blue
Above their heads were really looking through;
Just then a flash, a sudden roar above,
The red bolt sped to that same sheltering grove;

Limb after limb was twisted off and sent
Among the boys beneath the branches bent;
All were unhurt of that gay group, but one,
He lay a corpse, — it was the rich man's son.

The world said, Strange the red bolt was not sped
Upon some other's than his pleasant head;
That crowded household, had the deed been done,
Out of its inmates, might have given one.

Had human Reason had that bolt to throw,
Not that kind boy had felt the fatal blow;
He would have bade the fatal shaft transfix,
Out of the poor man's starving, needy six.
Then the poor father, though of one bereft,
Had felt he'd five bright little fellows left;
And Reason thinks, had he but ordered so,
All our best instincts had approved the blow;
One blest with plenty would have been alive,
And the poor household had the living five.

O! my dear boy! 'twas not for human wit
To say whose head Death's shining bolt should hit,
For then, methinks, my little blue-eyed boy
Had still been here to fill our home with joy.

The "Chadwick Knot" Brownfield's

THE LITTLE GENIUS.

THERE is a household that I know full well,
Where two fond parents love-cemented dwell;
In that sweet home, while it was fresh and young,
A beauteous boy of golden promise sprung;
But the fond bosom, where it first was pressed,
At length went up to throb among the blest.
Another came, and that beloved son
Found it as downy as the natural one.
The first had flown, like some enchanting bird,
But its sweet echoes still each bosom stirred,
And the new voice, in perfect harmony set,
Changed the old trio to a new quartette.

Whate'er life's toils, perplexities, and cares,
A happy home of buoyant hearts was theirs,
And had Religion not been there to check,
Joy's dancing life-boat might have been a wreck;
But she was there, and ruled the helm so well
That they were happy whatsoe'er befell.
E'en from the first the prophecy began
That that young boy would be no common man;
The fire of Genius, like Isaiah's coal,
Fresh from her altar, kindled his young soul,
And as along through boyhood he careered,

Fresh scintillations at each step appeared,
And feats of skill, by him contrived and planned,
Leaped into being from his cunning hand;
And young Invention, starting at his will,
Showed magic worthy of a veteran's skill;
And books allured, and learning had her charms,
And Truth bewitching clasped him in her arms,
And though, boy-like, of play and sport brimful,
He was a star in social life and school.
Unlike those strange, precocious things of earth
That come like Pallas, all equipped at birth,
Who, men in boyhood, dazzle earth, and then
Play out their manhood, and grow stupid men,
He, ever active, never, like a shirk,
Left intuition to perform the work,
Nor wished to find, however toil might frown,
A royal road to honor and renown.

Health, rosy goddess, by preëmptive claim,
Reigned in each fibre of his manly frame,
And seemed to say, as with a prophet tongue,
That that bright genius would not perish young.

Religion's spirit, like the falling dew,
Dropped on his heart and thrilled it through and
          through,
And his young being, with her spirit fraught,

Seemed all in harmony with the truths she taught;
The little altar that he'd reared to Heaven
Ne'er lacked his presence either morn or even,
And life with him, e'en while but yet a boy,
Was full of play, but fuller of employ;
Work, study, frolic, piety, and play,
All wreathed in harmony, filled each passing day,
And all believed, who used his life to scan,
That such a boy would be a useful man.

Ah! that home knew not how much of its joy
Sprang from the gift of such a noble boy;
For if high hopes had ever cause to start
And fill the chambers of a parent's heart,
'Twas these two bosoms, in whose down that boy
So oft had nestled for his feast of joy,
And, with life's sun declining in the west,
They hoped, in turn, to nestle in his breast.

Cold, shivering Winter had begun to show
Signs of relenting, with its frost and snow;
The snow-banks swooned, and frost's chill fetters
        broke,
And rills unnumbered into action woke;
First silver threads come trickling down the way,
Then others join, and down the hill-sides play,
Till, reinforced by swooning ice and snow,

They swell to torrents, and like torrents flow,
And rush and leap, resistless in their track,
Until they plunge within the Merrimack;
And others come that young Niagaras seem,
That plough their way and plunge within the stream,
Till the old river, from these fierce attacks,
Swells to the size of twenty Merrimacks,
And its green valley seems at length to be,
Not a green valley, but an inland sea;
And lo! at length, the swelling waters come
Within the precincts of that happy home,
And in scooped hollows fiercely plunging, make
In many a field full many a mimic lake.

Our little genius, merrier than a lark,
Had built his craft, and hastened to embark,
And, as commander, he began to make
A hasty voyage around the little lake,
But the young helmsman, steering from the strand,
Like Palinurus, never came to land.

That day at school the little boys discussed
The different ways that dust returns to dust;
Each tyro told how he'd prefer to die,
And gave his reasons, all substantial, why;
Each chose the way, whene'er life's journey ceased,
Whose sufferings were, in his opinion, least;

And little Henry told, at last, his views,
And what the mode of dying he would choose;
Methinks, to go within the crystal wave
Would be the easiest passage to the grave;
O! when I go, if God should think it best,
Let me be rocked within the waves to rest,
Where unassailed by sickness' ghastly train,
And all unscarred by violence or by pain,
I may lie down within the crystal deep
As calm and life-like as if fallen asleep;
Then, when fond love shall look its last adieu,
I shall not be a loathsome thing to view,
But pleasant object over which they'll bend,
And love to think of to their journey's end.

That very day, ere eve her dews had shed,
Henry was lying in his watery bed.

Had human Reason guided at the helm,
And been the Neptune of that watery realm,
He would have bidden Henry's little boat
Bear its freight safely o'er the lake afloat;
Then, when the frolic and the sail were o'er,
Bring the young mariner safe and sound ashore;
Or, if a victim must be taken, take
Some ragged boy and plunge him in the lake;
And man, wise man, without a moment's pause,
Had given the deed his heartiest applause.

And hast thou, man, the wisdom to divine
Which had been best, God's providence or thine ?
Who, though thou triest until the " crack of doom,"
Canst never pierce one inch beyond the tomb ;
Nor though with sages and with seers to guide,
Hast power to pierce one inch ahead this side.
'Tis not God's way, His glory to insure,
To deal His vengeance only on the poor,
Nor when he deals an unexpected blow,
Smite only those who're unprepared to go ;
Nor yet, whene'er he bids a mortal come,
Take but the stupid and the vicious home.
He sees each link of cause's endless chain,
And feels each pulse throughout his broad domain,
And knows exactly, by an errless test,
What Providence is wisest, kindest, best.
And the wise parent, howe'er sad, is awed,
And feels 'tis best to leave it all to God.

THE ONLY SON.

I KNEW a mother, polished and refined,
Grace thrilled her heart, and learning filled her
      mind, —
A model lady, modest, kind, and true,—

Beloved, admired by every one that knew.
She had one son, a bright and blooming boy,
To train whom rightly was her highest joy ;
Not weak and blind, 'twas with a lynx-eyed skill,
She watched his faults and trained his stubborn will,
Pruned each excrescence, checked each tortuous
    growth,
To make all vigorous and symmetric both ;
And all that saw, foretold, with seer-like joy,
A life of honor for that noble boy.
And that fond mother prayed and taught and toiled,
That her dear boy might not be praised and spoiled.

The child was ill, and round his weary bed
She bent and moved with quick and careful tread,
Watched every symptom, every light and shade,
And the best skill invited to his aid ;
And as she saw him daily fade away
And still grow weaker each succeeding day,
Earth's hopes, joys, treasures, all alike grew dim,
For if her boy died, all would die with him.
O ! how she prayed that her dear child might live, —
The sweetest boon that God had power to give !
But still he languished, still from day to day
She saw him sadly droop and fade away !
Till the sad truth before her seemed to ope :
Your boy must die, there is no longer hope ;

Then, in the blackness of her deep despair,
She bowed and knelt and shrieked aloud her prayer:

" God spare my child, — O ! spare my darling son ;
God spare my boy, — he is my only one ;
Take any blessing from me, O ! my God,
But spare my boy, and I will kiss the rod ;
Deny all else, whate'er the blessing be,
But leave my own dear darling boy to me.
I must not lose him, O ! withhold the blow —
O, spare the child — I cannot let him go."

She could not say, — Spare my beloved son, —
" Yet not as I will — let thy will be done, — "
And so God spared him, as the mother prayed ;
O ! 'twas a miracle, everybody said.
The kind physicians gave the matter o'er,
They'd done their utmost, and they could, no more,
And they had told her, — told her with a sigh,
Skill has done all, — your little boy must die.
And when God saved him, suffering, dying there,
The mother felt that God had heard her prayer.

And so he lived, — and twenty years from then,
That boy lay chained within a felon's den,
And justice waited at the outer door,
To swing him off and all would then be o'er ;

And but one joy was with her sorrows blent:
'Twas that her poor son died a penitent.

O! my poor boy, upon the bended knee,
With all our hearts, how warm our prayers for thee!
And then we prayed that God would let us give
Our own lives up, if our dear boy might live;
We dared not say, — We cannot spare our son,
But always added, — "Let thy will be done."
And when God took thee and refused our prayer.
We felt he did it to attract us there.

And ever since, we've felt it in the heart,
We soon shall meet thee, never more to part;
And then we think that God did hear us pray.
And gave the blessing in the heavenliest way.
We prayed that Charlie might continue ours,
To make life pleasant within home's sweet bowers.
The prayer was heard, — the blessing will be given, —
To bless life's future in our home in heaven.

BENEFIT OF AFFLICTIONS.

AH, me! how sorrow will the bosom scathe,
That is too wise to need the aid of faith,
To yield obedience to a blind command,

Or take a truth it cannot understand.
When sorrow comes, the bitter is complete,
Unintermingled with a single sweet;
The stoic WILL, with anæsthetic care,
May blunt the soul till it has power to bear,
Or time's attritions wear the edge of grief,
Till the sad heart-throes issue in relief.
It does not heed, or else it is to spurn,
The useful lesson sorrow gives to learn,
And so no crown is given him for the cross,
And no gain issues from the dreadful loss;
He loses, when affliction drops from heaven,
The sweetest lesson God has ever given.

O! sweet Affliction, when we use it right,
It brings a feast of unalloyed delight,
And in this life how few of all that weep,
The glorious harvest, sorrow offers, reap!
When mind gets tangled in the web of thought.
How sweetly faith can cut the Gordian knot!
When dear ones leave us, and from earth remove,
Faith whispers sweetly, it was done in love;
And what we cannot understand below,
Faith kindly comes and freely lets us know.
Our Charlie died; — the fact alone was plain,
The cause and purpose nothing could explain,
Till faith assured us it was done in love,

To bid us look to purer joys above.
Are earth's attractions fewer or less fair?
Heaven's are more numerous now that he is there.
One of the sweetest sources of your joy
Was sweet communion with your darling boy;
You need not lose it, — still commune, and this
Will help attract you to a home of bliss;
You've darlings yet, — let not an earthly love
Outdraw the ties attracting you above;
Another blow might be, in kindness, sent,
Another bond of earthly love be rent;
The traveller meets more dangers here below
Who moves in pleasure than who wades in woe.
Prosperity has led more souls astray
Than its black rival ever frowned away.
Our little ones, the source of so much joy,
Oft siren-like enchant us and destroy,
And our kind Father, full of pity, sees,
Strikes down the siren, and the captive frees.
When life goes well, how pleasant poor earth seems,
Fair as a landscape that we see in dreams;
And e'en the good man, without some rebuff,
Acts as if life were really quite enough.
But let him lose some dear and precious things,
Let wealth fly off upon its yellow wings,
Let his sweet children from his heart be rent,
Or dear companions into darkness sent,

And then he thinks of bright possessions lost,
And dreams of brighter on a heavenly coast;
And then he thinks of his dear ones above,
And then of Him whose very name is love,
And feels when he, on Jordan's further side,
Wakes with His likeness, he'll be satisfied.

THE MERCHANT.

I KNEW a man, and loved him as a friend,
And watched his history to his journey's end;
With a clear head and genial heart, he moved
Midst friends and kindred, loving and beloved.
The fields of Science and the fields of Art
Possessed few witcheries for his mind and heart;
He sought for knowledge, not the most or least,
'Twas not to him a penance or a feast.
So my friend fed on Science and on Art,
But to gain strength for what he had at heart;
And that he gained sufficient for the strife
That traffic brings along the path of life, —
Two objects always beckoned him before,
First to be rich, then liberal with his store:
By thrift and labor, study, toil, and care,
To gain the station of a millionnaire;
And both while gaining, and of wealth possessed,

To use it freely, making others blest.
Not love of fame inspired his heart alone,
For genuine kindness had, within, a throne ,
And to have wealth, and having, not to give,
Had made it misery, made it woe, to live ;
And with a heart as generous as his own,
Joy had died out to share his wealth alone.

Thus he began and wealth flowed in apace,
And streams flowed out earth's sorrows to efface ;
And though gain was not at life's board the least,
Yet Charity was the dessert of the feast.
But year by year trade multiplied affairs,
And added business brought him added cares,
And just inversely as his gains increased,
The pleasant dessert vanished at the feast.
Not that he meant, as long as he should live,
To lose the luxury that it gave, to give ;
But fortune's favors so like sirens smiled,
His hours were captured and his thoughts beguiled ;
And suffering found it harder every year
To tell its story and to gain his ear,
For whene'er going to the Merchant's door,
They found that business had gone in before.

All went on smoothly, — Commerce's merry sails
Seemed always filled with only prosperous gales ;

Gain came so flush, it took him night and day,
To count the sum, and stow the sum away,
Until, at length, with all his treasures there,
Men set him down a solid millionnaire.

And on he moved, as smoothly as a dream,
Down the gay current of life's merry stream;
Wealth filled his coffers ever brimming o'er,
And each new moment only added more;
Adversity ne'er mingled with his lot,
Till he had almost such a thing forgot,
And life, all lovely as the hues of even,
Seemed good enough, without a future heaven.
His earthly feast was so surpassing sweet,
He quite forgot some had but crumbs to eat;
And worse than this, he'd quite forgot that some,
E'en his near neighbors, had not e'en a crumb.
Thus 'midst the billows of old Traffic tost,
He did not dream how much he daily lost.

But God looked on with all a father's care,
And saw the dangers that beset him there,
And — out of pity, out of love, 'twas done —
Struck down his only well-beloved son;
And said, " Perhaps, if I remove a part
Of all the cares that cluster round his heart,
He will, once more, poor Sorrow's patron be,
And e'en, perhaps, may give his heart to me.

O! how the father staggered 'neath that stroke!
With a sad heart — alas! 'twas almost broke —
He tried, in vain, amidst affliction's blows,
To bear his burdens and endure his woes;
At last he roused him, and he said I can,
And I will be, from this good hour, a man.
And then, more deeply plunging in affairs,
He banished sorrow by his added cares,
And bidding business take each wish and thought,
His pangs were hushed and all his woes forgot;
Or if, perhaps, his sorrows, half suppressed,
Did sometimes grate harsh discord in his breast,
Seen on the canvas of his pictured bliss,
It only seemed an ugly cicatrice.
And life passed on as merry as a dream,
And gain came flowing in a yellow stream,
And then he thought, if he did think, how strange!
There are no poor folks! what has caused the
     change?
They used to come — whole flocks of ragged poor —
Around my warehouse and my mansion door,
And I would give them, till their sorrows ceased,
And always found that 'twas my sweetest feast;
I lose it now, — the dessert, once so sweet, —
We have no poor, and want is obsolete.
Poor man! — it never entered in his mind,

That want was near him, but himself was blind, —
Nay, within hearing, on her ragged bed,
A mother starved, and children cried for bread;
But time passed smoothly, princely fortune smiled,
And her rich treasures in his coffers piled,
And the poor rich man scarce, if ever, thought
He was not doing everything he ought.

But God still watched him, and he loved him so,
To make him blest, He struck another blow:
Storms dashed his ships upon the treacherous rocks,
Fires swept his stores and bankruptcy his stocks;
His princely fortune dwindled to a speck,
With but a pittance gathered from the wreck,
Yet with that pittance, freed from crushing cares,
He was far richer than our millionnaires;
He found joy's feast far sweeter than before,
And the old dessert on his board once more;
Want came around as plenty as whilom,
And found him in at counting-house and home;
His treasures now — he saw them up above:
His little boy was looking down in love,
And best of all, the Man of Sorrows bent,
And smiled upon him, wheresoe'er he went,
And he ne'er ceased, until life's final close,
To thank his God for those two stunning blows.

Affliction, O! thou messenger of love,
Sent down to bid us lift our thoughts above,
When thou didst come and rend the ties apart,
That bound ourselves and Charlie heart to heart,
The pulse of sorrow for an instant stopped,
And not a crystal from its fountain dropped.

When the cold lead, from Berdan's rifle shot,
Ploughs through his form, the victim heeds it not;
The nerves must rally and be brought in act,
Ere the brave man is conscious of the fact.

We saw him sick, and watched him night and day.
And saw him wasting, wasting slow away,
His languor spreading as his strength decreased,
And his breath shortening, till his breathing ceased:
And then we saw him lying, through the day,
A worthless thing, — a lifeless lump of clay.
We got a coffin, very rich and fair,
Of polished rosewood, and we laid him there;
Then bore him off, and gently laid him by,
In the green homestead where our dear ones lie,
And where, thank God, when He shall think it best,
We hope to go, and with them sweetly rest.
And then we turned and rode away, and this,
Without one kiss, — the usual parting kiss, —
Rode off and left him, nevermore to come,

And meet, or greet, or kiss us at sweet home,—
Rode off and left him rudely, vilely thrust
In the cold grave, to mingle with the dust.

But O! not yet our bosoms had begun
To feel the absence of our darling one,
Nor half appreciate, staggering 'neath the cross,
The fearful import of the dreadful loss,
Nor even feel the expectation vain,
That our dear boy might yet come home again.
But time moved on, and every moment brought
Some fresh memorial that our child was not,
Showed us some record upon memory's leaf,
That added anguish to our load of grief;
And, to this day, our bosoms, sorrow-tossed,
But just begin to feel how much we lost.

We might have plunged more deep in earth's affairs,
Assumed new duties, new pursuits, and cares,
Till all absorbed in every wish and thought,
We had our darling and our woes forgot;
But we could not,— God did it, and we meant
To find the meaning of the message sent.

With faith's keen eye, we followed the dear boy,
Through the dark valley, to his home of joy;
We saw him seated on his little throne,

All ready, waiting, for our darling one,
And then we gazed, if we might haply trace,
The fadeless charms that deck the Holy Place,
And tried to find the source of beauty there,
That made each object so exceeding fair;
And source of bliss within that realm of rest,
That makes each being so completely blest.
We found heaven's bliss and charms on every side
Were but the radiance from the Crucified,
And should that radiance vanish from its bowers,
Heaven would be dim as this poor earth of ours;
And while we gazed, our hearts seemed knit in
      love
With the pure spirits and their bliss above.
And then we felt 'twould cause a throb of pain,
To come and rove this dull, cold earth again;
And when we came, our dear old homestead seemed
Not half so pleasant as before we deemed.
And one sweet source of pleasure every day
Was sadly blotted, rudely swept away.

And now we oftener lift our thoughts above,
And earth seems now to have far less to love.
But all the charms, from earth's gay landscape riven,
Are now transported to the realms of heaven;
And oft we long to have the moment come,
When we and ours shall all get safely home.

And now we feel we've found the reason why
Our dear, dear Charlie had so young to die;
God grant we may not, whate'er else we do,
Lose both our Charlie and the blessing too.

THE PASTOR.

He was my Pastor, and I loved him well;
His teachings still within my bosom dwell,
And if I ever reach the fields of heaven,
I shall owe much to his wise counsels given.
His was a frame, strong, stalwart, hale, and vast,
And after Nature's manliest pattern cast.
His was a mind capacious, mighty, keen,
That grappled truths and fathomed what they mean;
And his a heart whose pulses used to play,
Sweet as an angel's, and as pure as they.
Like a huge train, his ponderous mind required
To be supplied with fuel and be fired;
But when it moved, there's nothing could attack
And stop the train, and throw it from the track:
The dust of error might obscure the rails,
He blew it from them and outstripped the gales.
Like a huge steamer on the sea of truth,
He ploughed the waves, however rough or smooth;

Calm as old Neptune, at the helm he sat,
And watched Truth's polestar, for he steered by
    that.
The wrecker Error might false lights employ,
To lure him on the breakers and destroy;
It could not lure him, for he saw and knew
Which lights were false, and which were right and
    true;
He knew the chart and every reef and rock,
And shelf and quicksand, to the very dock.

Not sour, morose, and sombre and severe,
He loved gay converse and he loved good cheer;
But, while unbending, never went so far,
He gave sweet duty either strain or scar.
Thus was our pastor to our hearts allied,
A boon companion and a prudent guide.

And so we loved him, — loved him, for we felt
He prayed for us, whene'er he meekly knelt; —
Loved, for we knew the mighty mind he bore
Dug from truth's mine the richest, purest ore; —
Loved, for his bosom used to bound or melt,
In harmony with the joy or woe we felt;
And last, we loved him, if for nought beside,
Because we could not help it, if we tried.

His youthful home was a most charming realm,
For he'd an angel with him at the helm,
And little cherubs, starting up between,
Made it a very, very hallowed scene.
But soon that angel took her upward flight,
And bore off with her many a ray of light;
And the young cherubs, robbed of one sweet nest,
Came warmly nestling in the father's breast.

Well I remember — though 'tis many years —
How the man melted to a child in tears,
And how the Christian, getting aid from God,
Bowed meekly down, and smiling, kissed the rod;
And though earth seemed all covered with a blight,
Heaven seemed more full of beauty and delight.

Time passed, and home, though still a sweet retreat,
Lacked one rich source of much that made it sweet,
When lo! an angel gliding to the realm,
Sweet as the lost one, mildly seized the helm;
And cherubs came, fresh cherubs from above,
And filled that home, full as before, with love.
But God appeared in kindness as before,
And filled that home with sighs and tears once more:
Two cherubs melted one by one away,
Like crystal dew-drops in a summer day,
And Mercy's angel seemed new founts to ope

Of manly patience and of Christian hope;
And they did drink, and by His presence awed,
Like parents wept, like Christians kissed the rod;
And when God rent those tender ties apart,
They felt Him saying, " Son, give me thy heart;"
And though earth's feast became less rich and sweet,
They now had manna fresh from heaven to eat.

The first two cherubs (how the young do grow!)
Had grown too old to be called cherubs now;
One was a man of no degenerate stock,
But a true chip of the paternal block,
Well-trained and taught in science and in art,
And with grace early planted in his heart.
He, full of vigor, full of hope, began,
Just at man's threshold, to enact the man,
And friend and kindred, full of hope and joy,
Looked to the future of that manly boy.

Away from home, but not from those that loved,
For Friendship found him wheresoe'er he moved,
And with " Excelsior" on his flag unfurled,
He now began to grapple with the world.
A loving grandsire standing at his side,
His steadfast friend, wise counsellor, and guide,
Health's buoyant spirit seemed his frame to fill,
And every fibre of his being thrill;

And had an artist wished a model, who
Might sit for health, the genuine and the true,
'Twould have inspired him with delight and joy,
To find so stalwart and robust a boy.

One day he drooped, and friendship thought 'twas best
The wounded one should have a day of rest,
Nor had a doubt that nought was needed more,
To bring him back as vigorous as before;
And still he drooped, yet none saw danger there,
Or aught was needed but a little care;
But still he drooped, yet no one deemed him ill
Enough to ask a kind physician's skill;
And still he drooped, till friendship thought it wise,
To call in skill to counsel and advise.
The grandsire came, and neighbors came, and still
None thought him other than a little ill;
But prudence whispered, — send the tidings home,
And let the father, if he pleases, come.
He came, he saw, and looked the matter o'er,
And thought his boy would soon be out once more;
As drooping flowers need but a little rain,
Or little sun, to blush and bloom again,
And so he needed only care and rest,
And in a short time he'd be convalesced;
And so he left, brimful of hope and joy,
To think no danger seemed to threat his boy;

And he went, therefore, to his childhood's home,
Where his own sire was waiting him to come,
Intending, when that duty should be done,
On his return, to call and see his son.
He went, he came, and, on arriving, said,
" How is my son ? " " Alas ! your son is dead ! "
" Dead ? God forbid " — the stoutest heart would
          melt,
To feel that moment what the father felt ;
A red bolt leaping from a cloudless sky
Were not more sudden than that he should die.
O ! how the father staggered 'neath the stroke,
And how the Christian from its mastery broke !
" And but for one sad thought," said he, — " but one,
I could, with rapture, say, ' Thy will be done.'
None thought him sick, — himself, or friends, or I,
While at that moment ill enough to die.
None thought him sick, and, therefore, none applied
The needful thing, and so, alas ! he died.

" All that I have, and all expect, I'd give,
If I could know, ' he'd a fair chance to live,'
'Tis that that kills me — that that barbs the dart,
That now is rankling in my bleeding heart.
O ! solve this doubt, and I'll be satisfied,
Although the first-born of my youth has died ;
I'll kiss the hand by which the blow was given,

Glad I can feel my darling is in heaven.
But O! these doubts the deepest anguish give,
There is a doubt, 'he'd a fair chance to live.'
This wounds the wound inflicted by the loss,
This plants a cross within the dreadful cross;
And if grace e'er can heal the dreadful sore,
This keener wound would rankle at its core;
And if it make the cross more light to bear,
This second cross will still keep crushing there."

Thus mourned the father, and is mourning yet,
That, " peradventure," he can ne'er forget,
And though time long has gathered round the doubt,
And spread its mists and twilight hues about,
Yet memory often sends its vision through,
Sees the dread doubt and feels the woe anew,
And sighs, " Alas! will nought the assurance give
That my dear boy had a fair chance to live?"

'Tis ever thus, methinks, 'tis ever thus,
When dear ones die, such fears will torture us;
Things that we could, but did not, might have proved
The very means of saving those we loved;
And things we did, we often have our fears,
Were just the ones that laid them on their biers.
Each may be true in all its fulness, still
We're but the agents carrying out His will;

The rock on which joy's vessel should be wrecked
Is conscious guilt in action or neglect;
The tender conscience feels the keenest stings
From what the common deems indifferent things;
The common conscience deems the guiltless man,
Who thinks and acts as wisely as he can;
The tender feels the guilt, if any, lies
Back of the act in not becoming wise;
And where's the man beneath yon azure sky,
'Gainst whom this charge does not most justly lie?
Few are the parents but would do their best,
To save the dear one nestling in their breast;
And fewer still who, in the retrospect,
Find no wrong done, no blunder, no neglect.
The most devoted, angel-hearted one
Sees most his faults and duties left undone:
The polished surface shows the stain or spot,
Where the unpolished and the dim would not.
Sin always seems to its committer's eyes
Of magnitude inversely as its size;
The little boy at the first moral stain,
Feels the intensest agony and pain;
When travelling further in the downward road,
Though huge as Atlas, he feels not the load;
The road to guilt grows steeper by degrees,
Till greatest loads are borne with greatest ease,
Till when a veteran in the fiend's employ,

He gets from sin his only thrills of joy.
Ah! weeping father, let it soothe the smart,
That these, your fears, denote an honest heart.

Ah! not a day, — nay, scarce an hour, has passed.
Since our dear Charlie gently breathed his last,
But thought, unbidden, in our bosom starts,
And sadly whispers to our aching hearts, —
Had this been done, or that been left undone,
You might e'en now have had a darling son ;
'Tis this makes sorrow's fountains overflow,
'Tis this adds anguish to our cup of woe.

Faith bids us bear and kiss affliction's rod,
And says, — be still, it is the will of God.
Has it a power to hush the dreadful thought
Of fancied errors we ourselves have wrought?
Has it a balm to soothe the soul that aches,
From its unmeant omissions and mistakes?
O! yes ; faith groups them to the chariot given
To waft our dear one safely up to heaven ;
But if the sentry falls asleep or strays,
And the grim monster enters in and slays,
No common faith, e'en with its heavenliest arts,
Can soothe the sorrows of the guilty hearts.
Old time may soothe, — it never can efface
What conscious guilt on memory's page may trace,

And God forgive, although the sinner may
Forgive himself not, till his dying day.

O! my dear boy, the fear will sometimes start,
That 'twas our fault that severed us apart,
Some well-meant act or some unmeant neglect
Were the dread rocks on which our joys were
          wrecked;
But thou, boy, know'st we had been glad to give
Our lives, our all, if thou couldst only live;
But 'tis a sorrow we expect to have,
Till we lie down oblivious in the grave.

Well, 'tis no matter, sorrow may annoy,
'Tis not so dangerous in this world as joy;
The whitest robes that spirits wear above,
Are made of sorrow by the hand of love,
And many happiest floated to the skies
On sorrow's tear-drops and affliction's sighs.

Then let us weep and think about our boy,
No tears of ours shall mar another's joy;
We'll weep alone, and tell our griefs the while,
And with our friends we'll always wear a smile.
Or if our sorrows will peep out beneath,
Out of those smiles we'll make an extra wreath;
We'll speak, if speaking of our little one,

Of something cunning by him said or done;
And while conversing, we'll be cheerful even,
And speak of him as our sweet boy in heaven,
And tell how much it swells our present joy,
To think we have had such a darling boy.

The burdened heart, though often it conceals,
Sometimes betrays the sorrow that it feels;
Grief, all unconscious of its tears and sighs,
Tells its tale oft to other people's eyes,
And one sad spirit midst the gay and glad,
May, without meaning, make the circle sad.

When we laid Charlie in our funeral bowers,
The sympathetic mingled tears with ours,
And friendship kindly gathered at our side,
And shared the griefs we had not power to hide:
And 'twas a solace mourners only know,
And many a pang was taken from our woe.
But the first gush, when sorrow calls for aid,
Has passed away, and the due offering made;
Henceforth, our hearts must, as the woe's our own,
Know their own sorrows and must bear alone.

Then let us weep, — it shall be silent grief,
Its history's written on no open leaf,
We'll try our best, no thrill of woe shall dart

Outside ourselves, to pierce another's heart;
And in all circles it shall be our care,
No gloom shall enter from our presence there.
Grief seldom injures, from its normal flow,
And tears but smooth the rugged path of woe;
They never injure, ne'er inflict a wrong,
Save when intruders where they don't belong;
But where they do, they're angels in disguise,
That bring down manna kindly from the skies,
And although weeping may endure a night,
Joy comes in bounding with the morning light.

Although we weep till we with Charlie sleep,
"Twill do no injury, 'twill do good, to weep;
The danger comes not, our own histories tell,
From loving earth too little, but too well.

We know Heaven has, within e'en earthly bowers,
Set all along the purest, sweetest flowers;
Home has its charms, though of one source bereft,
And little ones are in its precincts left,
And sure as Phœbus rises in the east,
We have an oftener than a daily feast;
And heartiest thanks we, to our Father, give,
That He still lets us with our dear ones live;
But O! methinks, when looking down below,
He says, "Come up, 'twill be no cross to go."

THE HAPPY FAMILY.

I HAVE two friends — I feel they're friendly yet,
Although for years we have not even met,
The nicest culture, both of heart and mind,
Has made them genial, erudite, refined;
Their home is decked with beauty, taste, and
  thought,
And made by them a most enchanting spot,
And social life gets many and many a gem,
And many a thrill of purest joy from them.
In public life, not giddy and elate,
He served with honor his old native state,
And that old state, out of her loyal hosts,
Called him to many of her highest posts;
And, wheresoe'er consenting to embark
On any duty, always left his mark;
And like a Goldsmith, with a skill inborn,
Attempted nothing he did not adorn.

She was a lady, — not by courtesy one,
The fact beamed out like sunshine from the sun;
Intelligence from every feature beamed,
And the soul's magic through each avenue streamed;
In form and feature, act and speech and air,
The graces clustered sweetly everywhere;

For culture seemed to shape each thought that stirred,
And then to shape each pure expressive word;
And taste, outspringing from the cultured soul,
Shed its bland influence and adorned the whole;
And harmless humor, in its merry play,
Tinged e'en the sombre often with the gay,
And gave to converse, when she bore a part,
So sweet a zest, it always reached the heart.

And they were Christians, both the man and wife,--
Pure Christians, both in theory and in life.
He was devout, in word and thought and air,
Without one tinge of the ascetic there;
She, ever smiling, shed good cheer about,
Without one glimmer of the undevout.

Young spirits flitted from yon azure dome,
And gayly lighted in this happy home;
One came and carolled many a roundelay,
Knit to their hearts, and then it flew away.
Another came, a little cherub thing,
To chant the lays the first had ceased to sing.
Love, writhing yet with sad bereavement's smart,
Took the young comer to its opening heart;
And when at length the new-formed ties had twined,
And the new cherub in its heart was shrined,
The little stranger sang its farewell strain,
And left home writhing with its woes again.

Another came, pure as a flake of snow,
Ere sorrow's tears had ceased, alas! to flow.
Joy's merry pulses now began to play,
Before, alas! poor sorrow's died away;
The parent feels the noblest, brightest son
Can't fill the void left by the buried one;
The soul ne'er makes a harmony half so fine
As when joy's notes and sorrow's notes combine;
Nor lives a life so lovely and so sweet,
As when the two, to check each other, meet.
The loveliest picture artist ever made,
Had not all light, but mingling light and shade;
So, to my friends, should this fresh love-bud stay,
And bless their household to their dying day,
The little ones, whose stay was made so brief,
Would ever live on faithful memory's leaf,
And so life's future, onward to its even,
Will be made up of mingled earth and heaven;
And when well weighed according to their worth,
Heaven in the end will swallow up the earth.

O! how they prayed that this young bud might bloom
    In adult sweetness ere it reached the tomb!
And how they prayed that by this blessing awed
They might more wholly give themselves to God!

And that their love for this fresh blessing given
Be so much added to their Sire's in heaven!
O! how they watched, each mental bud to find,
From the rich mould of childhood's opening mind,
Or to behold the tender outshoots start,
Warmed into being by the virgin heart!
And how harmonious, more and more each day,
The soul's machinery seemed to work and play!
And how they found, as loving parents can,
Proofs that the boy would live and be a man!
Two little ones, that God had kindly given,
Just won our hearts and then went up to heaven,
God still is good, — He sends this little bird, —
So sweet, so lovely — O! He'll spare the third;
But few the homes where death has never come,
And from the circle has not taken some;
And fewer yet where, at the Master's call,
The monster comes and rudely slays them all.
Besides how health in every feature lives!
And grace and beauty, strength and vigor, gives;
And every day parental visions can
See fresh precursors of the coming man, —
Some gift or power that Nature would not give,
If 'twere not meant the little one should live;
And when the boy's a little rough and rude,
He feels the augury for long life is good.

So these fond parents watched, by day and night,
For each new augury that could give them light,
And found enough, they almost thought, to give
The sweet assurance that their boy would live;
They'd minds too strong to think they could not lie,
And their boy could not, like the others, die, —
And hearts too loving not to hope, alas !
That signs show sometimes what will come to pass.

'Twas not because he was their only son,
He seemed so lovely and so bright an one ;
Each mental outgrowth and each moral shoot,
E'en from its birthday, bore the sweetest fruit ;
And his gay physique, at its birth, began
The perfect model of the future man,
And they said sometimes, Can the thought be true
That this dear boy is given us for the two ?

The one who's felt the anguish of the smart,
Caused by the blow that sunders heart from heart,
Will fear and tremble to his journey's end,
Lest, like the first, a second should descend.
All know their dear ones may be torn away,
The mourner *feels*, as well as knows, they may.

And so they knew, not only knew, but *felt*,
Their snow-flake might at any moment melt ;

But as " All's well " the present shouted out,
And the gay future echoed back the shout,
The loving parents, captured with the spell,
Joined in the chorus and the shout " All's well ; "
For with the cultured, howe'er trained and taught,
The wish is often " father to the thought,"
And wisest minds, in many a trusting hour,
Like Samson, find that they have lost their power.
And so they slept, — the husband and the wife, —
For lo ! their dear one had a charmèd life.

And just such quiet in each parent's breast
Had lighted there, and built its downy nest ;
And doubt and fear, by many a false alarm,
Had lost the power of doing good or harm.
And while they strove with every power and thought,
To teach their darling as he should be taught,
And tried to make him, by the surest plan,
A hearty Christian and a useful man ;
Just then disease, insidious demon, came,
And, like a vampire, lighted on the frame, —
At first so gentler than a Zephyr's breath,
Love's eye, though piercing, scarcely dreamed of
        death. ·
They watched for days, watched every changing hue,
And saw each symptom as it rose and grew,
Till, as if with a new suspicion caught,

Each looked as if to read the other's thought;
Nor dared to whisper what they really felt, —
That their pure snow-flake was about to melt.
God spare our boy; O, spare our darling son!
Yet not as I will, but Thy will be done.

God heard their prayer, — took their young love-
    bud home,
And bade the parents to prepare to come.
He heard their prayer and answered it full soon,
He took the child and gave a heavenlier boon;
And, to prepare them for a home of joy,
Gave them an angel for a helpless boy.

O! how God watches o'er His ransomed ones,
And wisely chastens whom He calls His sons;
And when He wants a polished stone to place
In His fair temple of abounding grace,
He smites again, and puts them where their hearts
Shall feel the friction adverse life imparts:
A moment only Christians will despond,
Ere they will see a brighter scene beyond.
So the fond parents, staggering 'neath the loss,
Soon saw light beaming from the dreadful cross.

How sweet the magic that was wont to run
Through the sweet ties that bound them to their son!

'Tis sweeter now a thousand times for this,
The ties reach now to realms of perfect bliss.

Had their boy gone to some fair sunny isle,
Where they would meet him in a little while,
They, night and day, would heartily prepare,
To get all ready for the journey there ;
And now they'll try, with ardor and delight,
To get all ready for the upward flight.
God saw how hearty was the effort made,
And so vouchsafed to grant them further aid.

Wealth was not theirs, yet fortune sometimes smiled,
As if to make him its adopted child,
And hope would sometimes whisper to the mind,
That fortune might be in their future kind,
And it may be its siren voice was heard,
And touched their hearts with many a flattering
        word.
God saw the danger, greater day by day,
And, like a cobweb, swept it all away ;
Then how their hearts rose up to yonder height,
With scarce a mote to check their upward flight !
And just as tourists to old Windsor haste,
To see the scenes of splendor and of taste,
And ere admitted, walk the grounds about,
Or view the splendors of the court without,—

All things that please them are the things akin
To the rich splendors they will see within ; —
So while these mourners for admittance wait
Among God's works. this side the pearly gate.
The objects now they think about and love
Are those most kindred to the ones above.

And were they happy? Never more than then,
When their hearts felt in all its force, *Amen!*
When having found earth's dearest objects riven,
They found it easier to mount up to heaven, —
They'd fewer ties to bind them down to this,
They'd more to draw them to a home of bliss.

Are they still happy? They'll the answer say,
Who're with them, — see them, — hear them day by
		day :
Had fortune still upon their pathway smiled,
And God had never taken wealth or child,
A life of ease its meshes might have twined,
Till rust had spoiled his highly-cultured mind,
And gorgeous luxury with Circean art,
If not transformed, might yet have stained his heart :
But now the young flock to his classic seat,
And drink pure manna, sitting at his feet.
Thus he beloved, for his assistance shown,
Lights up their minds by flashes from his own,

And from the richness of his heart, imparts
His moral sweetness to their youthful hearts;
And she a magic scatters o'er the whole,
From the o'erflowing sweetness of her soul;
Thus twofold joy upon their board is spread:
They're feeding others and themselves are fed,
And while imparting unto others light,
They keep their own souls active, pure, and bright.

Are they unhappy? Go, apply the test,
And tell me where there is a home more blest;
The Hill of Zion yields unnumbered sweets,
This side her fields, this side her golden streets,
And they've the promise in that happy home,
Of both this life and that which is to come.

This is a scene to which I often turn,
It has a lesson that I fain would learn;
God grant we may the lesson's bidding do,
Without the facts to prove the truth anew.
Experience is, as all things serve to show,
The best instructor we can have below,
And wise is he who his experience reads,
And every lesson that it teaches, heeds;
But wisest he who studies not alone
His own, but others' added to his own.

There is one question I can ne'er conceal,
Why was I spared one dreadful blow they feel?
I know Religion does more sweetly shine
Within their bosoms, than it does in mine.
I know it well, and say it with a sigh.
They live far higher above the world than I.
Why, then, that blow that was by Wisdom dealt,
Unfelt by me, by those fond parents felt?
Perhaps Omniscience, looking from on high,
Saw they could bear it better far than I,
Or that the picture would be more divine,
Wrought in their bosoms, than if wrought in mine;
And yet, alas! whate'er the cause may be,
'Tis naught that wakens any pride in me.

THE ENGLISH FAMILY.

THERE is a good man whom I love to meet,
As I do, daily, in the busy street,
And have, sometimes, when 'twas within my power,
Been to his home to spend a social hour.
And never, never have I met him yet,
But I felt better after I had met;
He is my senior, yet to judge him by
His buoyant heart, he is as young as I,
And till my Charlie took my heart from me,

I was, at heart, a younger man than he;
I never meet the good man in his walks,
I never listen to him as he talks,
But I feel better, feel instructed even,
And feel like lifting my sad thoughts to Heaven.

I never saw him when he seemed to wear
A sombre aspect or a gloomy air;
Smiles always play on his expressive face,
Which sorrow's self is powerless to erase;
Yet one can see, both by his words and mien,
That he's seen sorrows and knows what they mean.
That queenly isle, by all things noble decked,
We sometimes scold, but oftener far respect,
And things full often in time's course unfold,
That prove we have abundant cause to scold,—
That queenly isle, he loves, adores her yet,
And that fond mother he can ne'er forget,
Her honors often, often have been shed,
Upon his noble, but untitled head,
And all her glories, in his heart inwove,
Claim even yet the incense of his love.

In early manhood, with a hopeful breast,
He'd seen afar this empire of the West,
And hither came, an English home to find
Akin to that which he had left behind.

'Tis sweet to see how his old English love
Is in the web of Western progress wove;
He sees our faults perhaps more keen than we,
But sees our merits plain as we can see,
And when there's discord that will rise sometimes
Between his native and adopted climes,
'Tis sweet to see how his large heart expands,
And takes within it both the rival lands;
He knows, though two, the nations are but twins,
He lauds their virtues, but reproves their sins;
And if war should, between the nations, spring,
And stern defiance at each other fling,
To fight 'gainst either, he'd be very loath,
But yet I know he'd gladly die for both.

The hand of fortune, by his magic, thrilled.
With richest gifts his spacious coffers filled;
And to the island o'er the stormy main
He soon returned to seek sweet home again.
There, with a mind well cultured, pure, and chaste,
His was a home of elegance and taste,
Where fortune's sons in social life could blend,
And stern misfortune's always find a friend,
And where wealth never breathed a word or thought,
That would set harshly in the poor man's cot;
And should misfortune, armed with vengeance, come,

And sweep all bare in that delightful home,
No retrospect in wealth's career would plant
A single sorrow in the home of want.
God looked from heaven, and dearly loved to shed
His choicest blessings daily on his head;
His home was sweet with wealth all strown about,
Would it be still as sweet a home without?

And so God tried, — He swept away his wealth,
And left him nought but honor, hope, and health.
Farewell, dear England, fare thee well, sweet home;
Land of the West, to thee again I come;
I'd gladly linger on my native shore,
Until, alas! life's fitful dream is o'er,
But duty becks, and who her voice obey
Find hers a thorny, but a flowery way,
And that her pathway always leads to bowers
Bedecked with thornless and immortal flowers.

And now old ocean, with its waves and foam,
Divides his island from his Western home,
He's left the first, and stormy ocean past,
He, with his dear ones, nestles in the last;
While round him one her white arms sweetly flings,
And like the ivy round her old oak clings,
While, like a shoot in all her virgin growth,
Another clings and twines around them both.

Ah ! happy trio, keen misfortune's smart
Has but disturbed the pulses of the heart ;
E'en now those gay and fluttering pulses beat,
If not as boisterous, yet, methinks, more sweet.

One son, their only, now just stepping o'er
The threshold set at manhood's opening door,
All lit with hope's and health's bewitching smile,
Still stayed and dwelt within his native isle ;
A boy of promise, all were wont to say,
Who'll make his mark upon the world some day,
And ere at last he lays life's sceptre down,
He'll set some gems in virtue's earthly crown,
And if signs fail not, he will write his name
On the bright scroll of honor and of fame.

If there was one more fondled than the rest,
In the soft down of that domestic nest,
It was that boy so cultured, so refined,
So pure in heart and so acute in mind.

The boy, far oftener than the girl, will get,
I scarce know why, to be a household pet,
And girls themselves take hold with heart-felt joy
And help install him as the petted boy,
And home is never quite so full of bliss,
As when, within it, there's a boy to kiss.

True, 'tis a sight not seldom to be met,
That some sweet girl is made the household pet,
And yet, methinks, more often home elects,
As household pet, one of the sterner sex.

Parental love, like other loves on earth,
Is gauged not always by the object's worth;
'Tis not unfrequent stronger for the boys,
Whom vice debases and whom crime destroys;
And pets are seated on their household thrones,
Not most or oftenest from the brightest ones,
Nor yet because the little ones can boast,
They're thought the brightest or are loved the
    most.
Not that dear group round that domestic hearth
Loved that boy *thus*, — they loved him for his worth,
Not as a pet, to frolic with and play,
To kill the moments of the passing day,
Not as a little plaything of a son,
To fill up ennui with a little fun;
But the sound granite, solid, polished, dressed,
Where manhood's structure will securely rest,
The little tree that, with a vigorous root,
Begins, e'en now, to bear the sweetest fruit,
And one that will in life's career be found
No barren plant, no cumberer of the ground.

A steamer came, — and each that used to come
Brought them fresh tidings from their English home.
O! how their hearts went fluttering at the thought
Of what the tidings this fresh steamer brought;
The dear ones there, — are they alive and well?
Wait for the letters, they'll the answer tell.
They broke the seal, and read, delighted, till
It said, " Dear Willie is a little ill,
But do not worry, for the case is plain,
We'll write next steamer that he's well again."
The steamer came; the letters came and said,
" Dear father, mother, sister, Willie's dead;
His last faint prayer was uttered for the three,
So dear, so loving, now beyond the sea,
And the last thoughts that faintly struggled through
The gathering twilight, seemed to be of you.

God bless the father, — so his dear ones said, —
'Twill kill him when he hears that Willie's dead;
Ah! 'twas not so, — though heart-broke at the loss,
He bent submissive 'neath the heavy cross;
God had been with him and prepared his heart,
And grace now came and kindly soothed the smart,
And faith so sweetly told him that his boy
Was roving now in realms of heavenly joy,
That although cheered when others came to cheer,
And soothed at Friendship's sympathetic tear,

He needed naught to soothe his stricken breast,
Nor aught that might give comfort to the rest.

'Twas sweet to see the good, kind father try
To wipe the tear from each co-weeper's eye ;
To see him sit and on the virgin sheet,
Write down his thoughts, so gentle, kind, and sweet,
So full of comfort and so full of joy
About dear Willie, his now sainted boy,
And how delightful 'twas to think that they
Should be with Willie, at no distant day,
And how, perhaps, the little boy was given,
To gain their hearts and draw them up to heaven :
Thus would the good man often write and say,
As if he had no cross to bear but *they.*

There's many an oasis in this desert earth,
Where pleasures spring of most surpassing worth.
The good man finds, from earth's intensest ills,
The sweetest nectar of delight distils ;
The bad man finds from earth's best blessings, flow
The keenest anguish and intensest woe ;
And most men lingering at some point between,
Find earth to be a very checkered scene.
The bitterest sorrows get their bitterest gall
Out of the bosoms into which they fall ;
And if 'tis joy that out of sorrow starts,

It gets its sweetness out of human hearts.
The spark produces quite a different scene,
That strikes the mountain and the magazine;
And whether sorrow be a good or ill,
Bides the decree of the recipient's will.
Vice comes as powerless to the virtuous mind,
As rays of sunlight falling on the blind,
And holy thoughts dropped down from paradise,
Would be rank poison to the heart of vice,
And virtuous hearts in their divine employ,
Get out of all things, howe'er saddening, joy,
And feast far oftener, thankful and devout,
On things within them than on things without.

Thus 'tis no marvel that the good man's home
Is the bright spot where gladness loves to come;
Although not wealth, with its attendant care,
They yet possess sufficient and to spare,
And if one sorrow in their bosoms live,
'Tis only this, — that they've no more to give.

Go to his home, — you'll see it, at a glance,
That 'tis a home of taste and elegance,
Not grand and gorgeous, as the wealthy boor
Piles up his stuff to prove he is not poor,
But such as people of refinement feel
Makes home bright, cheerful, pleasant, and genteel:

Books find an entrance, of the choicest kinds,
And then beam forth like sunbeams from their minds;
And knowledge written and unwritten comes,
And finds apt scholars in this best of homes;
And social converse is all brightly lit
With scintillations of his sense and wit;
And there's an altar where their pure hearts leave
Religion's offerings every morn and eve.

I did not know the pleasant group before
The shipwreck came, and Willie was no more,
And therefore know not, if before it, they
Were the same joyful spirits of to-day;
And yet I doubt not but in heart and mind
They were as gentle, affable, and kind,
But as the rose out of the driving storm,
Gets sweeter sweetness and a lovelier form,
So out of sorrow's almost poisoned bowl,
The little group gained many a grace of soul,
And one who'd known them in the days whilom
Would say their present is a happier home.
And since I've felt how human hearts can ache,
Until they feel as if about to break,
I sometimes fancy that his heart was rent
When sad affliction's thunderbolts were sent,
And that whenever sorrow is in view,
'Tis not with *one* heart, but he feels with *two*.

When Charlie died, who always loved to greet
The kind, good man, whene'er they chanced to meet,
And when the tidings entered through his door,
That his young friend would never greet him more,
He seized his pen, and, like the breath of flowers,
Sent his heart-breathings to combine with ours;
And so, in harmony, as they came along,
They soothed our sorrows sweetly as a song.
O! sweet the balm, the sympathizing heart
Pours in the breast that feels affliction's smart;
A kindly word costs nothing to bestow,
But may take many a bitter pang from woe.

"Poor Willie died, — Have you been blessed for
    that?"
Said I, as we in social converse sat.
"O! *yes*," said he, ('twas an emphatic *yes*,)
"'Twas a remembrance sent to me to bless;
I'm sometimes glad, sometimes 'exultant' even,
That my dear Willie is a saint in heaven.
Though dread the blow that sundered us in twain,
I would not dare to call him back again;
I'm now. sweet thought, at life's dim afternoon,
And shall rejoin my dear, dear Willie soon;
Things that looked dark. look now no longer dim,
For I live better when I think of him;

And if I'm saved, I shall both feel and know,
How much I'm debtor to that boy and blow."

This is the story, doubt it if you choose,
Would it were carolled by a loftier Muse;
Yet howe'er rude, unskilful, and uncouth,
One thing rely on, — 'tis the sober truth.
I think it over, write on Memory's chart,
And with my own I shrine it in my heart,
And while they're there, no impure wish or thought
Can find admittance to the hallowed spot.

How sad the truth that lessons meant to save
Must be learned often o'er a dear one's grave,
And to unite us in a world of bliss
We must be rudely torn apart in this.
O! blest the man who, when afflictions smite,
Gets from the blow a harvest of delight,
But doubly blest whose heart is guided so,
He reaps the harvest, but without the blow.

THE GENIAL CHRISTIAN.

FIVE days ago, — five, at the time I write, —
Two friends came in to see me just at night,
A man and wife, and 'twere but truth to say

I never saw a happier pair than they.
Genial, kind-hearted, liberal, frank, and free,
You could not meet them and ascetics be;
You saw the sunshine o'er their faces play,
And could not part and carry none away.

We had not met, as we were wont to meet,
For some few days, in ferry-boat or street,
And so they called, kind-hearted friends, to see
If I were ill, or what the cause might be.
'Twas sweet to greet them at my home and hearth,
Because I loved them, for I knew their worth.
His was a heart so loving, kind, and true,
No act of kindness he'd refuse to do;
His was a judgment accurate and acute,
At whose decisions slander's tongue was mute,
So uncorrupt, all California might
In vain essay to sway him from the right,
And so kind-hearted, 'twere no boon to live,
If sorrow sighed and he had nought to give,
And all his life long, to its very end,
Each good cause deemed him its undoubted friend;
His mind so active, vigorous, strong, and clear,
He could not live and be a cipher here,
And in life's mart, amidst the bustling throng,
He made his mark where'er he passed along,
And works of science and the charms of Art,

Had a sweet shrine within his liberal heart,
And e'en Invention, starting at his will,
Took magic shapes beneath his plastic skill;
Social and genial, friendship could not come,
And find no welcome at his happy home;
That home seemed made to overflow with bliss,
Enough for others and for him and his,
And all attracted to that home were sure
Of something pleasant, polished, rich, and pure.

Just at life's prime, he ne'er before had stood
So strong for work, so ripe for doing good,
So running o'er with kindness' overflow,—
Such was my friend but just five days ago.
This morning tidings came to me that said,
"That pleasant friend, you loved so well, is dead;"
He died unwarned, not wasted, worn, and wan,
Died as he wished, — died with the harness on.

And then I thought where among all I know
Could death have struck a bitterer, keener blow?
Or could have thrown one of his venomed darts,
And pierced more loving and more sorrowing hearts?
Methinks, had he, all his barbed arrows hurled,
Chance-aimed among the busy, bustling world,
Few would have fallen, whoever they might be,
More bright for action and for thought than he;

None could have fallen and heartier tears be shed
O'er the green velvet of the sleeper's bed.

O! 'tis not strange that any one below,
At any time, should feel the monster's blow.
He strikes at random, seeming, without aim,
Or as rude boys shoot anything for game:
A harmless sparrow flitting through the wood,
Or busy robin carrying home its food,
Or if some chance should happen to suggest,
They'd fire the death-shot in its unfledged nest;
And there's no rule that Reason could devise,
Or research find with its acutest eyes,
Which seems the one, comparing facts with facts,
By which the monster in his butchery acts.
Spirits from bodies stalwart, firm, and strong,
Mount up to heaven and join the happy throng,
And burdened spirits break, with joy, away
From their poor, leaky, shattered homes of clay;
Look where we will, at whate'er point we stand,
Travellers are starting for the spirit land.

Farewell, kind friend, to-morrow they will bear
Thy form to Greenwood and they'll leave thee there;
And when fond love has reared the marble stone,
And chiselled there the dear name, Atkinson,

Whene'er at Greenwood, 'twill be always sweet
To thread the paths and see thy green retreat,
And breathe the prayer, God grant it be not vain,
That we may meet our pleasant friend again.

THE YOUNG PATRIOT.

How ceaselessly God's glittering armory opes,
And the bright shafts lets fly at human hopes!
E'en as I write, an echoed bolt is sped,
And a young patriot's numbered with the dead.
In wealth's soft cradle he'd been fondly rocked,
In love's soft bosom he'd been sweetly locked,
And all that could by wit or wealth be done,
Were found among the assets of that son;
And he repaid them, O! how well repaid,
For all their kindness, all their love and aid;
Each throb of care or mite of treasure spent,
Came back with usury to the hearts that lent;
And as Sorrento, in all stages, sees
Buds, blossoms, fruits upon her orange-trees,
So these fond parents saw in his young mind,
The boy's, youth's, man's developments combined;
Ripe fruits were hanging in the moral bower,
While buds formed, swelled, and opened every hour.

He was a student, not in name, in *fact*,
And proved in theory not alone, but act ;
And when at length his college life was done,
And he departed hale and twenty-one,
Not a diploma, but his well-trained mind,
Sufficed to prove him erudite, refined ;
For one as well might walk gay Flora's bowers,
And not inspire the perfume of her flowers,
As be with one so cultured and refined,
Nor feel the influence of his liberal mind.

We'd met but twice, but twice sufficed to show
He was a person one would love to know.

Among the last young voyagers from Yale,
Who, for life's trip, had set the merry sail,
Was that young man, around whose noble brow
Yale's classic garland worthily rested now,
Of truth's broad sea he'd studied well the chart,
Rocks, reeves, and quicksands, — knew them all by
        heart,
And now at last that college lustrum's gain
Must bear the test of life's colossal strain ;
None feared that knew, nor ever dreamed of less
Than that the issue would be found success ;
And so it was, — e'en ere he joined its strife,
He gained success, and sealed it with his life ;

Unswayed by wealth, undazzled with delight,
He laid his life down at the beck of right,
As much a martyr as if stricken dead
By the fierce plunge of Berdan's screaming lead.

While yet within his Alma Mater's walls,
His country's shrieks came echoing through her halls.
And his young heart with quicker pulses beat,
To throw himself obedient at her feet;
He felt with Horace, at his country's cry,
How sweet, how glorious it would be to die!
And when at length, with bosom all aglow,
Yale wreathed his brow, and, smiling, bade him go.
Like Pallas leaping out of Zeus's head,
He leaped from Yale's and marched with martial tread.

That proud old ship, the gallant Arago,
A perfect life-boat both in calm and blow,
Takes the brave patriots, with a mother's care,
To waft them — waft them — ah! they knew not
        where;
No matter where, provided 'tis to stand,
And meet the foeman of their native land.

Ah! fond affection with a quivering lip
Thanked God that boy was in so safe a ship,
And felt almost, amidst old Ocean's strife,

That ship was surety for the dear one's life;
But ere that steamer had been out a day,
Death came on board for plunder and for prey,
And of the thousands in that good ship piled,
Took but that hero, learning's foster-child.
Home, for a moment, stood in mute despair;
It seemed all midnight with no sunlight there;
And not till Faith came up, her tale to tell,
Could the fond inmates utter, " All is well."

No greener wreath had 'twined around his brow,
Than genuine merit is intwining now,
Nor greater good could he have done his land,
Than peril life to lend a helping hand,
E'en had he lived, amid the battle's smoke,
To mow down thousands with his sabre's stroke.
He's the true hero, he's his country's friend,
Whose part's well acted to the drama's end.
And so love felt, and faith assisted love,
And so the parents looked for aid above,
And though heart-broken at the dreadful loss,
Love's healing beams came streaming from the cross:
That cross, at which their hero-boy had given
Himself, his all, to justice, truth, and heaven;
All now seemed bright, except the shadow cast
On poor self sitting at her sad repast.

No honest effort God e'er failed to bless,
Though oft it seem far, far this side success,
As prayer, unanswered, in the mode we pray,
Full oft is answered in God's better way;
So love now sees, with faith's pure light supplied,
Success stood waiting where their dear one died,
And though defeat in all he'd hoped and dreamed
Writ on the tombstone o'er his ashes seemed,
Love still sees victory crowning what he'd done,
Not that they'd pictured, but God's nobler one.

O! yes, be sure, when merit's tale is told,
That you'll find Sterling with the names enrolled,
And progress' mission was more nobly done,
For the brief drama acted by that son.

Not to the realms that merry fancy fills
With her gay witcheries woven as she wills,
Have I been roving something sweet to find,
To fill the void that Charlie left behind.
I've walked through Nature, and her buds and flow-
    ers
Lay thick as snow-flakes after winter showers,
And fruits, all ranging from the bud to blush,
Lay thick as hail 'neath every tree and bush,
And plants and trees at every stage from birth
Lay livid corpses on the lap of earth,
And grace and beauty all o'er nature spread
Lay marred or scarred or numbered with the dead;
And in earth's workshop, down beneath our feet,
Creations perished ere one half complete;
And in life's mart, where all for conquest press,
Defeat was seen far oftener than success,
And of the years allotted here to men,
How few used up their threescore years and ten;
And when our Charlie bade poor earth adieu,
And up to heaven on his young pinions flew,
It seemed so like the good God's usual way,
We had no murmur or complaint to say;
We felt it must be not alone not wrong,
But a sweet note in God's harmonious song.

OUR CHARLIE.

PART SECOND.

OUR CHARLIE.

PART SECOND.

O ! who that e'er received from heaven a little bud
    of love,
To see it like a dew-drop melt and sail to realms above,
But oftentimes has asked himself, with many a tear
    and sigh,
Why should such fairy little things in life's young
    morning die ?
Why should they come, with hope and joy these
    throbbing hearts to thrill,
And then fly off and leave a void that nought can
    ever fill ?

A mourner who is trembling yet 'neath sad afflic-
    tion's smart,
But with a mind convinced 'twas right, and with a
    chastened heart,
Has pondered o'er the question much, Why should
    our children die ?
And jotted down upon these leaves full many a
    reason why,
And not a reason of them all, but to the thoughtful heart,
Takes many a bitter pang away from sad affliction's
    smart.

WHY SHOULD THE YOUNG DIE?

THE sweetest gardens here below, the fairest earthly
    bowers,
Are not the landscapes gayly decked with only adult
    flowers.
To make an Eden like the first, each hue and form
    and size
Of floral gems must mingle charms to make the
    paradise.
The little green and tender stalk that issues from the
    roots,
The little stems that start from it and form the lat-
    eral shoots,
The velvet leaflets and the leaves of finest texture
    wove,
That gayly flutter in the breath that whispers through
    the grove ;
The little buds of tiniest growth and microscopic
    size,
Almost unnoticed and unseen by all unaided eyes,
The larger buds that earlier yet their way begin to
    push,
And have arrived to almost flowers upon their parent
    bush,
And those just opening to the light and gayly hold-
    ing up

A load of beauty and of sweets within their little
    cup,
And full-blown flowers in adult bloom, among whose
    varying hues,
The golden beams of sunlight play upon the spar-
    kling dews, —
All these their beauties must combine, and into
    harmony bring,
Before earth's sweetest landscapes rise and loveliest
    Edens spring.
Select the brightest, gaudiest gem of all that flowery
    train,
And then with such, and only such, adorn the lovely
    plain,
Instead of flowers, a single flower, the sweet parterre
    would grace,
Instead of charms, a single charm would play o'er
    Nature's face ;
The loftiest, or the sweetest, or the softest mono-
    tone,
Can ne'er one stave of music make, unaided and
    alone.

Look up to yonder vaulted sky and view each glit-
    tering gem
That He, who made them all, has set in night's
    bright diadem ;

Select the brightest, purest one, in its aerial march,
And pin, with such, night's curtain up, to yonder
    spacious arch,
'Twould mar the bright and glorious scene spread
    out before the eye,
And take a thousand charms away from our own
    gorgeous sky;
Variety that never tires, but gives us something
    new,
Would then be blotted from the sky and spread a
    sameness through;
The stars would then be all alike, without a sepa-
    rate name,
And every little inch of sky be everywhere the
    same.
Those brilliant stars, whose names are known, and
    on whose disks we gaze,
The little snow-white nebulae, that form our milky-
    ways,
With those of every hue and size, between the two
    extremes,
Are gems on which the rudest gaze, and Science
    looks and dreams.
This makes the sky that glorious page, so gorgeous
    round about,
Which loftiest science cannot read and still be unde-
    vout.

'Tis sweet to stand in summer-time and look the
 landscape through;
With scenery like in every part, 'twould be a dis-
 mal view,
But boundless in variety, the man of taste admires,
And though he gazes, year by year, he never, never
 tires.
The hills, the plains, the groves, the meads, and
 waving fields of grain,
The flocks and herds that rove and feed on every
 hill and plain,
The little ville, the country church, the farmer's
 barn and cot,
All, all in gay variety, the verdant landscape dot.

Select the brightest feature now of all, that makes
 it fair,
Sweep off the rest, and leave but this monotonously
 there,
The warmest lover Nature has, would, in a moment,
 tire,
And her devoutest worshipper lose every spark of
 fire.

'Tis sweet to see the fleecy flocks along the landscape pass,

And rove around the hills and vales and clip the
      verdant grass;
For happiness and innocence and sweet content are
      there,
Without a single fear of woe or single thought of
      care.
Behold them slowly moving round sometimes in
      single pairs,
Sometimes in lines, sometimes in ranks, sometimes
      in solid squares;
Sometimes they gather, as they feed beside the
      brooklet's brink,
Sometimes within the pebbly bed go gayly in and
      drink,
Sometimes, beside a shady fence or shady tree or
      bush,
They chew the cud, or look, or doze, or into slum-
      ber hush,
And when the sober, timid things find something to
      alarm,
'Tis fun to see them leap the walls and scamper o'er
      the farm,
And huddle in some corner, where they safely may
      remain,
Until their fright is o'er, and they can go and feed
      again.
Let such a sweet and pleasing scene be banished
      from our farms,

And rural life would be deprived of some delightful
    charms ;
But yet, in such a scene as this, there's one defect,
    alas !
There is another thing required to give the *coup de
    grace*,
For lo ! among the feeding flocks, the sober serious
    dams
Must have, dependent on their loves, their lambkins
    and their lambs ;
And while their sober mothers do whate'er is to be
    done,
The little lambs must frisk and play and add the
    glee and fun.
O ! he who e'er has stood and gazed upon a summer
    day,
And seen them gambol, leap, and run, and gayly
    sport and play,
And seen the mother oft look up, and with her
    well-known bla,
Assure the little fellow near that she's the real
    ma.
No man, methinks, that has a heart, but feels a
    thrill of bliss,
To see a scene as innocent and beautiful as this,
And feels, with all the magic thrills that such a
    vision brings,

That flocks without, and with their lambs. are very
    different things.

Where is the spot, the sunny spot beneath the
    swelling dome,
One half as sweet and half as fair, and half as blest
    as home ?
'Tis there, from earliest infancy, our purest joys
    were found ;
'Tis there the spirit woke to life and first begun to
    bound :
'Tis there. whenever we were plagued or vexed
    with earth's affairs,
We always came and always found a solace for our
    cares :
'Tis there, whene'er in social life fair friendship's
    bonds unwove,
We always fled and always found the richest
    draughts of love ;
O ! it was there, that everything beneath the golden
    sun,
That sweetens life, or brightens life, or gladdens
    life, begun ;
And where our tastes and modes of thought and
    habits took their rise,
And where our souls received the food that gave
    them shape and size ;

And we, in fine, whatever we in after-life become,
Are always, and shall ever be, embodiments of
    home ;
And just as much and long as we shall love our-
    selves on earth,
So much and long we e'er shall love the homestead
    of our birth.
'Tis for these reasons, earthly homes, however homely,
    glow
With brighter charms and richer joys, than any spot
    below.
However large, however small, however young or
    old,
The little group of loving ones, the happy homesteads
    hold,
The memory loves to travel back, wherever we may
    roam,
And walk among the pleasant scenes we used to see
    at home.
But still, e'en home, however sweet, will lack a
    thousand charms,
That has no little prattlers there in its parental
    arms.
The tender bosom understands you well, when you
    declare
Your home is happy, but alas ! it has no baby
    there.

The choral song of home, sweet home, has some
  enchanting notes,
That cannot be expressed by aught, but by the tiniest throats;
The full and perfect harmony of joy upon the
  heart
Is only felt where there's a voice attuned to every
  part;
An absent voice was ne'er supplied by substitution
  yet,
For O! the song of home is marred by any one's
  falsette.

Among the endless forms of life, all o'er our planet
  spread,
The father of it all has put the human at the
  head.
And although frailty writes its name on everything
  we do
And think and say and will and plan, 'tis notwith-
  standing true;
And though 'tis we that make the boast, who're of
  the species " man,"
Yet we're the ones of all the world who know it
  and who can.

I might go on, and volumes write, and not exhaust
  the theme,

To prove that man's supremacy is not a baseless
    dream ;
But all I'll say is simply this : if progress, since the
    fall,
Has added aught to human bliss, 'tis man has done
    it all.
There's not a living thing on earth, that wishes or
    aspires,
To be a thing or do a thing, an inch above their
    sires,
But centuries hence, if centuries come, when earth
    shall pass away,
They will be found exactly what we find they are
    to-day ;
Or if improved in strength or size, or health or
    beauty, still
They'll be indebted for the change to plastic human
    skill.
But though we search from east to west, and search
    from pole to pole,
And find poor fallen man the best and noblest of
    the whole,
God did not choose, when he resolved to carry out
    his plan,
To take, because his noblest work, and stock the
    earth with man ;
But as, in Flora's lovely realms, among her gems we
    trace

Ten thousand times ten thousand forms of beauty
  and of grace, —
So when Jehovah's fiat came, life started into birth,
And spread in rainbow loveliness all o'er our mother
  earth,
So that, when looking from on high, He can enrap-
  tured see
All o'er his vast unbounded realms unbounded har-
  mony,
And know how much 'twould mar the scene to
  banish from his plan
His little animalculæ, as well as lordly man.

'Tis harmony, all harmony, that throughout Nature
  springs,
And not a discord ever jars upon her faultless
  strings ;
Those seeming discords that perplex and so annoy
  us here
Grow harmonies on Nature's strings, before they
  reach His ear.
And that unbounded harmony that thrills the Al-
  mighty mind
Has in it minor harmonies all perfect in their
  kind ;
And even the minutest ones are, of themselves
  alone,

As perfect as the general one, e'en to its tiniest
    tone ;
And everywhere the searcher finds, wherever he has
    trod,
This beautiful analogy runs through the works of
    God.

Our race was never meant to form a single mono-
    tone,
But a grand harmony all attuned to Nature's grander
    one ;
God might have made us all adults, as Adam was,
    and then
Have peopled earth, this beauteous earth, with only
    full-grown men.
If childhood must to manhood grow, and this is
    Nature's plan,
He might as well, had He thought best, have made
    the boy a man,
And then, instead of toiling years, in getting up the
    hill,
Where stalwart manhood wields his power with vigor
    and with skill, —
And when, perhaps, but just begun and fairly set in
    play,
The fiat from Jehovah comes and summons him
    away, —

Man might have sprung, Athena-like, with adult
    armor on,
And to the manly work of life, without preparing,
    gone;
But then among the harmonies of God's harmonious
    plan,
There would have been a discord felt when coming
    on to man.
For wheresoe'er we mortals look, we see at every
    breath,
Attached to everything below, are birth and growth
    and death;
O! how 'twould mar the harmonies, the whole and
    lesser both,
To strike from any single link the principle of
    growth!
O! no, the grand analogy that runs through all
    God's plan,
'Twould be absurd to think, alas! would disappear
    in man.

Could we, from some aerial height, inspect the scene
    below,
And see, upon the stage of life, its actors come and
    go,
Among the untold witcheries that on the planet
    live,

Each little inch of time would have its representative.
Just on the eastern edge of life our little ones would
    peep,
And on their tiny feet and hands among the minutes
    creep,
Like those two cherubs Raphael's brush 'neath that
    Madonna traced,
That Dresden has, with pious care, within her gal-
    lery placed.
And far upon the western edge, close on existence'
    brink,
Old age would walk on tottering feet and just about
    to sink,
And all between the two extremes, at every inch
    from both,
We should behold each moment's true development
    and growth;
And all transition's lights and shades in all the dis-
    tance through,
And everything that time with man has power on
    earth to do;
In fine, see every changing phase of size and hue
    and mould
That human nature can assume and into which unfold;
O! where's the bosom does not feel how fair and
    fresh and new
The lovely panorama is of such a charming view?

But look again at yonder scene and see how wonders
    start,
Take off your vision from the whole and fix it on a
    part.
See how the same variety has left its magic trace,
Yet all in perfect harmony, upon the human face;
However strong resemblances the gazer's eye may
    strike,
There are no two in everything in all the world
    alike.
In yonder artist's studio, the products of his art
Are not unfrequent just the same alike in every
    part,
But Nature always unconstrained throws her crea-
    tions out,
So that each thing's identity, though sometimes
    brought in doubt,
Though sometimes dim and indistinct as if about to
    die,
It never wholly can escape the expert's practised
    eye.

O! yes, methinks that bliss above and happiness
    below
Must, since in essence so alike, from kindred foun-
    tains flow,

And if we seek the sources whence our sweetest
    earthly feast,
Our hearts would fondly testify the social not the
    least.
'Tis said the blessed ones above find added rapture
    even,
Whene'er they see a lost one start upon the road to
    heaven ;
And 'twould be strange if it awoke no added thrill
    to this,
When that new spirit safe arrived within a home of
    bliss ;
But stranger yet, if when that guest unites in
    Heaven's employ,
The happy spirits do not feel an extra thrill of
    joy.

O ! heaven, methinks, must be a place where just such
    charms appear
As fill the ransomed soul with joy e'en while it lin-
    gers here,
And that the sweet variety, that all so dearly
    love,
To please the ransomed spirits there must deck the
    realms above.
And so God speaks, and tender ties are every mo-
    ment riven,

And those we love so much below are taken up to
    heaven ;
Sometimes He takes the hoary sage whose work is
    nobly done,
Sometimes, in duty's mid career, the strong and
    vigorous one,
Sometimes He smites the ripened youth just entering
    manhood's door,
And full of heart and full of hope he falls to rise no
    more,
Sometimes he smites, in childhood's days, our daugh-
    ters and our sons,
But oftener, far, than all the rest, He takes our lit-
    tle ones ;
And as He takes them one by one to holier courts
    above,
They give to heaven's variety, new beauty, bliss, and
    love,
And when He wants to fill a place unfilled among
    the blest,
He's always sure to take the one that will adorn it
    best.

Then is it strange, since children are the sweetest
    blessings given,
That God should take our little ones and place them
    safe in heaven ?

Or that, to make the world above most beautiful and
    blest,
Should call our little ones away far oftener than the
    rest,
Or should, to make heaven seem to us most charming
    and most fair,
Transport our little ones above to help attract us
    there ?

Dear Charlie, we accept the thought, and shrine it
    in our breast :
God would not sure have taken thee, had he not
    known 'twas best, —
The best for us, the best for thee, and best for all
    above,
For now the happy ones in heaven have one more
    thing to love.
For in that glorious world above, as surely as in
    this,
'Tis true, that added things to love give added thrills
    to bliss ;
And, Charlie, though nor eye nor ear, nor heart of
    man, can know
What things the Father has prepared for those he
    loves below,
We *do* know now *what* spirits live within that happy
    sphere,

Because they're just the little ones we loved and
      fondled here ;
And as we know what joy they caused in home's
      divine retreat,
We feel the bliss of heaven must be, beyond con-
      ception, sweet.

Methinks, dear Charlie, thine must be intenser thrills
      of joy,
Since thou didst go to Paradise while yet a spotless
      boy.
And could I cease to feel the weight of this sad
      crushing cross,
And wipe away, from memory's page, the record of
      that loss, —
Had I the power to bury self beneath oblivion's
      wave,
And all self-interest sweep away from little Charlie's
      grave,
And, without weighing in love's scales how much the
      loss may be,
Weigh, in the scales of faith, how much the gain
      has been to thee, —
Methinks, instead of shedding tears of sorrow for our
      boy,
We should be shedding, every day, the gushing tears
      of joy.

O ! sometimes, when the vision opes and flings the
    real out,
And shows the triumphs of our boy unclouded by a
    doubt,
The tears of sorrow for our boy e'en while they're
    dropping stop,
Or turn to tears of gladness when the little crystals
    drop ;
And until self steps in again and breaks the magic
    spell,
We think of our dear boy in heaven and feel that
    all is well.
And thus alternate day by day we write, leaf after
    leaf :
To-day we write a page of joy, to-morrow one of
    grief ;
And oftentimes we long to have the glorious morn-
    ing come,
When self itself shall have a feast with Charlie at
    his home.

THE NEW SONG.

THERE is a song the ransomed sing, — a song of love
    and joy,
The fresh spontaneous outburst of their heavenly
    employ.

'Tis called the " new," for as the charms of love and
 truth unfold,
The song takes in fresh harmonies and so it can't
 grow old.
'Tis called the " new," because as oft as new-born
 raptures start,
The fresh performer comes attuned exactly for the
 part ;
'Tis called the " new," because, as long as endless
 ages roll,
The ransomed ones will sing the song and never sing
 the whole ;
'Tis called the "new," for truth and love of every
 shape and hue
Are ever twining in the song and keep it always
 new,
And until truth and grace and love shall all their
 stores unfold,
That same " New Song" shall still be fresh and
 never shall grow old.

EACH NEW-BORN SPIRIT APPEARS AT THE RIGHT TIME.

METHINKS, 'twas when the ransomed ones within
 their courts above
Were singing, and they chanced to touch a tenderer
 strain of love,

The tender notes, like drops of dew, were quivering
    into play,
All ready for some cherub's throat to mingle in the
    lay,
When Charlie oped the pearly gate and with his
    new-strung lyre,
Stepped sweetly up and took his place among the
    heavenly choir.
'Twas just the part for Charlie's voice, the part for
    Charlie's heart,
And O! how sweet the darling boy performed his
    destined part!
O! then, how sweet the strain was played, how
    doubly sweet 'twas sung,
When sounded on his little harp and carolled by his
    tongue!
For if there was among the charms in his pure na-
    ture wove,
A grace more sweet than all the rest, it was the
    purest love.

Sing on, my darling boy, sing on, I'll not disturb a
    note,
I almost hear the melody from thy melodious throat.
Perhaps, when we are done with earth, and life's
    short journey through,
We may, beside our Charlie, stand and join the
    chorus too.

E'en now, in spirit, we are there beside thee every
    day,
And hear thee sing, and sing ourselves less sweet
    than thou, the lay;
And then we feel, while listening to the music from
    thy tongue,
How sweet it is and blest it is to be transplanted
    young.
'Tis not the titled and the proud, the learned and
    the wise,
That learn the easiest and the best the language of
    the skies:
The babe that never spoke a word while in its
    brief sojourn,
Goes right to speaking there, because there's nothing
    to unlearn;
And that dear boy, who never ceased to love his
    mother best,
Is almost fitted, at the first, to mingle with the
    blest.

EACH HAS HIS MISSION EVEN IN HEAVEN.

METHINKS, that Reason shows the fact without the
    fancy's aid,
God has a mission in this world for everything that's
    made;

And 'twere absurd exceedingly to think it can
    be so,
That though man lives beyond the tomb, his mission
    ends below.
The tome of God tells everywhere of heaven's un-
    fading joys,
But side by side it tells about its pure and blest
    employs.
O! yes, methinks, when we have passed life's fitful
    journey through,
We shall have thrilling joys to feel and pleasant work
    to do.
The bliss of heaven, however rest may in its essence
    lurk,
Would lose full many a thrill of bliss without a touch
    of work ;
Of all the forms of punishment inflicted here below,
'Tis solitude, pure solitude, inflicts the deepest woe,
But still it drops full half its pangs and half its ter-
    rors too,
By giving to the solitaire a little work to do.
The spirit, when it mounts on high, must grow a
    different one,
If that can be a blissful spot where nothing's to be
    done.
And if, for it would seem absurd to have one doubt
    of this,

The social is in paradise an element of bliss,
The beings there must be engaged in some divine
        employ,
Whose products are the elements of one another's
        joy,
And fond Affection, with itself, the question will dis-
        cuss,
If our dear lost ones e'er extend their ministries
        to us.

HEAVEN'S REVEALINGS.

When God reveals the mysteries He wishes us to
        know,
He does not fill the picture up and every feature
        show,
He gives the outlines only oft, because He deems it
        best
That our own powers and faculties may try to find
        the rest.
Methinks, He never would reveal a hidden truth or
        doubt,
That we, with our own innate skill, had power to
        solve without.
He always helps the weakest mind in every trial
        made,

And hearty effort everywhere is sure to get his aid.
He's told us much about the heaven where He for-
  ever dwells,
But 'tis by symbols He portrays the most of what
  He tells;
He leaves to us, with all the powers that He himself
  has given,
Out of the symbols He has shown, to form our views
  of heaven;
And though we may not group them right, however
  wise and shrewd,
We always, in the effort, find enough to do us
  good.

He's given us hints, nay, more than hints, *revealings*
  meant to show
Our angel ones have ministries that reach sometimes
  below;
And then He leaves the precious truth in all its
  rainbow hues,
For us to group, as fancy bids, and for our profit
  use,
And fond Affection seldom fails, when contemplating
  here,
To feel the fact and find enough to comfort and to
  cheer.

EACH FINDS HIS PROPER PLACE IN HEAVEN.

Howe'er alike we mortals are upon a hasty view,
We've powers and tastes and aptitudes of every
    shade and hue ;
And thus in all the walks of life, of every changing
    phase,
There always is some person found just fitted for the
    place.
And half the ills and half the crimes and half the
    sorrows here
Arise because so many a man gets jostled from his
    sphere ;
For he's the surest to succeed and surest to be
    blest,
Who's in the place and does the work for which
    he's fitted best ;
But when we leave this mortal coil and on new
    pinions fly,
Alighting midst the happy ones in mansions in the
    sky,
There'll be no veil about us then, though it be ne'er
    so thin,
To help us seem to be without what we are not
    within.
For nothing but our characters, developed while
    we're here,

Will prove our own identity within that happy
 sphere,
And like the needle to the pole, the spirit of the
 blest
Is sure to find the mission there for which he's fitted
 best ;
And so no jar or discord can in any corner lurk,
But perfect harmony unites the actor and his work.

I love to think what mission is to our dear boy
 assigned,
I think it must be something sweet, exceeding sweet
 and kind ;
I know just what he was below, — he's just the same
 above,
And it must be, — I *feel* it must, — his ministry is
 love.
When sorrow sighs with broken heart and tears
 begin to play,
We know he'd go with sunny smiles and kiss the
 tears away ;
And if a honeyed drop of love could melt some
 heartless one,
That honeyed drop would sure distil and so the deed
 be done.

DO THE SPIRITS OF THE DEPARTED ONES VISIT US HERE?

As, when the boy, while yet a lad, goes gayly out
    to roam,
And seeks in some far-distant clime a fortune and
    a home,
However rich or learned or wise or honored be his
    lot,
He ne'er forgets, however small, his humble native
    cot, —
He recollects his playmates there, the rustic girls
    and boys,
And never ceases to retaste their rude and simple
    joys;
And childhood's reminiscences make his old native
    hearth
The sweetest spot, the purest spot, the holiest spot
    on earth.
And young life's pleasing retrospects appear so pass-
    ing fair,
He'd leave a palace to sit down in that domestic
    chair;
And earth's *elite*, he'd bid good-by, with heart brim-
    ful of joy,
To meet again the rustic friends he played with
    when a boy.

And none but he who has no heart or has a lack
    of brain,
But loves to think of early scenes and visit them
    again.

It is this truth that makes us feel, when earthly ties
    are riven,
Our dear ones love to think of us when they are safe
    in heaven ;
And if they love to think of us, they'll dearly love
    to come,
And visit friends and scenes they knew, when in an
    earthly home.

O ! such a faith, although it were on airy nothing
    built,
Would keep the heart in which 'tis shrined from
    . many a stain of guilt ;
But if 'tis built on heavenly truth, the faith and fact
    combined
Would pour more sweetness in the heart, more
    brightness in the mind.

O ! it must be that our dear boy, who used to love
    us so,
Does sometimes come on angel-wings and visit us
    below.

Perhaps he drops a pleasant thought to soothe the
    grief we feel,
Or brings a sweet and healing balm our wounded
    hearts to heal;
Perhaps he brings a floweret plucked the other side
    the tomb,
That gives a pleasant hue to death and robs it of
    its gloom;
Or whispers, with his angel-tongue, Dear Mother, I
    am near,
And fondly thinks, because she smiles, she must his
    whispers hear.
And then, perhaps, he flies around and visits all the
    rest,
And whispers some enchanting thought in every
    throbbing breast;
And then, perhaps, we smile because we feel an inner
    joy,
And then he thinks, because we smile, we know our
    darling boy;
And then, perhaps, he kisses us, as was his merry
    way,
When he went either off to bed or went away to
    play.
Perhaps our hearts *did* know our boy, and by mys-
    terious thought,
Communed with him, and talked with him, and yet
    we knew him not.

We cannot, with these eyes of ours, however keen
    and sound,
Behold a spirit as we see material objects round,
And it may be that spirits, when commissioned here
    below,
See nothing but the spirits of the ones to whom they
    go.
Howe'er this be, one thing is true, if spirits do ap-
    pear
Among old scenes and with old friends, to hold sweet
    converse here,
It is not through the senses they their messages
    impart :
They whisper them within the mind, they tell them
    to the heart;
And though we catch new thrills of joy and many a
    pleasant thought,
We know not whence, by whom, or why, the pleas-
    ant things were brought ;
And self-communings, out of which such pleasant
    fruitage starts,
May be but converse going on between them and
    our hearts.
And when we think of those we loved all safe en-
    throned in bliss,
And feel that Jordan's farther bank is lovelier far
    than this,

'Tis not perverting common sense or lowering Fan-
    cy's powers,
To think the scenes from yonder world, the spirits
    bring to ours.

If, while on earth, 'tis such a feast to be with those
    we love,
Perhaps we can a greater have when they are
    throned above.
While here encumbered with the flesh, with sorrows,
    doubts, and fears,
Bewitching us with smiles sometimes and saddening
    us with tears,
'Twas not all honey that distilled, sometimes a sting
    was born,
Nor all were roses in the way, sometimes there was
    a thorn;
And so the pleasant feast of love, like every earthly
    one,
Was sometimes of a dainty short, or sometimes badly
    done.
But O! how pure, how peaceful now are our dear
    ones above!
If we have converse now with them, it must be one
    of love;
And if it prove not one of joy, when on our table
    placed,

The fault is a corrupted heart or a perverted taste.
But O! the banquet of delight that he, unceasing,
    shares,
Who keeps his heart and keeps his mind in harmony
    with theirs!

No tongue can tell what pure delight would be to
    mortals given,
If they were more in harmony with those who live
    in heaven;
Those bright celestial visitants would in our pathway
    fly,
Or we should walk and talk with them along the
    starry sky,
And heaven and earth would be so near, and like
    each other then,
The angels would be, every day, the visitants of
    men.

HEAVEN.

O! WHAT is Heaven? the anxious heart full often
    says and sighs,
And Echo, in her covert hid, O! what is Heaven?
    replies;
And yet from Heaven's own Delphic shrine responses
    come to show

That 'tis a holy, happy place, where sorrows never
          grow,
And tell us, too, that in the midst of its unbounded
          joys,
The spirits keep their rapture up by sweet and pure
          employs.
But all the rest, the filling up, all gently touched
          and traced,
God has not in that lofty tome of heavenly wisdom
          placed ;
Imagination takes her brush and traces vale and
          hill
And tree and flower and happy ones, according to
          her skill.
But had the God who made it deigned the picture
          to portray,
We might have seen upon what plan he takes our
          friends away,
And understand, it may be, what His providences
          mean,
By cutting down the old and young and every age
          between.
Perhaps the different grades of work in yonder holy
          sphere
Need actors who've reached every grade of earthly
          training here.
The babe, one little moment old, the sage, a hun-
          dred years,

May work the best of all the rest in their allotted
    spheres.
If Christ must needs have lived and died and suffered
    want and woe,
Ere he could feel and sympathize with mortals here
    below,
So we, if we shall work with them when we're trans-
    ferred above,
Must here have just the discipline to do the work
    of love;
No more or less, but just enough, of discipline pos-
    sessed,
To help the actor do the work that God assigns him
    best.
A tender babe may win a heart as gentle as a
    dove,
While, if a man, he could not fire that stubborn
    heart with love.
Full many a boy has spoke so sweet and looked so
    mildly up,
The beastliest father was subdued and dashed away
    his cup;
But had that boy but been a man, with logic's keen-
    est art,
He had not swayed that father's mind or ever reached
    his heart.
To train the young idea right and teach it how to
    shoot,

Requires the powers and aptitudes exactly made to
    suit ;
The hoary sage, however learned or good or wise or
    kind,
Is quite unfitted now to train the young and tender
    mind.
'Tis not because he would disdain to do an act so
    small,
But that he cannot do it right or cannot do at all.
The velvet touch of childhood's hands upon the
    mother's cheeks,
A thousand tender thrills of love to her fond bosom
    speaks ;
Let forty years of stubborn time its velvet softness
    kill,
That hand upon the mother's cheeks would wake no
    gentle thrill.
We think of Moses in his ark so beauteous, sweet,
    and fair,
And think of tenderness and love in perfect harmony
    there ;
But when a man on Sinai's brow, we stand and look
    with awe,
And fancy paints around his brow the thunders of
    the law ;
And now the foundling is a sage, the boy a hero
    grown,

And Amram's babe is now the heir to haughty
  Pharaoh's throne ;
And although trained with royal care in Egypt's
  richest lore,
He cannot win affection now as easy as before.
The stalwart father tries to soothe his sick and suf-
  fering boy,
And lifts him gently in his arms and tries to give
  him joy ;
But in his mother's warm embrace he loves to lie
  the best,
For there's more softness in her arms, more down
  within her breast.
The stalwart arm and iron nerve make no soft downy
  bed,
For that poor suffering languid boy to lay his aching
  head.
If love could win a stubborn soul that is on mischief
  bent,
Not Peter, John would surely be the helping spirit
  sent ;
If ponderous logic only could the sceptic's doubts
  o'erthrow,
Not sceptic Thomas, reasoning Paul would be the
  one to go.
And when the timid Christian shrinks at power's
  demoniac frown,

'Twould be a Luther's ministry to come in kindness
    down ;
And if the truth in sweetest tones would aid the
    trembler best,
Melancthon's spirit would glide down and whisper in
    the breast.
And since there are uncounted grades of mind and
    heart below,
To which, upon their ministries, the happy spirits go,
'Twould seem there should be grades like these,
    among the blest above,
To fit them to discharge the best those ministries of
    love.

Yes, it must be that God assigns to my beloved boy
Some lovely mission that secures and gives the purest
    joy ;
And when we come to see it all and understand it
    right,
And read his history, line by line, in heaven's clear
    crystal light,
'Twill only seem a magic thrill 'twixt Charlie's birth
    and death,
Or inspiration wafted down upon an angel's breath ;
And had it been more short or long, or gentle or
    intense,
So sweet a bud of paradise had never sprung from
    thence.

WHY WAS HE TAKEN?

Alas! why was so dear a boy, so loving and beloved,
From our fond hearts and arms and home at such
   an age removed?
We ask these questions every day along life's weary
   way,
And contemplation furnishes new answers every day;
And every hour's experience brings something new
   to light,
That serves to show that Charlie's death, e'en when
   so young, was right.

This world was never meant to be, with all its fruits
   and flowers,
So very, very dear to us, to make us call it ours;
'Tis but a life estate we have in anything below,
And we must leave it any hour the owner bids us
   go.
And all we really gain of earth with all our magic
   powers,
Is what we weave to character, and that is really
   ours;
It matters little what the world may offer or refuse,
It only matters how the gifts that God has given
   we use.

If life were all, and after death, in lifeless dust we
    blend,
Our lives would not be then as now, a simple means,
    but end.
'Twould be the voice of Wisdom then with all our
    skill and powers,
To get earth's sweetest cup of bliss and cull her
    loveliest flowers,
And always keep before our eyes this very simple
    plan,
That if we can't get all the world, get all the world
    we can.
But since this is not all of life of which we're here
    so fond,
And all that's really worth the name is that which
    lies beyond,
And could we see and weigh this life through all its
    changing scenes,
'Twould serve to prove 'tis not an end but only just
    a means.
And all the harvests that we reap of gladness and
    delight
Are incidents of doing things and using things
    aright ;
For if this life were meant for joy and nothing but
    for this,

God gives the rough material which we're to change
    to bliss,
And e'en the purest, sweetest things, that on our
    planet grow,
We may convert, just as we please, to pleasure or
    to woe.
The farmer ploughs and plants and sows and tills the
    fertile plain,
His object is not ease and joy, but 'tis a crop of
    grain ;
But though the harvest is the end and object of
    employ,
Yet, at each honest blow he strikes, he gets a feast
    of joy.
And when the harvest crowns his toils, the honest
    farmer still,
Who tries to turn it all to joy, will turn it all to ill;
Because the harvest's chief design is not for fun and
    glee,
But life s support, while we prepare for immortality.
And if, while feasting on the fruits and drinking
    from the bowl,
We had a feast of reason too and had a flow of
    soul,
'Twas not alone or chiefly that the viands tasted
    good,
But 'twas because we used them as our father meant
    we should, —

To feed these natures we possess, the earthly and
divine,
And make them both in harmony grow, develop and
combine.
But just suppose, among the rest, a savory dish is
placed,
We dearly love, because it is in harmony with our
taste ;
And though the dish were nutritive and healthful, and
combined,
In due proportion with the rest for body and for
mind,
But feast upon that favorite dish too freely and
alone,
Until a slave to appetite, and health is overthrown,
And if the ills *that* slavery brings break not the
oppressor's sway,
The last resort of wisdom is to take the dish away.

The gifts of God, to bless our race, are every moment new,
As genial as the beams of heaven and gentle as the
dew ;
And yet not one of all the train, since this round
earth has stood,
Has e'er produced, when used by man, its full
amount of good,

Till 'tis a truth that man has placed in verity's loft-
    iest niche,
That there's more safety in the world in being poor
    than rich,
For human greatness is so weak and human nature
    such,
We always love the things we have, too little or
    too much ;
And when too little, we, alas! neglect them or
    abuse,
And when too much, we worship them and all the
    blessing lose ;
And when the wisdom that inspects, and never, never
    errs,
Sees what effect each blessing has upon our characters,
Sometimes it takes the things away whene'er it deems
    it best,
Sometimes it leaves to let it sting and rankle in the
    breast ;
And blest is he who, having found his dearest idol
    slain,
So acts that from the dreadful loss, he gets a world
    of gain ;
But doubly blest the man who sees his errors and
    amends,
Ere yet the fiat's spoken and the dreadful blow de-
    scends.

We loved our children, love them still, and shall for-
　　ever love,
And hope when parting here below to meet them all
　　above ;
And since those snatched from our embrace are safe
　　on yonder shore,
We shall not love our children less, but Him who gave
　　them more.
Indeed, we cannot love too much, provided it be
　　wise,
For in a weak and doating love the real danger
　　lies ;
The only love for things below that wisdom would
　　applaud,
Is that embracing what He gives and reaching up to
　　God.
Methinks, we should love everything that God to us
　　has given,
Not only for its real worth, but that it came from
　　heaven.
If friendship gives, and we despise, whate'er the gift
　　is worth,
Because we say we should not love the grovelling
　　things of earth,
We show a lack of common sense too silly to de-
　　fend,

And lack of common gratitude to that kind-hearted
    friend.

The earth was given to us by God to foster and to
    use,
But e'en Religion oft steps up to slander and abuse,
And says that earth and everything upon this good
    round earth ;
Are only bubbles that will burst and prove they're
    nothing worth ;
Nay, worse than that, — they're but a load 'neath
    which the pilgrim bends,
And often falls e'en in the path that straight to
    heaven ascends,
And God is told, who gave us earth so perfect and
    complete,
We do not deem it worth a son and stamp it 'neath
    our feet ;
True, as an end 'tis vanity, — the whole there is of
    earth,
But as a means, Eternity can only tell its worth.
Earth has enough to show us heaven and teach us
    how to win,
And life's the time and time enough for us to do
    it in.
O ! then I'll love this beauteous earth, that God has
    deigned to give,

And love this life as long as God shall deign to let
　　me live;
And whether feasting on his gifts or writhing 'neath
　　His rod,
I'll try to love whatever comes, because it comes
　　from God,
For O! I know, if wisely loved, whatever here is
　　given,
'Twill bring a joyous harvest here and blissful one
　　in heaven;
And O! the more intense we love the blessings He
　　imparts,
Intenser love for Him who gave will thrill our grate-
　　ful hearts.

This theme we ponder day by day, though dimly
　　understood,
And ah! the more we think of it, the more it does
　　us good;
For each successive look emits an extra ray of light,
And more and more it serves to show that Provi-
　　dence was right;
And when we sigh, " Our boy is gone!" as we full
　　often sigh,
Our faith and thoughts by mutual aid find many a
　　reason why.

The world has grown unnatural now, and he that
    passes through
With comfort and success, alas ! must grow unnatural
    too.
The social strings that nature made and into harmony
    wrought
Have been by self all disarranged and into discord
    brought ;
The governor of this strange world, with all its light,
    is self,
And pretty much the whole he wants of those he
    rules is pelf ;
And were the bonds of social love to keep him from
    his prey,
'Twould take them in its ruthless hands and rend the
    bonds away,
And ravage earth with fire and sword for that old
    Tyrant Self,
And fill his gaping coffers up with plunder and with
    pelf,
Or on his altar sacrifice e'en happiness and health,
To gain that grossest, poorest gift that fortune gives
    us, — wealth.

And 'tis to such a world as this, our children must
    belong,
If they are left us long enough to join the motley
    throng ;

And they must always be with them in all their
    tastes and ways,
Or else, while mingling with the world, be martyrs
    all their days;
For though there are who're happy here, who live
    above the race,
They're only those who've giant wills and thrilled by
    sovereign grace.

O! then when our beloved ones are called away so
    young,
And our sad hearts, at every pulse, in agony are
    wrung,
Some reasons might, at every search, start up before
    the eye,
To show 'twas best, and how 'twas best, our little
    ones should die ;
And though full many a reason be ideal, dim, and
    crude,
'Twill always do the mourning one a wondrous deal
    of good.

Our blue-eyed boys and black-eyed girls so trusting,
    pure, and sweet,
How would they this unnatural world with all its
    vagaries meet?
How would they battle with the world amidst its
    noise and strife,

And cut a smooth and pleasant path through rough
    and stubborn life?
That honeyed sweetness, that distils and captures
    every heart,
Must first grow acid, ere it stands the ferment of
    life's mart;
That simple trust that in our breasts feels ne'er a
    throb of fear
Must sceptic grow to meet the world so false and
    insincere;
The guileless heart that loves so well, without one
    selfish thought,
Must love less ardent where it loves, and feign where
    it does not, —
And that which Nature made to act so delicate a
    part
Must drop all Nature's pretty ways and use the wiles
    of art,
And for that little tender thing so loving, pure, and
    sweet,
Must be a hardy Ishmaelite in cunning and deceit,
Or bundle of affected wit and elegance and grace,
And gain by some sly *ruse de guerre* a victory o'er
    the race, —
In fine, to gain the most below and at the least ex-
    pense,
Must grow far worse than now in fact and better in
    pretence.

O ! how the questions will within the weeping bosom
    start,
And throw a shadow or a gleam of sunshine o'er
    the heart:
Would those dear ones, at whom Death's lance has
    been so rudely hurled,
Have e'er been rude and coarse enough to battle
    with the world?
Or if they would and gained, beside, success's high-
    est prize,
Would not the boon have been obtained at too much
    sacrifice?
Or was there not some unseen taint within the dear
    one's vein,
That would have plagued him all his life and caused
    a life of pain?
Or moral idiosyncrasy, whose care and cure would
    ask
More thought and skill than we should e'er have
    given to the task?
Were we to search, who've seen cut down our loved
    ones in their bloom,
And laid away like loathsome things within the silent
    tomb,
We might behold the sunlight play among the tears
    we shed,

And wreathing many a rainbow round the little
    sleeper's bed ;
And should full many a reason find and many a
    cause espy,
Why 'twas a blessed, blessed thing, our little ones
    should die.

That dwarf on whom deformity has left so many a
    trace,
We scarce could recognize him as belonging to the
    race ;
That weary cripple tugging on, with crutches or with
    canes,
And who must step and hobble on, with greatest care
    and pains ;
That pallid youth, whom Phthisis now has robbed
    almost of breath,
And kills by inches, dying on a lingering, living
    death ;
That beggar-boy, in filth and rags, the badges that
    he wears,
Who lies and cheats and begs and steals and for the
    dessert swears ;
The tourist in mid-ocean wrecked, beneath an open
    sky,
Where thirst and hunger wring his soul until 'tis
    sweet to die ;

The soldier, maimed and hacked and bruised, with
    little left behind,
Except a torso with, alas! a shattered heart and
    mind; —
Like those of whom I've sung above and those I
    might below,
Of every grade and every shade of vice and want
    and woe,
Our little ones, had they but lived, might, in the
    lapse of time,
Have been the children of disease and woe and want
    and crime ;
But now love's hand, love's velvet hand, has all in
    kindness come,
And lifted up the tender ones, in all their sweetness,
    home,
Where want and woe, disease and crime, can never
    more annoy,
Nor anything can change or check a single thrill of
    joy ;
And if with faith's unclouded eye we take an up-
    ward view,
And see as plain as aught on earth the glorious fact
    is true,
The tear would dry, the sigh would hush, and sor-
    row light to joy,
To think about our angel girl or more than angel
    boy.

But when poor weeping self comes in all staggering
    'neath the cross,
And thinks, with all the pangs it brings, about the
    dreadful loss,
The sigh would swell and heave again, the tears
    begin to flow,
And all the fresh-born happiness be changed again
    to woe.

'Tis ever thus, — when God afflicts to make his own
    obey,
'Tis self that feels the blow the most, for self has led
    astray.
He never robs the industrious to give the lazy food,
And ne'er afflicts the innocent to do the guilty good;
And though He crush our little ones 'neath His
    almighty arm,
He does it often for our good and never for their
    harm ;
'Tis but uprooting tender plants in nurseries here
    below,
To set them in a sunnier clime to strengthen, bud,
    and blow.

'Tis true, God sometimes chastens men not for their
    good alone,

To plant reform in other hearts as well as in their
    own;
So kind is He, because He sees the unknown future
    through,
He never chastens more than one, where only one
    will do.
The curses heaped on Arnold's name, with earth's
    contempt and hate,
Have doubtless saved full many a one from both his
    fame and fate.

HOW GOD AFFLICTS.

When God afflicts, the blow he deals is very seldom
    dealt
In such a way that 'tis by none but by the victim
    felt;
He seems to want the healing balm affliction can
    impart,
To heal the one at whom He aims and many a kin-
    dred heart;
It seems to be the essence of our Heavenly Father's
    plan,
To strike the blow and use the rod as little as He
    can;
But when He strikes, 'tis His desire the blessing
    from the blow

Should do as much and go as far as it can do and
    go.
He made the mind with enginery of plastic power
    and skill,
To spread the healing balm abroad in harmony with
    His will.
Old History takes the record up of folly, tyranny,
    crime,
And hands it on from sire to son adown the course
    of time ;
The social heart takes up the sigh from sorrow's
    gloomy hearth,
And bears the dreadful telegram about the listening
    earth ;
And most of all, the ties of kin, the sweetest here
    below,
Bear on the saddening thrill and melt the hearts to
    which they go.
And thus by all these magic means, and countless
    thousands more,
He sends the balm from heart to heart and wafts
    from shore to shore ;
And all the fruits of Right and Wrong, and good
    and evil lie
As beacon-lights which men and states can guide
    their actions by ;
And so but one correcting rod and one paternal
    blow

Suffices to induce reform in many a heart below ;
And though chastising, evermore, in Providence will
    lurk,
'Twill ever be, while time shall last, our Heavenly
    friend's "strange work."

Why should He snatch our little ones from fond
    affection's arms,
When just beginning to put on their most bewitch-
    ing charms?
How oft the question will come up, Why should our
    children die?
And gleams of sunshine often flash and show some
    reasons why.
The little ones so pure and sweet were sent us from
    above,
Dependent for their all below on faithful earthly
    love ;
If faithful, theirs is earthly joy as well as heavenly
    bliss,
If faithless, then the dear ones lose the world to
    come and this.
And then the weeping parent feels, and says it with
    a sigh,
O! if their all depends on me, 'tis better they should
    die.
There's so much, in *my* case, of self to censure and
    condemn,

It shows how much I might have wronged or failed
    to do for them;
This head of mine and heart of mine and body that
    I wear,
All show the tokens of abuse or lack of skill and
    care.
The honest parent oftentimes, however much he tries,
Knows well his vigils will relax and culture grow
    unwise;
And almost *fears*, e'en when he tries the very best
    he can,
To train his girl for womanhood, or boy to be a
    man.
'Tis fearful to receive a soul that God has made and
    given,
And train it so 'tis wretched here and fails to get to
    Heaven.

Why should He take our little ones just sent us from
    above,
Whom we have just begun to aid and just begun to
    love,
And who, themselves, have just begun their infantile
    employ,
To make their little cup of life a little cup of joy;
And while reclining midst the down of love's divine
    embrace,

Have just begun to think the world a very charming
　　　place ?

If those dear ones could always in that downy bosom
　　　rest,
And every breast on which they'll lean would be
　　　affection's breast, —
If fortune would forever smile and never wear a
　　　frown,
And sickness never plant a pang within that bed of
　　　down, —
And if this world of ours would seem, all through its
　　　brief career,
As pleasant and as sweet a spot as we esteem it
　　　here, —
Far fewer glimpses of the truth would meet the
　　　inquirer's eye,
To make the thing a little plain and tell the reason
　　　why.
The broken fortunes that succeed the hasty heels of
　　　gain,
The shattered hearts and ruined minds that mingle
　　　in the train,
The perjured bosoms that invite within their pleasant
　　　nests
The aching head, and plant a sting within the trust-
　　　ing breasts,

And countless throngs of ills beside whose venomed
    curses ope,
And crush the flowers of human joy and blast the
    buds of hope, —
All these things come up, every day, to fond Affec-
    tion's eye,
And whisper in its listening ear a thousand reasons
    why.

Why should He take our little ones, who've just
    begun to live
The lovely lives that He has deigned mysteriously to
    give ?

If life were all, designed for us, and Jordan's farther
    bank
Were nothing but a gloomy spot or nothing but a
    blank,
We might, indeed, the question ask, and ask it with
    a sigh,
How can a God, whose name is love, bid little chil-
    dren die ?
And lesser light than now appears would aid us from
    above,
To show a God who thus decrees can be a God of
    love.

When faith has vital power enough to show our little
    ones,
Just as they are in Paradise upon their little thrones,
And see what rapture thrills their hearts within those
    realms of joy,
Without a single moment's pause or tincture of
    alloy,
And see what fair and beautiful and sweet and lovely
    things,
That move around so gracefully upon their golden
    wings ;
Methinks, we should not heave a sigh nor shed a
    single tear,
Nor wish the darlings back again to spend a moment
    here.
Or if a sigh, or if a tear, or if a wish, arise,
'Twould be to have the time arrive to meet them in
    the skies.

If life is but the nursery that God has kindly
    given,
To train up souls, immortal souls, for happiness and
    Heaven,
Why should He snatch our little ones who've just
    begun to grow
To show so much of loveliness and charm our home-
    steads so, —

And show in every little bud and every little shoot
The infant germs of loveliness and sweetest moral
    fruit ?

If earth were all the paradise where deathless plants
    may grow,
And Heaven were not so genial as this dimmer
    Heaven below ;
Nay, if it were not brighter far and sunnier far than
    this,
For deathless spirits to expand and ripen into bliss,
When we stand weeping round their beds to see our
    dear ones die,
We might with reason look to Heaven and ask the
    reason why.

Behold the little infant plants that in their nurseries
    stand,
And shoot aloft so prettily all o'er their native land,
'Tis not the loftiest of these plants, transplanted out
    of these,
That grow the best and look the best and make the
    nicest trees.
The little tender infant plants whose roots are only
    threads,
That cling with but the slightest hold within their
    native beds,

Uprooted and transported where they're meant to
    grow to trees,
The loveliest, fairest, fertilest, of all the rest, are
    these.
And though a tree may sometimes thrive, removed
    and set with care,
And grow as well as smaller trees, 'tis very, very
    rare ;
And in this moral nursery, Earth, where little spirits
    come,
And form that jewel character and go to Heaven,
    their home,
'Tis not the loftiest spirits here, most erudite and
    wise,
That make the brightest, happiest ones, transplanted
    to the skies.
The little one that only lights within this world of
    ours,
And plucks a little gem or, two within its thorny
    bowers,
Flies gayly up to paradise, — God's image yet com-
    plete,
Untouched by anything below, excepting what is
    sweet ;
For that unsullied excellence that pleases Heaven is
    not
So much the product of how much we gain on earth
    as what

Achievement, howe'er great or small, has merit or
    has none,
Weighed not alone by what we do, but what we
    might have done.
The widow's mite, though so minute, was worthier
    of regard,
Than all the gorgeous charity of any rich Girard;
For although millions measured his, the princely gift
    was small,
When weighed against the widow's mite, because
    she gave her all.
And when the little child goes up before the great
    white throne,
With but its little nosegay decked, its little moral
    one,
He'll look as fair and be as sweet and have as much
    of love
As he who wears the proudest wreath of moral flow-
    ers above.
With all that wafts a mortal up to yonder realms of
    light,
There's much that presses down again and checks the
    upward flight;
And while we're gathering flowers below to weave
    our heavenly crown,
We're gathering more of earth each day that serves
    to press us down;

And though long life cull heavenly flowers, each
    moment in the way,
'Tis just as sure to find earth's thorns and pluck
    them every day;
And nought but grace, abounding grace, that guides
    and checks and warns,
Prevents a man from gathering here, instead of flow-
    erets, thorns.
O! yes, methinks, to enter Heaven, for which the
    ransomed yearn,
The aged veteran has much more he must unlearn
    than learn;
And when he goes to taste the joys that thrill all
    hearts above,
And midst the pure inhabitants to do the work of
    love,
The ugly moral knots and twists, an earthly growth
    has given,
Must be untied and straightened out to enter into
    Heaven;
But when the little child goes up, all tender, pure,
    and sweet,
And roves the fields of paradise and walks the
    golden street,
A single breath of heavenly love, a single touch of
    grace,
Would every little spot remove and every stain
    efface;

No ugly spot or tortuous growth is left on heart or
    mind,
Nor e'en the slightest touch of ill leaves any trace
    behind.
And when to Heaven's pure studies there the new-
    born spirits turn,
The little ones have nought to do but set them down
    and learn,
While age so long to errors wed, to earth-born habits
    given,
Must first unlearn and shake them off, ere studying
    truth in Heaven.
The ransomed soul that stays on earth for threescore
    years and ten,
And mingles in the scenes of life among his fellow-
    men,
Must carry through yon pearly gate, to Heaven's un-
    fading plains,
Some little faint dissolving views of moral spots and
    stains ;
Or if not so,—if spots and stains that gate forever
    bars, —
The ransomed ones, though pure and clear, must
    carry in the scars.
The *Man of Sorrows* even yet his bleeding wounds
    displays,
The loveliest sight in paradise on which the blessed
    gaze,

And shall the ransomed, who have been by sovereign
    love forgiven,
Bear no memorial of its power when they appear in
    Heaven?
O! yes; for though in Paradise, that pure and holy
    place,
There'll be no spot or wrinkle there on any child of
    grace,
Methinks, the shadow of the past upon the golden
    floor
Will show, though so angelic now, just what they
    were before,
And then portrayed in all its truth the contrast serves
    to prove
What love has done and at each glance awakes new
    thrills of love;
But when the little child goes up so pure and fair
    and sweet,
If there's a little shadow falls beneath his merry
    feet,
It must be very faint indeed, it must be very fair,
And on the golden pave of Heaven be scarce a
    blemish there.
Beside the rainbow oft is seen a secondary glow,
Almost as bright and gay and pure and beautiful a
    bow,
And if beneath our Charlie's feet a shadowy image
    lies,

It must be like a cherub boy who roves in Para-
    dise ;
For O ! dear Charlie, though removed to yonder
    spotless sphere,
Thou canst not be much sweeter there and purer
    there than here.

Of all the truths in truth's domain, the richest and
    the best
Is this, that God desires to make his erring children
    blest ;
And as He knows each vital thread of which the
    soul is wove,
And which the one that thrills with hate and which
    the one with love,
And which the little quivering thread that, by His
    touch inspired,
Will call out from the human heart the moral fruit
    desired,
If gold's the weight that keeps us down, the glitter-
    ing prize is riven,
And then we plume our lightened wings and sail
    away to Heaven ;
If pleasure is the polar star by which life's tide we
    stem,
He clouds our sky and then we take the star of
    Bethlehem ;

If children are our idols, O! He lays them 'neath
    the sod,
And then we have no idol ones between ourselves
    and God;
And if poor earth is all we want, some pleasant
    thing is riven,
That makes earth seem with all its charms a little
    less like Heaven;
And if a single chastisement that God has ever
    sent
Has failed of wakening in the heart the sweet emo-
    tion meant,
'Twas never that He touched a cord unsuited to the
    thing,
But we had got it out of tune or paralyzed the string.
The fruit-tree springing from the earth, and from a
    vigorous root,
Will surely bear, if there's no foe to intercept the
    fruit.
The goodness of our God, that drops so sweetly from
    above,
Wakes in the heart, when 'tis in tune, the finest
    thrills of love;
And yet, though feasting every hour upon his boun-
    ties given,
Man is a rebel and a foe to all that's dear to
    Heaven.

And then, to catch the untuned heart, He wakes a
    harsher strain,
Till the poor sufferer feels the pang and tunes the
    strings again.
Ah! mourner for a darling child, whom God has
    called to die,
Is there no light from all these thoughts that tells
    some reasons why?
Ah! look within and read your heart and all its his-
    tory scan,
And weigh the changing lights and shades impartial
    as you can,
You'll find, perhaps, since kindness failed to give the
    blessing sought,
He sends, alas! some chastisement by which the boon
    was brought;
And if this fail, like those before, to bring the golden
    grain,
Beware lest, out of purest love, your Father smite
    again;
And each successive providence in love's alembic
    passed
May grow more frequent and intense and crushing
    to the last.

FAITH.

A VOICE from Nature's mellow tongue, a message
    from above,
In accents plain as angels use, proclaim that "God
    is love,"
And yet from many and many a crash in Nature's
    grand career,
And many and many a providence that brings a sob
    and tear,
There comes a harsh, discordant voice, there comes
    a mournful wail,
That whisper to the sorrowing heart a very different
    tale,
And Reason, with its boasted skill and boasted power
    of thought,
Is powerless, with its two-edged sword, to cut the
    Gordian knot.
'Tis true, we feel He must be kind in so much good
    He's given,
And that love sometimes shows its face in His af-
    flictions even,
But oftener far, when sorrow comes and wraps us in
    its pall,
We cannot see a hand of love or heart of love at
    all.

We cannot feel, at such an hour, without the aid of
    grace,
" Behind a frowning providence He shows a smiling
    face."
'Tis only Faith can purge the heart and make us
    really feel,
The dreadful blow that makes us writhe was only
    meant to heal, —
'Tis only Faith can clear the eye and help us look
    above,
And see through all earth's clouds and storms the
    truth that " God is love."
Until Faith aid, however bright the distant prospect
    seem,
'Tis but a dim Apocalypse, a very pleasant dream ;
But when Faith comes in all its power, and sets its
    beams in play,
The mists disperse, the gloom dissolves, and all is
    bright as day ;
The Heaven to which the pathway leads, in which
    it bids us go,
Seems real, as if just ahead within these realms
    below.
When dear ones die and we, alas! are staggering
    'neath the cross,
There's nothing in this weary world alleviates the
    loss ;

The dreadful truth, daguerreotyped in every act and
  thought,
Is that we had an angel once, but now we have him
  not ;
And every act and every look and every vision
  come
And bring the lovely image back, in all its witchery,
  home ;
And then we sit and weep and sigh and ponder and
  reflect,
And call up all the pleasant scenes in life's short
  retrospect,
And howe'er sweet, they've lost the power to make
  us gay and glad,
And ah ! the sweeter they were once, the more they
  make us sad.
We think of days and months and years, all brimming o'er with joy,
Because so filled with sweetness by our darling girl
  or boy ;
But now time lags with snail-like pace, and all looks
  dark and drear,
Because those little messengers of gladness are not
  here ;
And then we think how we were wont to wait and
  watch and pray,
To see new buds of promise swell and blossom every
  day,

And how we daily, fondly hoped, our dear one's
  pretty name
Would sometime stand upon the roll of usefulness
  and fame;
And then we say, ah! Halcyon days! and feel, because so bright,
Their setting sun has left us 'neath a pall of darkest
  night;
And then we think of home, sweet home, so Eden-
  like before,
When the young prattlers sang and laughed and
  scooted round the floor.
The song is hushed, the laugh is o'er, and prattler-
  less each room,
And, save poor sorrow's sighs and groans, 'tis silent
  as the tomb,—
Far gloomier than it would have been, had it ne'er
  brimmed with joy,
From that enchanting little girl or love-bud of a
  boy;
And then we think of all we did to aid and guide
  and cheer,
To make him good and wise and kind and merry-
  hearted here,
And sometimes fear, however much we tried to aid
  our son,
There might be acts we did not do, but which we
  might have done.

We think how much we watched his health, and
    fancied all along
The course we took to aid and train would make
    him firm and strong;
But, looking back, we shudder now to think of many
    a way,
By which we might have saved our boy to cheer our
    home to-day,
And sometimes think of many an act in purest kind-
    ness done,
We then thought wise, but now we fear it was an
    unwise one,
Or some ungentle deed we did that sudden passion
    woke,
Or some unkind rebuke we made or hasty word we
    spoke,
Or sweet request we thoughtlessly refused our little
    boy,
That might have thrilled with many a sweet, his
    little cup of joy,
Or some indulgence we allowed because he begged
    us so,
We were not wise or firm enough to kindly tell
    him no;
And so all through the buried past we bid the fancy
    run,

And gather up the memories of our dear, darling
      son,
And whether to the gay or sad the fancy chance
      to go,
It always brings a keener pang to thrill our cup of
      woe.
There's nothing comforts, nothing cheers, and nothing
      soothes our grief,
And silence, like a raven, sits upon life's current leaf;
And then we call for Reason's aid and bid it look
      about,
And try to make the matter plain and solve each
      lingering doubt.
We think how short is human life, how swift the
      moments fly,
And had he lived however long, how soon he'd have
      to die,
And since time first began to take our daughters and
      our sons,
By far the most of all our graves have been our little
      ones;
That children drop like Autumn leaves and strew
      the velvet ground,
But Time, that slew, comes like a friend and heals
      the ghastly wound,
That we can see the havoc made by vice, where'er
      we go,

And life all pleasant at the first becomes a life of
    woe ;
That ruin, in unnumbered ways, like its great author,
    roams,
And with its heedless chariot-wheels, rides over
    hearts and homes ;
That friendship, the divinest boon that God has sent
    below,
Oft, Judas-like, betrays its friends, and grows our
    deadliest foe ;
That health, that rosy messenger from Heaven, its
    native bower,
Though sent to all, scarce visits one with all its bliss
    and power ;
For when we're breaking Nature's laws, the ruddy
    goddess flees,
For in the train of broken laws there always comes
    disease,
And rebels against Nature will, in one continual
    strife,
Be murdered, piecemeal, inch by inch, at every step
    through life ;
And 'tis a truth exceptionless that never had a
    pause,
That every man's a sufferer from breaking Nature's
    laws ;
That wild Ambition fires the soul to gain the glit-
    tering prize,

It fails, or gaining, finds the joy Ambition promised
    lies ;
That Avarice, unsated fiend, whose rallying cry is
    " More ! "
Makes most, grown richer, every hour feel poorer
    than before,
Till the poor miser, having grown so hollow-eyed and
    gaunt,
Pines on from lack of care and food and dies at
    length from want ;
And appetites and passions swarm like locusts here
    below,
Destroying every pleasant thing and scattering want
    and woe ;
And that gross despot, grovelling sense, with his de-
    basing train,
Stands keeping vigil, everywhere, to rivet on his
    chain.
All these, alas ! and myriads more too numerous to
    be sung,
All must encounter every hour who're not promoted
    young.

Thus while with Reason's eagle eye we're passing in
    review
These Scyllas and Charybdes, strown life's fitful
    journey through,

A momentary thrill of joy is for our solace given,
To think our boy escaped them all and landed safe
      in Heaven;
But O! 'tis but one ray of light that flashes through
      the gloom,
Unbroken night rebounds again from little Charlie's
      tomb.
The little face that smiled so sweet and made all
      bright before,
Lives but on faithful memory's leaf and in this
      bosom's core
No magic, Reason can bestow, or potence lend the
      sight,
Can make his Heaven seem real gain and make his
      loss seem right;
'Tis not till Faith comes kindly in, and with her
      magic wand,
Parts the dim veil 'twixt Heaven and earth and
      shows us all beyond,
And makes us feel so plain we *know*, without the
      sense of sight,
That what God does, whate'er it be, is good and
      just and right;
And more than this, when gauged and tried by love's
      divinest test,
Whate'er he does, severe or kind, it must be for the
      best;

And when, with faith to aid and guide, we've looked
the vision through,
Till all the film of doubt is gone and we can *feel* 'tis
true,
And God's unerring sovereignty and Heaven's un-
fading bliss,
And that there is an endless life awaits us after
this,
And when the ties that bind us here shall one by
one be riven,
The good will feast forever on the endless bliss of
Heaven —
When all these truths, ideal now, shall into real
grow,
And seem as destitute of doubt as things we see and
know,
The pang of sorrow that we feel at losing such a
boy,
When touched by grace, will be but thrills of purest
heavenly joy.

When captured by the charms of faith, the head and
heart unite,
And both can banquet at her board with profit and
delight,
And life and death, disease and health, and loss and
gain shall be

The perfect notes when all combined that make
    Heaven's harmony;
Then, when our prattling innocents fly off to yonder
    shore,
And shed the sunshine of their love on home, sweet
    home, no more,
The only sigh of sorrow then from feeling's fount to
    start,
The only pang of anguish then to rend the aching
    heart,
Would be the sigh, would be the tear, would be the
    pang of pain,
That we should never see or hear our darling ones
    again;
And when we take in all the truth, the sorrow for
    our boy
Is more than paid, a thousand times, with little Char-
    lie's joy;
And when we can lay self aside, though staggering
    'neath the rod,
And feel the deed was done in love, because 'twas
    done by God, —
The God that spread yon dome of blue and pinned
    it up with stars,
That move around in magic dance without mistakes
    or jars, —
Who traced the shrubs and trees of earth and beau-
    tified the gems,

By stringing richest jewelry upon their boughs and
    stems, —
Who made the boundless universe around, below,
    above,
And wrote upon it everywhere the beauteous motto,
    "Love;"
Or if His wrath, instead of love, appears our hopes
    to scathe,
'Tis but another formula of heavenly love to faith,
Who made these wondrous frames we wear so curi-
    ously wove,
These minds of ours to meditate, these hearts of ours
    to love,
And these undying souls within, which, when the
    body dies,
Will live and seek companionship above the starry
    skies, —
'Tis such a God who did the deed, who took our
    Charlie home,
To sing the song and rove the fields above yon starry
    dome,
To study all his wondrous works as spirits do above,
And most of all and best of all, the lessons of His
    love.

While thus we look and thus we think and ponder
    on the act,

And read it with the eye of faith and feel it as a
    fact;
Our bosoms heave with wild delight that He whose
    name is love
Should deem it best that our dear boy should live
    with Him above,
And that 'twould add new thrills of bliss to Heaven's
    unbounded joy,
That Charlie should an angel be, instead of little
    boy;
And that to make e'en Heaven itself, more beautiful
    and fair,
He came to us and took from us our little Charlie
    there.
And now no longer sweetening earth, by his bewitch-
    ing love,
He draws us up and makes it sweet to lift our
    thoughts above,
And when we quite forget the past and cast our eyes
    before,
To look with faith's unclouded eye to yonder "shin-
    ing shore,"
And feel the truth in all its power that it portrays
    so plain,
That there's the spot where we shall meet our little
    boy again;
Our struggling bosoms leap for joy and we're com-
    pelled to say,

"Fly swifter round ye wheels of time and bring the
    welcome day."
O! when on prospects such as these our meditations
    run,
The heart looks up brimful of love and says, "Thy
    will be done."

THE PAST.

Ha! restless spirit, dost thou yet stand shuddering at
    the cross,
And rove around and weep among the memories of
    thy loss?
O! linger still, for much of all the good that we've
    amassed
Has come from lessons that we learned by talking
    with the past;
Success and failure both alike have choicest things to
    give,
And good and bad have wit enough to teach us how
    to live;
For though along the buried past the wisest ones
    will throng,
There's such a thing as lingering there and studying
    there too long.
The limit of our stay should be to get but just the lore

That may suffice to help us live more nobly than
　　before ;
All else were lumber from the past except the moral
　　food,
To strengthen minds, to sweeten hearts, and do the
　　spirit good ;
But he that lingers in the past, where no sweet
　　floweret blooms,
Is sure to be like him at length who dwelt among
　　the tombs.
But yet, methinks, the danger is that earth's unthink-
　　ing throng
Will linger there not long enough far oftener than
　　too long ;
And while they're there, their thoughts, alas ! will be
　　so vague and crude,
They scarcely get a single thing that really does them
　　good,
And so there is a double loss that pierces through
　　and through,
They lose the darling of their hearts and lose the
　　blessing too.

O ! yes, till weary life goes out with all its days and
　　years,
We shall go back to Charlie's grave and water it
　　with tears,

And so 'twill keep remembrance fresh and let it
    not grow dim,
For although he's so far from us, we're fast ap-
    proaching him.

TEARS.

Yes, mourning parents bend above your lost one's
    little bier,
There is a spell from Paradise that quivers in a
    tear,
For O! the tear the heart sends out, all pure and
    bright and warm,
Will melt the soul in tenderness and never do you
    harm.
The struggling soul that finds at last its sins are all
    forgiven,
Ne'er starts, without a flood of tears, upon the road
    to Heaven.
The new-born bliss forgiveness brings, the crystal
    flood employs,
To show the depth and loveliness of its diviner joys,
'Tis better far, our Father says, in his unerring
    tome,
To be within the mourner's cot than in the revel-
    ler's home;
The haughtiest heart, the proudest heart, the guiltiest
    heart will melt,

If anywhere where tears are shed and keenest anguish
    felt ;
Though Sorrow has a shaft to wound, she has a balm
    to heal,
She has a dreadful pang to bear and pleasant thrills
    to feel,
But never till she's tried her powers and every trial
    failed,
And every bulwark round the heart she could assail,
    assailed,
Does she the sword of justice draw and in the cul-
    prit thrust,
Or e'en beneath her vengeful heels she tramples him
    to dust.
O! Sorrow has a mission here, the sweetest ever
    given,
To melt the heart till it will take the signet seal of
    Heaven ;
But if she fail, with all her powers, to cause the heart
    to feel,
Or fail to soften it enough to take the signet seal,
Or if the bosom still remains unthrilled and unde-
    vout,
'Tis that it takes in other things and leaves poor
    Sorrow out ;
O! then let us let Sorrow in until her mission's
    through.

And she has done us all the good she has the power
    to do.

Ah! mourner, do not dry your tears, but let them
    freely flow,
For from so pure a crystal fount the sweetest flower-
    ets grow;
O! check them not, the tears will cease when Sor-
    row's work is o'er,
And 'twould not benefit the heart to stay a moment
    more.

'Tis true she tarries longer where she's kindly asked
    to stay,
And where the heart communes with her and hears
    her every day,
But, then, she'll plat a crown for him and take away
    the cross,
And leave a gain enough to pay a thousand times
    the loss;
And round the wounded spirit's brow entwine a gar-
    land, wove
Of faith and hope, and that bright gem, the best and
    greatest, love.

SABBATH-SCHOOL INCIDENT.

'Twas in the little Sabbath School where Charlie
    used to go,
And he was seldom absent there, because he loved
    it so, —
And though as merry as a lark through all the live-
    long day,
And foremost in the merry ring whene'er they met
    for play;
And if in farce or comedy, whichever part he bore,
He always acted well his part and always caused a
    roar;
And when he wore his soldier-hat or took his sword
    or gun,
He made, for one as small as he, a great amount of
    fun;
And old or young or grave or gay or lively or
    severe,
Were always glad, exceeding glad, to see our boy
    appear;
For it was known to every one who knew our dar-
    ling son,
Where'er he came that there would be some pure
    good-natured fun;
For Charlie had a fund of sense and fund of mother
    wit,

And often made a sage remark and oft a happy hit,
And home, *our* home, was never made so gayly to
    rejoice,
As when it rung from room to room with little
    Charlie's voice ; —
But though a merrier boy than he you'd find not,
    if you search,
He was a perfect model boy at Sabbath School and
    Church :
His open manly countenance and smiling cheerful
    face
Seemed always quite in harmony with business, time,
    and place,
And never did our darling son, in act or word or
    air,
Commit the slightest breach of right or strict decorum
    there ;
And when he saw a boisterous boy or thoughtless
    girl depart
From rules of strict propriety, it always pained his
    heart,
And many a time his mild blue eye ran o'er with
    tears, alas !
When some rude girl or ruder boy disturbed the
    little class.

It was the last fine Sabbath-day, when Charlie was
    to meet

The last fleet hour that he, alas! would occupy that
    seat;
Intently as the busy bee the rosy nectar sips,
He'd drunk in every thought and word that left the
    teacher's lips;
He'd heard the girls their hymns repeat, the boys
    their lessons say,
And when the teacher knelt in prayer, he knelt with
    her to pray;
And when the little boys and girls had sung their
    pleasant airs,
He joined his rich and mellow voice in sweet accord
    with theirs, —
O! never was a happier boy, we always used to
    say,
And never was he happier than he was that Sabbath-
    day.

Their business now was almost done, the session
    almost o'er,
But 'twas their custom ere they went to sing a little
    more,
When Charlie said, "Please let us sing, Miss Spear,
    before we go,
'I want to be an angel,' for I love to sing it so."
'Twas sung, and his sweet mellow voice helped sing
    the favorite strain,

He sang, but with that little choir he never sang
     again;
He had his wish, — a few weeks more and all earth's
     ties were riven,
And Charlie was an angel-boy among the blest in
     Heaven.

It is not strange a little child, who dearly loved to
     sing,
Should choose that favorite little air, for 'tis a charm-
     ing thing;
But when I think its words and thoughts and honeyed
     notes combined
Were so in harmony with his pure and gentle heart
     and mind;
It is a very pleasant thought that when he took his
     flight
From that retreat of innocence so brimming with
     delight,
He went off singing, as he flew, the same sweet
     melody,
"I want to be an angel," and he went to Heaven
     to be,
And then, methought, on new-born wings, I saw our
     Charlie soar,
And enter through the pearly gates upon the golden
     floor,

Still singing, but a little changed to suit the spirit-
    land,
"I *am* a little angel-boy and with the angels stand."

INCIDENT.

His little sister and himself were at their usual
    play,
And Charlie seemed more learned and wise than was
    his wont that day:
He talked of secular affairs as wisely as before,
And then began to show his fund of theologic lore;
He talked of earth and sea and air and of the starry
    sky,
And how God hung the curtain up and pinned it up
    so high;
He told her how God made the world and told how
    long it took,
And how, before 'twas finished quite, old chaos used
    to look;
He told her how He scooped the bed and put the
    ocean there,
And how He makes the lightnings flash and bellow
    through the air;
He told her how he formed the sun and made it look
    so bright,

And how He put in gas enough to furnish earth with
　　light ;
He told her how He made the moon and hung it in
　　the air,
And how and why He made the man who's always
　　sitting there ;
He cleared up all the mysteries how man was made
　　and why,
And what they'll be and where they'll go, when they
　　shall come to die. —
For Charlie, in Theology, was just as orthodox
In all his views of sacred truth as Calvin, Huss, or
　　Knox,
And when his logic failed to bring the true solution
　　out,
He always had another way by which to solve the
　　doubt.

He told her God had power enough to lift this world
　　and all,
And toss it in the air as we can toss a rubber ball ;
He told her nothing here below was from his knowl-
　　edge hid,
And God could see the smallest act that anybody
　　did, —
And all the marvels he could tell or wondrous things
　　could say,

He told his sister while she sat and listened on that
  day,
And Helen heard him talk and talk, till she was
  almost awed,
To hear him talk so learnedly about God's works and
  God,
And said to Charlie, leaning on her elbow on the
  floor,
As if she never even dreamed he knew so much
  before, —
" How is it, Charlie, that you know (and here she
  gave a nod)
So much as you have told about the works of God
  and God ? "
And Charlie answered gravely as a judge upon the
  bench, —
" I do not know, except it be because I've studied
  French."

CHARLIE AT THE COMMUNION.

'Twas one of those sweet Sabbath-days when those
  that love the Lord
Are wont to gather round His board obedient to His
  word, —
When none but those who think they've met a
  Saviour from above

Are wont to come and gladly take the symbols of
    His love,
And Charlie to his mother said, as sweet as cherubs
    say,
"Dear Mamma, let me go with you and sit with you
    to-day."
"But 'tis Communion," she replied, "when children
    all retire;
No sermon's given nor organ played nor singing by
    the choir."
"But let me go, for Christ, you know, bade little
    children come,
And I'd much rather go with you than stay, alas!
    at home."

And so we went, and Charlie went, all sparkling with
    delight,
And watching every word and act throughout the
    simple rite;
And when they prayed, he joined in prayer, and
    when they sung, he sung,
And when the pastor rose and spoke, he on each
    accent hung.
O! how he watched the minister while breaking up
    the bread
And pouring out the sacred wine which looked so
    pure and red!—

And when they took the bread and wine, how calm
    he looked to see,
And seemed as if he wished to say, O! is there none
    for me?
It seemed as if his little heart was perfectly in tune
With what a Christian's ought to be when going to
    commune.
And so delighted Charlie was, that when we went
    away,
He said, "Dear Mamma, let me come on each Com-
    munion-day,
I love to sit with you, Mamma, upon that little seat,
For everything appears so calm and everything so
    sweet ;
I hope that you will always let your little Charlie
    come,
'Tis so much sweeter staying here than 'tis to stay
    at home."
And when assured that he might come, I can't de-
    scribe the joy
That wreathed the face and lit the eye of our
    beloved boy.

Ah! little dreamed we, that when next around that
    festal board
We should sit down to celebrate the sufferings of our
    Lord,

The little cherub at our side would from our hearts
    be riven,
And sit down sweetly at the side of Him he loved
    in Heaven.

We thank thee, Heavenly Father, for the honor
    Thou hast done,
To let our only son sit down beside thine only Son.

Seems this a trifle to our minds? it seems not so to
    ours,
'Tis one of sweet remembrance's enchanting little
    flowers;
It is a flower that never fades, but which unceasing
    gives
A sweet aroma to the heart as long as memory
    lives;
And this delightful incident will ever serve to show
That Charlie's heart was tuned for Heaven, while he
    was here below;
And howe'er gay and full of fun when in a merry
    mood,
He dearly loved to be among the gentle, pure, and
    good.

And now on each Communion-day, when gathered
    at our place,

The little fellow seems to come and show his smiling
    face ;
And as we take the bread and wine that show a
    Saviour's love,
We long sometimes to take them new with our dear
    boy above,
And think if 'twere so sweet below to sit beside *us*
    even,
What ecstasy 'twill be for us to sit with him in
    Heaven.

CHARLIE AT ST. PETER'S.

THE one who's been beyond the sea and travelled
    and explored
The almost countless realms that deck old Europe's
    checker-board,
Will ne'er forget how, everywhere as busily as bees,
Officials used to hail him with " Your passports, if
    you please."
And if a city was in sight or village came in view,
A passport only oped the gate and let the traveller
    through ;
And when he entered a hotel for food or sleep or
    ease,
Ere getting either, he must hear, " Your passport,
    if you please."

And if beneath Italian skies and midst Italian scenes,
He went to see with curious eye what all her magic
    means,
He found almost at every turn official beggars stand,
And crying, " Passport, if you please," thrust out the
    eager hand.

And little Charlie had seen this repeated o'er and
    o'er,
Since first he set his little foot upon a foreign shore,
Until he almost thought that when two persons came
    in sight,
A passport was the only thing to make the meeting
    right.

'Twas when our tour was lengthened out and reached
    as far as Rome,
That we, one day, were roving round beneath St.
    Peter's dome;
Our little boy and little girl were gayly running
    o'er
From side to side, from end to end, upon the mar-
    ble floor,
While looking at the wonders there, stood little
    groups around,
Who felt, if 'twas not holy, it was really magic
    ground.—

A man of dignified address and very lofty mien,
Apart, of course, from all the rest, was in the tran-
      sept seen,
And any one, with half an eye, would know him
      from that isle,
Where 'tis a sin to crack a joke and ungenteel to smile,
And worse than all a thousand times, where he might
      chance to go,
To look at one or talk with one whose rank he did
      not know.

But Charlie, never noticing such trivial things as
      these,
Stepped up to him and gently said, "Your passport,
      if you please."
Sir Dignity looked round surprised, but as he saw
      the child,
With pleasure flashing in his eye, Sir Buckram really
      smiled,
And, without knowing what he was, — a peasant or
      a peer,
He said, "My boy, to tell the truth, I have no pass-
      port here."

Is this a trifling incident? O! nothing can be truer,
But 'twas a pleasant beam of light that beautified
      our tour;

And it will be a retrospect that ne'er will cease to
  give
A thrill of pleasure to our hearts as long as we shall
  live, —
That, with his sunny, merry face, our Charlie could
  beguile,
And melt a frigid Englishman until compelled to
  smile.

WHERE IS HEAVEN?

WHERE is that fadeless Paradise where God has
  built His throne? ·
And where He sits in majesty approachless and
  alone?
The contemplative soul looks up and, with a heart-felt
  sigh,
Attempts to fancy where it is within the starry
  sky,
And sad bereavement, with its tears all gushing down
  its eyes,
Cries, Tell me where my dear ones are, — O! where
  is Paradise?
They tell me Heaven is full of love and running o'er
  with joy,
And bliss ecstatic is the fruit of its divine employ,

And beauty reigns without alloy all o'er the happy
        place,
And every form of loveliness and every form of
        grace,
And they that rove around the realm are unre-
        strained and free,
And are as happy and content as blessed ones
        can be,
And it may be that this and all God teaches should
        suffice,
Till we get there, to know about the things of
        Paradise ;
Yet wounded spirits, from whose hearts beloved ones
        are riven,
And who have gone, they feel assured, to happiness
        and Heaven,
Will ask themselves, will ask the learned, will ask
        the Book of Love,
O! where is Heaven, that blissful place, within the
        realms above ?

The mother, when her only son has gone away to
        roam,
Feels very anxious till she knows that he has found
        a home,
And yet her anxious hopes and fears have not their
        mission done,

Until assured her son has found a sweet and happy
    one,
Nor then is free from anxious thought and many a
    fear and care, —
She wants to know not only *what* that sweet home
    is, but where;
Then with the map upon her knee, the mother
    ceases not,
Until she's searched it through and through and
    found the very spot,
And then one less uncertainty being left her to
    annoy,
She plants herself upon that spot and looks upon her
    boy;
So, when our dear ones flee away and we, with tear
    ful eyes,
Look up and try, alas! to trace the travellers to the
    skies,
We feel intensest thrills of joy, if, in the starry air,
We can select some azure spot and feel that Heaven
    is there;
Then 'twould be easier with that point in yonder
    blue arch given,
Upon imagination's wings to speed our flight to
    Heaven.

The glittering hosts that gem the sky beneath the
    swelling arch

Are, day by day and night by night, forever on the
    march,
And planets, stars, and satellites appear to shoot and
    fly
Around one common central point, far distant in the
    sky;
And though around each central sun, its own fair
    planets move,
And satellites *their* planets gird, each in its destined
    groove,
Yet every bright and central star, with all its glit-
    tering train,
Is sailing round the centre of God's limitless do-
    main,
And there, methinks, (it must be so,) amidst the
    starry skies,
Right in the centre of it all, must be that Paradise.
And there Omnipotence sits down upon His great
    White Throne,
And holds each globe within its orb unaided and
    alone,
And though in millions far too great for finite minds
    to read,
And sailing some at snail-like pace and some at light-
    ning speed;
And though their orbs run every way, like huge
    eccentric things,

As though all space were rudely piled and filled with
    golden rings,
Yet though these orbits cross and twine in countless
    shapes and ways,
And form to every eye, but God's, a giddy, tangled
    maze, —
And though these heavenly travellers fly, within their
    several spheres,
In rounds that take sometimes a month, sometimes
    ten thousand years,
And comets, rocket-like, shoot out among those
    countless orbs,
Without one jar, although their flight a thousand
    years absorbs, —
Yet not one single satellite, one planet, or one star
Has e'er received, since they began, one unintended
    jar,
And beauty and sublimity, enchanting and divine,
Start forth in all their loveliness, whene'er they sail
    or shine.

And thus God sits in majesty within that happy
    place,
The centre of uncounted worlds that fill unbounded
    space ;
And that unfading Paradise is, O ! how sweetly !
    wove

Of everything in all these worlds the happy dwell-
　　ers love,
And whatsoe'er is beautiful and good and sweet and
　　fair
In all these worlds that sail around, its archetype is
　　there ;
And when the good from all these spheres go up to
　　swell Heaven's host,
They'll find the things they loved within their native
　　planets most.

And there the Triune God sits down, its centre and
　　its soul,
And sees each atom and each world throughout the
　　boundless whole,
While round him in ecstatic groups the white-robed
　　spirits stand,
His ransomed children, all safe home, within the
　　promised land.

STUDIES OF HEAVEN.

Come, mourner, come, and let us on Imagination's
　　wings
Sail up, alighting midst this host, before the King of
　　Kings ;

Where'er you look, above, below, or at each angle
    round,
Majestic beauty, grandeur, grace, fill full the hallowed
    ground ; —
See how the globes in graceful curves of faultless
    beauty move,
Each rolling on in majesty in its aerial groove,
In curves of every shape and size that Mathematics
    sweeps,
With speed as various in degree as wondrous Motion
    keeps.
And yet, O ! how harmoniously they shoot and float
    and roll,
Without a single jar or clash throughout the bound-
    less whole !
And how the gorgeous spectacle, evolving something
    new,
Brings out of this unbounded maze new mazes into
    view !
And change on change shall never cease all through
    the magic whole,
While long eternity shall through its endless cycles
    roll,
And never through eternal years just such a scene
    as this
Shall meet the gaze of those that look from that sweet
    home of bliss.

For lo! the scene is shifting yet, e'en while we stand
　　and gaze,
And now and now and now and now evolves a new-
　　formed maze;
And now the great Artificer, perhaps, holds out His
　　hand,
And out of nothing forms a world of air and sea and
　　land,
And hurls it out among the rest without endanger-
　　ing one,
In graceful curve within the sphere of its predestined
　　sun, —
In just the right direction sent and right momentum
　　given,
To have it lodge within the path designed for it in
　　Heaven, —
And then, perhaps, a silver moon which, from his
　　fingers hurled,
Flies out and takes its destined path around its des-
　　tined world, —
Or golden ring that sails away exactly where 'tis
　　sent,
Till it begirts, like Saturn's ring, the world for which
　　'twas meant;
And soon as these new bodies gain their stations in
　　the sky,
And in their new-born orbits have begun to sail and
　　fly,

The starry hosts all o'er His realms the song of wel-
    come sing,
And all his children shout for joy till Heaven's old
    arches ring.

And so the Godhead every day bids novel magic
    start,
With some new thoughts to fill the mind, with some
    new thrills, the heart;
The groupings of created things, so changing to the
    view,
Are constantly regrouping and producing something
    new,
And new creations, every hour, meet their admiring
    gaze,
Each, grand, and making still more grand the uni-
    versal maze;
And when our lost ones leave poor earth, on angel-
    wings they soar,
And love-attracted gayly light on that enchanting
    shore;
There everything Jehovah does His happy children
    view,
Both when he groups created things and when creat-
    ing new.
He shows them how that wondrous power that New-
    ton sought and found

Draws everything to everything the universe around;
He shows them each phenomenon in Nature's wide
  domain,
That sages sought and toiled to find, but sought and
  toiled in vain;
And how the little tiny seed, dropped heedless in the
  earth,
Is made to warm and swell and burst and gayly start
  to birth;
And how all over Nature's face, in garden, field, and
  grove,
Each little fibrous thread is spun and into foliage
  wove;
And how each thing that vegetates, whate'er the
  species be,
Has just the leaf, in form and size, of such a plant
  or tree;
And how each opening bud, when kissed by air and
  sun and dew,
Expands, like its own kindred flower, in fragrance,
  shape, and hue;
And how the tints awaked to life that on the petals
  blush,
Are always just the tints and hues belonging to that
  bush;
And how, although the queenly rose has countless
  tribes and castes,

The normal idiosyncrasy through each gradation
    lasts ;
And how each plant and tree and flower, when
    touched by human skill,
Grows fairer, lovelier, sweeter far, and healthier for
    each thrill ;
And how it is that every blow that well-aimed effort
    gives,
In fairer forms and lovelier charms and sweeter
    fruitage lives.

He teaches all the lofty truths that learned chemists
    teach,
And all those grander, loftier ones, that lie beyond
    their reach ;
And what the powers in Nature's own great labor-
    atory lurk,
And what the wonders they produce and how the
    wonders work.
He shows them all the higher truths the Mathe-
    matics solve,
And those, to us, high mysteries that Numbers can
    evolve ;
And how the Science, so sublime when only viewed,
    as man's,
Mounts up to those sublimer heights by which God
    acts and plans.

He shows them those mysterious frames they used
    on earth to fill,
And all that seems so marvellous in beauty, strength,
    and skill;
And how, although so curious made, a sluggish lump
    of clay
The living spirit entered in, and set it into play;
And how the heart, with giant' power, sends out the
    purple flood,
To carry to each atom there its own appropriate
    food;
And how it is the unseen soul its own ideals sends,
Until they come out real from the actor's finger-
    ends;
And how the soul's imaginings are vitalized and
    flung,
In all their vast variety, from off the plastic tongue;
And how one soul its magic flings like odors from
    a flower,
Until another spirit, thrilled, obeys the charmer's
    power.

He tells them why He let the fiend within young
    Eden go,
And sow within its virgin bowers the seeds of sin
    and woe;

And why as long as earth shall roll He lets the seed
    be sown,
So that not one forevermore should get to Heaven
    alone.

He tells them why His love permits a vicious squalid
    home
To curse earth's unborn innocents for centuries yet
    to come ;
And why the father's eating grapes should, like a
    stubborn wedge,
Pierce down through future years and set the chil-
    dren's teeth on edge ;
Why He permits the ignorant sire neglect the tender
    minds,
And the poor children live and die, coarse and unlet-
    tered hinds ;
And why the vicious home has power, with its pes-
    tiferous breath,
To scatter 'mong the coming crowds disease and
    shame and death.

He tells them how that sacred book, in which are
    kindly given
The most we know of endless life and all we know
    of Heaven, —
Whose spirit must inspire before a single human
    breast

Can throb within that home of joy where all are
　　　good and blest, —
Is yet a Book unknown to most, unless 'tis kindly
　　　brought
By those who very seldom do one duty as they ought ;
And why it takes, to publish it to earth's remotest
　　　coast,
The sacrifice of self and gold, — two things we love
　　　the most.

He shows them what the reason why the wealth and
　　　joys of earth
Are scattered, it would almost seem, inversely as
　　　man's worth ;
He shows them why earth's good and ill, like shower
　　　and sunshine fall,
Without respect to character and equally on all ;
And why the moral tares and wheat are left alike
　　　to grow,
Although the yellow harvest be all dwarfed and
　　　blasted so ;
And why He lets the monster death in freak and
　　　frenzy slay
Whome'er he meets or wheresoe'er he meets them
　　　in the way ;
And, like a maniac, fiercely hurl his poison-pointed
　　　lance,

As if entirely purposeless or hurling it by chance;
And why, lest human science should succeed to
    thwart His skill,
He has a thousand, thousand ways, his mission to
    fulfil;
And why, unlike the serpent, which alarms before it
    springs,
The monster oft gives no alarm until he plants his
    stings;
And like rude boys that club and stone the ripened
    fruits and green,
He smites down infancy and age and at each hour
    between.

He tells them why the world lived on with but a
    flickering flame,
For full four thousand years and more before Messias
    came;
He shows the leaden power of guilt upon the fallen
    race,
And how it is the weight drops off, when touched by
    sovereign grace;
He shows how Love can bring pure gold from only
    worthless dross,
And make clear sunshine chase away all mystery
    from the cross;
And this must be – methinks it must — the sweetest
    scene above,

The centre of the beautiful, the centre of all love,
Round which the ransomed oftenest group, on which
　　　they oftenest gaze,
And out of which draw deepest draughts of rapture
　　　and amaze.

He tells them how the voice of prayer, when wafted
　　　up to Heaven,
Brings down, to soothe the sorrowing heart, the
　　　welcome word " forgiven," —
And prayer, around whose workings here such mid-
　　　night mysteries steal,
Which human logic cannot solve but ransomed
　　　hearts can feel,
Though hooted here by human wit, will prove the
　　　brightest gem
Of all the bright and glittering ones in love's grand
　　　diadem ;
An angel brighter than the train that on their mis-
　　　sions wait,
It takes the heart's petitions up and opes the pearly
　　　gate.

There's mystery writ on all below, whate'er the
　　　object be,
And there's no greater, mistier one in all the world
　　　than we ;

'Tis strown all o'er the outer world and in each sense
    that finds,
And there's a mystery in the way it takes it into
    minds,
And mystery in the processes by which we take the
    whole,
And change it into nutriment to feed the deathless
    soul ;
And mystery on mystery would all earth's joys
    derange,
Were 't not that familiarity wears off whate'er is
    strange.
But up in yonder world of bliss, as in this world
    below,
There are, and always will be, things the spirits do
    not know,
But fast as they can master truth and go to some-
    thing more,
The Heavenly Teacher lifts the veil and helps the
    truth explore, —
And long as God's eternal years shall through their
    cycles sail,
Truth shall be ever throwing off her dark mysterious
    veil,
And fast as spirits can move on in progress's swift
    career,
The mists and clouds that veil the truth will melt
    and disappear.

Were I to paint a paradise in such a world as this,
That would produce the sweetest kind and greatest
          sum of bliss,
'Twould be where all that walk its bowers are pol-
          ished and refined,
And there is one perpetual feast to feed the heart
          and mind; —
Not one all smoking on the board, all ready and pre-
          pared,
Without one effort of a guest by whom 'tis to be
          shared,
But which the guest must dig and reap, and gather,
          cull, and glean,
And after doing all the rest attend to the *cuisine.*

Where'er we mingle with the race, we always find
          it true,
That they are not the happiest ones who have the
          least to do;
And human progress does not move so merrily and
          fleet,
Where man has little else to do except to pluck and
          eat.

'Tis not beneath the warmest sun nor in the gayest
          zone,

Where Nature has, with liberal hand, her choicest
    blessings strown,
Where with the least amount of work and least
    amount of care,
The dwellers have enough to eat and all they want
    to wear, —
'Tis not in such a sunny clime, in such a gorgeous
    place,
That we should seek and hope to find the noblest
    of the race.
The chilly air and rocky shore and sterile vale and
    hill,
Which Agriculture's hardy sons inspire, subdue, and
    till, —
'Tis there the one who goes and seeks by far the
    oftenest finds
The healthiest frames, the purest hearts, the loftiest,
    strongest minds.
The normal state of haughty man, though at crea-
    tion's head,
Is this, that every man below must work and earn
    his bread ;
And not a man, from Adam down, whate'er his sta-
    tion be,
Has broke the law and yet escaped the solemn pen-
    alty.
The worker gets a feast from both, the banquet and
    employ,

The idler, too, may get his bread, but lose the extra
    joy;
No matter what the man possess, a hovel or a
    throne,
God's choicest blessings never fall upon an idle
    drone.

O! in that upper Paradise where Charlie's living
    now,
With his sweet harp within his hand and crown upon
    his brow,
I know there must be all they want for one per-
    petual feast, —
Enough of what the loftiest want, enough of what
    the least;
But yet I do not think the feast smokes on the table
    there,
Without, upon the feaster's part, a single thought or
    care.
I do not think that God permits a drivelling moral
    drone,
To take a seat beside His board or bow before His
    throne,
From that blest fund where all they need and all
    they wish is given,
The spirits get a full supply to banquet on in
    Heaven;

But yet, to get the richest feast in those enchanting
    bowers
Requires the constant exercise of all the spirit's
    powers.

I love to think that my dear boy, at every step
    above,
Finds some new truth to think about and some new
    thing to love,
And, unlike China's Buddhist Priests, — who think
    the height of joy
Is where there's not one wave of thought nor ripple
    of employ, —
My Charlie, in his home of bliss, at every step and
    turn,
Finds some new beauty to admire and some new
    truth to learn,
And that his little crystal mind, so active and so
    bright,
Is ceaselessly expanding there and gathering skill and
    might ;
And that kind heart, so sweet below, grows sweeter
    far above,
Where everything it feeds upon is beauty, goodness,
    love ;
And as he goes from truth to truth and lifts the
    sable pall,

That mystery throws o'er virgin ore, he understands
    it all;
And from the crude materials in Beauty's circling
    arms,
The sweet inventor hourly weaves fresh novelties
    and charms.

Dear boy, while bee-like flitting round in Heaven
    from gem to gem,
He gets the sweetest nectar from the Rose of Beth-
    lehem;
He recollects the story well, without a comma's
    loss,
About that wondrous, wondrous Babe that suffered
    on the cross;
He'd seen the little Jesus oft beneath St. Peter's
    dome,
He'd seen Him in the Vatican and every church at
    Rome;
He'd seen him almost everywhere that He had been
    to search, —
In almost every gallery, and palace, tower, and
    church;
And when returning home again, our merry little
    one
Still saw that same mysterious Madonna and her
    son;

And now the very central charm of that enchanting
    scene
Is that same Babe of Bethlehem, that humble Naz-
    arene.
The *Man of Sorrows*, who alone the dreadful wine-
    press trod,
Is now the central point in Heaven, enthroned a
    very God;
And though His tender bosom here was wont to throb
    with joy,
Whene'er he heard us tell the tale of Mary and her boy,
Yet now that he beholds the child on glory's topmost
    height,
His throbbing bosom overflows with wonder and
    delight;
But when he sees that Heaven itself, that pure and
    happy place,
Has not a charm, but lo! it is the radiance from His
    face,
And as, if yonder glorious sun were blotted from its
    sphere,
'Twould blot out every pleasant thing of love and
    beauty here,
So should that Blest One veil His face or from the
    scene remove,
There would be nothing left to charm and nothing
    left to love;

And thus from Charlie's mild blue eyes the tears of
    rapture run,
That he can rove that glorious place with Mary's
    spotless son.

And so upon the wings of thought we daily mount
    and fly,
And view the scenes of Paradise with Faith's de-
    lighted eye ;
And if we find a ray of light from some undoubted
    source,
That might direct the mind aright in its aerial
    course,
We take it with a grateful heart, all brimming o'er
    with joy,
And fly on buoyant wings aloft to find our sainted
    boy.

God has some shining rays of truth about Heaven's
    glories given,
And out of these we try to weave our little Charlie's
    Heaven ;
And as his pure and tender heart is graven on our
    mind,
And every pleasant angel-trait is in our memories
    shrined,
We have materials all supplied to paint his home of
    joy,

And midst its groves and in its bowers, our little
    cherub boy;
And often as we think and gaze in meditative
    mood,
It never seems to do us harm, — it always does us
    good.

IS IT A BLESSING TO HAVE HAD SUCH A BOY AND THEN LOST HIM?

When the pure love-flake fell from Heaven, what
    rapture filled the heart!
When it dissolved and rose again, how very keen the
    smart!
That smart is rankling in our hearts with all its
    anguish still,
And has the rapture in our breasts forever ceased to
    thrill?
We never shall forget the pangs while we remember
    aught,
And shall the rapture at the gift be evermore for-
    got?
O! no, the rapture that he gave, and still his mem-
    ory gives,
Will live and thrill our hearts as long as he that
    woke it lives.

But the keen anguish from the blow that rent the
    ties in twain
Will only throb a few short years till we shall meet
    again ;
And thus the bliss excels the woe from Charlie's
    birth and death,
As much as long eternity exceeds a fleeting breath.

THE BLESSING.

THE gentle dews of eventide that sail so soft below,
That light on every living thing and set it all aglow,
That string with pearls the blades of grass and set
    the leaves with gems,
And crown the velvet shrubs and trees with spar-
    kling diadems ;
And when the morning sun comes up and Nature
    looks as fair
As if an angel had been down and scattered jewels
    there,
The glittering dew-drops, solar-kissed, on new-born
    pinions rise,
And while we're gazing, disappear and seek their
    native skies ;
The day-god kissed, and up they rose on tender new-
    born wing,

But did not bear the blessing off that they had come
    to bring, —
The velvet verdure, dew-kissed, has a greener man-
    tle o'er,
And every floweret wears a smile diviner than
    before ;
And could that landscape tell its thanks, 'twould all
    the summer through
Keep singing every day and night how much it owes
    the dew ;
So, like a genial drop of dew sent sweetly from
    above,
Our Charlie came, a precious gem, to fill our hearts
    with love, —
So sweet, the love-beams from his face made happi-
    ness more bright,
And fringed each cloud of sorrow with a more than
    golden light ;
And most our hearts were thrilled by his, so pure
    and so refined,
And our minds brightened daily with the brightness
    of his mind, —
And as the florist grows more pure by talking with
    the flowers,
So from sweet converse, day by day, his spirit
    sweetened ours.

But God looked down,—we thought He frowned,
    but now we know he smiled,—
And sent some little cherubs down to bear aloft our
    child;
And, like a crystal drop of dew, kissed by the morn-
    ing sun,
Unseen by all but angel-eyes, sailed up our darling
    one;
And so the love-beams from his face have vanished
    quite away,
But not a single little thrill he ever set in play;
And home, e'en now, though full of tears, has many
    a gem of joy,
The fruits of those few fleeting years so hallowed by
    our boy;
And although frailties, errors, stains, will with our
    pleasures come,
Among the dear and pleasant things that cluster in
    our home,—
Yet if a heavenly visitant should in our home ap-
    pear,
Methinks he'd say, from what he saw, "An angel has
    been here."
Our very beings and our boy's have so together
    grown,
He'd find, perhaps, some traits of his transplanted
    to our own;

And as the air all odorless breathes through earth's
    lovely bowers,
And then comes out and passes on all redolent of
    flowers, —
So would he find that our sweet home wears a more
    charming air,
Because our little sainted boy left so much sweet-
    ness there :
He'd see in oil and photograph, in many a hallowed
    place,
The picture of a little boy with just the sweetest
    face ;
And, though its archetype not here in our domestic
    bowers,
He'd, by its very features, know the little one was
    ours.
He looks within our heart of hearts and on his little
    throne,
Sees, midst the life-throbs fluttering there, our sainted
    little one ;
And many a little pleasant thing that visitant would
    trace
Back to that charming little boy that wore that
    pleasant face.
O ! yes, as long as we shall live, 'twill be a source
    of joy,
That God, though for so short a time, gave us so
    sweet a boy ;

And if we ever reach the skies with all our sins
      forgiven,
And look to see what angel 'twas attracted us to
      Heaven,
'Twill be the one who came to earth and won us by
      His love,
And then flew up attracting us to follow him above.

FRUITS OF AFFLICTION.

How sweet the fruits of grief can be within the
      humble breast,
How Sorrow can, if used aright, make its recipient
      blest !
Affliction's rude, untender hand, if we but kiss the
      rod,
Grows velvet, as we grasp it tight, and leads us up
      to God ;
But e'en the softest hand she has grows calloused to
      the one
Who will not say or try to say, " Thy will, O God,
      be done."
God's yoke is easy to the neck, and burden — it is
      light
To those who freely take them up and wear and bear
      them right,

While those who will not take the yoke, nor yet the
 burden bear,
Will have more crushing loads to take and galling
 chains to wear;
For oftener upon sorrow's wings than gladness' wings
 we fly,
And light among the ransomed ones above the starry
 sky.
Prosperity, Calypso-like, with all its merry cheer,
Oft captivates the noblest minds and firmly chains
 them here;
Affliction smites, and then we learn how impotent is
 earth,
And then we feel that we must seek for things of
 nobler worth;
And then we find how wise He was, more plainly
 every day,
Both when He gave the little gem and took the gem
 away,—
The giving and the taking both are tokens of His
 love,
To show how charming, even here, the spirits are
 above;
And if so happy even here 'twas almost death to
 part,
What bliss 'twill be in Heaven to live, united heart
 to heart.

DO SPIRITS VISIT US HERE?

Is it a myth of some wild bard that unseen spirits
    walk
Among old scenes, and with old friends in sweet
    communion talk?
And though we know not, while immersed in trials,
    toils, and cares,
Our wearied spirits oftentimes are soothed and calmed
    by theirs;
And when, 'midst doubts and fears, alas! through
    devious ways we grope,
They come unseen, but not unfelt, and whisper joy
    and hope.

Time was, so says the Book of God, when spirits
    did appear,
And held communion with their friends who still
    were lingering here;
And that the spirits come to earth and mix with
    mortal men
Is not a whit more difficult in modern times than
    then.
When through the senses that we use for all life's
    work below,
A record's made on memory's scroll, it ne'er will let
    it go, —

And when life's fitful dream is o'er, and we depart
    at last,
'Twill still, in every tracery, bear the record of the
    past.
Each sense will die, whene'er the work of this fleet
    life is through,
For in the life beyond the tomb there's nought for
    it to do ;
For every power of all the powers that go to make
    a soul
Will be as fresh and bright as now, while endless
    ages roll, —
Nay, more than that, *more* fresh and bright, more
    vigorous and devout,
At every forward step it takes or problem it works
    out.
God makes us social beings here with interests inter-
    wove, —
I do not think 'twill be so here and not be so
    above ;
This world would be a dreary place, if insulated
    each,
And no electric spark of love from heart to heart
    could reach,
And Heaven would be no Paradise and Paradise no
    Heaven,
Were that electric current which unites the spirits
    riven ;

Communings here from soul to soul are made to ebb
    and flow
Through those mysterious unseen ducts called senses
    here below, —
These, like the ducts of proud old Rome, all wrecked
    and ruined, spread
O'er earth's campagna where repose her silent moul-
    dering dead;
But when a spirit freed from earth a sister spirit
    meets,
And holds sweet converse as they walk along the
    golden streets,
They need no sense to go between to bring and
    carry thought,
For truth is automatic where rude matter holds it
    not.
The spirit here, within its clay, gets snugly out of
    view,
And through the senses, sends abroad the false as
    well as true, —
But there, transparent as the air, if falsehood brings
    a mote,
The dullest soul in Paradise can plainly see it float,
And, therefore, 'tis a metaphor we utter when we
    say,
That beings with each other talk within the realms
    of day;

The spirits up in Paradise are what they seem
    to be,
For character, and nothing else, those blessed beings
    see.
If spirits have to tell their thoughts or others know
    them not,
Then there, as here, there's such a thing as coun-
    terfeiting thought;
And so among those happy ones that through those
    mansions flit,
There may be those, as here below, who play the
    hypocrite.

If spirits are above the sky transparent as the light,
And every moral lineament is all portrayed to sight,
Will it not follow that among the good and great
    and blest,
Whate'er one knows is known and seen and felt by
    all the rest ?

Go to that wondrous thing of Art by Raphael's pen-
    cil traced,
The brightest, sweetest, richest gem of all earth's
    works of taste ;
The slightest glance reveals the fact that 'tis a gem
    of Art,
That, once imprinted, always charms and captivates
    the heart ;

But he that drinks in all its charms must come and
    come and come,
And new discoveries every day are added to the
    sum ;
And though each charm was e'en at first as open to
    the view,
We had to gaze, how oft! and long before we saw
    it through.

In Heaven, no less than on the earth, there must be
    different grades,
And acquisitions even there of different hues and
    shades ;
For though transparent as the air, e'en to its finest
    thread,
They cannot learn the lesson there unless the les-
    son's read, —
Like the *chef d'œuvre* of Raphael's brush, or like a
    learned book,
They can't be mastered by a glance or by a hasty
    look.
One hour of social converse with the spirit of Saint
    Paul
Would show a thousand, thousand charms, it would
    not show them all ;
And though transparent as the light and open to the
    view,

It might consume a thousand years to read its beau-
    ties through.

O! when our little cherub rose and soared to fields
    above,
I know he must have looked for John and talked
    with him of love;
And save with Him whom all adore, admire, and love
    the best,
He talks with John and those like John, far oftener
    than the rest.
But tell me, does our Charlie not sometimes come
    down below,
And walk with us and talk with us who used to love
    him so ?
Our thoughts go daily up to him while roving midst
    Heaven's bowers,
And does he never come to us and rove with us in
    ours ?
Our spirits daily mount to him within his happy
    sphere,
And does his spirit ne'er come down and calmly join
    us here ?
Who doubts the pure ones think of us ? and what is
    thinking there
But going out and visiting the objects of their
    care ?

God fills all space and, therefore, nought where'er the
    objects lie
Can ever be beyond the reach of His all-seeing eye,
But disembodied spirits, like embodied ones below,
Must list, to hear, must look, to see, and learn a
    thing, to know;
And everything on memory's map inwoven and in-
    wrought,
Whene'er they wish, they go to see upon the wings
    of thought;
The laws of mind are always like, whate'er the
    actor be,
Both when encumbered with the flesh and when
    entirely free.

When thoughts like these come o'er our minds, we
    feel it must be so,
And Charlie does come home to see the ones he
    loved below;
We think that Reason is not shamed, nor Common
    Sense abused,
To say that spirits walk the earth exactly as they
    used.
Nor do I think that 'tis a weak and superstitious
    thought,
By dreamy musing conjured up or silly fancy
    wrought,

That, sometimes, in our tears we've felt an inner
    peace and joy,
That must have been the heavenly fruit of converse
    with our boy.

ALL MYSTERIES EXPLAINED IN HEAVEN.

I LOVE to think that when I to my Father's house
    return,
There'll be so many glorious truths that I shall have
    to learn;
There'll be so many mysteries unfathomed here below,
That I shall have to fathom there and study till I
    know;
And things that here seemed strange or wrong,
    within Heaven's clearer light,
Prove pure and faultless harmonies and all exactly
    right;
And that the ills that checker life and shorten and
    annoy,
Were but the seeds, the germs, the buds of Heaven's
    unending joy,
And that had one been blotted out or one had never
    been,
Life would have been a meaningless and inharmonious
    scene.

I love to think that every jar upon my heart-strings
    here,
That caused my breast to heave a sigh or eye to drop
    a tear,
Is but the tuning of those strings, so dissonant and
    wrong,
That I might be prepared to sing Heaven's high and
    holy song.

I love to think, in yonder world, one element of
    bliss
Will be to fathom and unfold the mysteries seen in
    this ;
And everything that pains us here and everything
    that grieves,
And every blight and mildew dropped on hope's ex-
    panding leaves,
And every hoary frost that came to our domestic
    bowers,
That nipped the buds or killed the leaves or scathed
    the merry flowers,
Will prove to be the richest gifts our Father could
    have given,
The seedlings of the sweetest charms attracting us to
    Heaven ;
And all the good and ill of life, its pleasures and its
    pains,

Its smiles and tears, its hopes and fears, its losses
and its gains,
That seemed so chance-directed here or meaningless
or wrong,
Were but the prelude to prepare for joy's immortal
song.

I love to think, when I sit down, if I shall sit
above,
The good and ill of life will seem alike the gems of
love ;
And I shall see exactly why, to draw my heart to
joy,
My Father had to snatch from me my darling little
boy.

I love to think the time will come when I shall see
and know,
That it was best, and why 'twas best, that mysteries
reigned below ;
And that within the field of truth, spread out on
every hand,
So much we saw or could not see or could not
understand ;
And it may be that it will prove (the strangest thing
of all)
That, though with minds of so much power, our
conquests were so small.

I love to think that I shall know how God, with err-
    less skill,
Could harmony from discord bring and happiness from
    ill,
And make the very wrath of man, howe'er demoniac
    even,
Work out the kind designs of love in gathering souls
    to Heaven.

I love to think that I may find our finiteness in
    this
May work out joy, intenser joy, within the world of
    bliss ;
The sweetest thrills of heavenly joy in bosoms up
    above
Must be the thrill that flutters from the living pulse
    of love ;
And filial love is ne'er so great and ne'er so pure
    and sweet,
As when the child sits learning at the teaching
    father's feet.
Could we the mysteries all explain and facts and
    truths discern,
And all we've ever got to learn by thought and
    study learn,
Methinks, 'twould wipe out faith entire, — the sweet-
    est viand given

To feed the deathless soul below and make it pant for
  Heaven.
But whatsoe'er the reason be, though veiled from
  human sight,
Faith, that celestial beam from Heaven, shows 'tis
  entirely right;
And sweet the thought, when we get home to man-
  sions in the sky,
We shall sit down among the blest and learn the
  reason why,
And every sorrow that we shared, and anguish that
  we felt,
Will into tokens of His love and boundless kindness
  melt.

O! yes, though mysteries throng my way and truths
  conceal their mien,
And pain and sorrow make poor earth a sad and
  dreary scene,
So much intenser, purer joy will thrill my ransomed
  breast,
When I shall see both that it was and how it was
  the best.

O! let me then, whate'er betide, without a doubt or
  fear,
Believe our Heavenly Father guides our tottering
  footsteps here,

And that the humblest, trusting one, is surest to be
    right,
Who walks among earth's dreariest scenes by faith
    and not by sight, —
Then, though our dear ones — *dearest ones* — are from
    our bosoms riven,
And our young prattling innocents are summoned
    home to Heaven,
I'll try to *feel* until the time when I shall *see* and
    know,
That it was love and only love that dealt the stun-
    ning blow.

STAY IN LONDON.

'Twas when we had our hasty home in that gigantic
    town,
All gray with age and bright with youth, the pride
    of England's crown,
Where Virtue stands where'er you go with blessings
    in her arms,
And Vice, beside her, woos her dupes with more
    than rival charms, —
Where wealth goes staggering 'neath the weight of
    its own money-bags,
And want, gaunt starveling, begs its crusts in scant
    and fluttering rags, —

And all extremes of good and bad within old London
    dwell,
That make her seem sometimes a Heaven and seem
    sometimes a Hell;
And there we lived and passed the hours, midst
    beauties ever new,
We wandered all her galleries and gardens throug'
    and through.
We went to see her palaces and mounted her old
    towers,
And travelled through her lovely parks and walked
    among her flowers;
We went to Kew and Sydenham, that brightest
    earthly gem,
Excepting Chatsworth that adorns old England's
    diadem;
We went to her old abbey where uncounted travel-
    lers tread
The marble aisles among the graves of England's
    honored dead;
We went to that enchanting pile beneath whose
    graceful wings
Her Lords and Commons congregate as well as
    Queens and Kings,—
And all these things on memory's leaf are written out
    so plain,
The picture never can grow dim or e'er go out
    again,

But midst these charming retrospects, so full of
    genuine joy,
The image always seems to stand of our enchanting
    boy ;
We hear his little pattering feet along the marble
    floor,
We see him gayly darting round through every
    opening door, —
We hear him calling Helen, as he saw some work of
    art,
Which chanced to catch his little eye and thrill his
    little heart ;
For feasting was no feast to him, however well sup-
    plied,
If Helen did not share it too, delighted at his side ;
No matter what, no matter how, no matter when or
    where
Our retrospects, the little form of our dear boy is
    there.

We go in memory back again to Madam Tussaud's
    court,
Where London tourists always go for pastime or for
    sport,
And little Charlie's always there, as merry and as
    gay
As when he asked a figure there to tell the time of
    day, —

And when the figure did not speak, he, with a little
    pause,
Came up and told us what a boor the stupid fellow
    was;
"I asked the man what time it was, and though I
    know he heard,
He did not even notice me nor say a single word."

We go in memory back again, and gayly rove
    around
In Kensington, that beautiful and almost fairy ground,
Around the lawn and through the grove and round
    the silver lake,
All swarming with aquatic birds of every form and
    make;
But Charlie always seems to rove amidst the magic
    scene,
With merry face and laughing eye and manly form
    and mien,
And calling Helen, Helen, in his sweetest, manliest
    tone,
Whene'er he found a pretty thing he would not have
    alone.
There he and Helen and the nurse — I see them
    plain as day —
Went out and spent the pleasant hours in merry sport
    and play;

I see them with the drinking cup to dip from yonder
    spring,
And basket with a liberal lunch of some delicious
    thing.
Anon, I see him standing there with something in
    his hand,
Among the noisy feathery tribes as thick as they
    could stand, —
When suddenly a hungry duck to little Charlie run,
And seized from out his little hand, his but half-eaten
    bun,
And off he waddled toward the lake with Charlie in
    his track,
And gliding in the water, gave a self-complacent
    " quack ; "
Then Charlie cried and then he laughed to see the
    creature run,
And sail away so far from land to eat his stolen
    bun.

It is a vision of the fact just as the fact occurred,
When Charlie's bun within his hand was stolen by
    a bird, —
And ever after while he lived and spoke of Kensing-
    ton,
He used to tell about the duck that came and stole
    his bun.

One day, while seated by a boy, — an English boy, —
    to look
And see the pictures in a little English picture-book,
From page to page they looked to see the reptiles,
    beasts, and birds,
And called them all exactly like, the designating
    words:
The Robin and Canary-Bird, the Serpent and the
    Fox,
The Fish, the Lamb, the Cow, the Goat, the Buf-
    falo and Ox;
And Charlie and his little friend pronounced them all
    the same,
Until they turned another leaf and to the Monkey
    came;
"Why that's 'a hape' upon this leaf," said little
    Johnny Bull,
But Charlie almost split his sides with laughter brim-
    ming full,
And looking toward his English friend, he, in a merry
    tone,
Cried out, "Pray tell me what's 'a hape,' I never
    heard of one."
And ever after, when he saw a monkey or an ape,
He, with a merry smile, would say, "See, Helen,
    there's 'a hape.'"

PARIS.

E NCHANTING Paris, where's the man that ever saw
　　　thy charms,
Whose Memory did not always clasp the vision in its
　　　arms,
And he who visits Europe's shores will always take
　　　good care
To visit Paris oftenest and stay the longest there.
Our home on rue de Rivoli was where we used to see
Those gayest grounds this side the skies, the gay
　　　Tuileries;
And when the children wished to go within the
　　　grounds to play,
'Twas nothing that they had to do but go across the
　　　way;
And, therefore, hours and hours they'd play, those
　　　happy little ones,
Among the Gallic girls and boys and white-capped
　　　Gallic *bonnes;*
And there they used to study French among the
　　　merry throngs,
Until they talked as well as they and sung their little
　　　songs;
And now when all these scenes come up on Mem-
　　　ory's pages traced,

Our Charlie is the central charm upon the canvas
    placed;
The gay policeman knew him well when coming
    near his beat,
And used to call him "Petit Sharl," whene'er they
    chanced to meet;
And on that same policeman's face you'd see a
    smile of joy,
Whene'er he saw him cross the street, — that little
    Yankee boy;
And they would talk, and "Petit Sharl" declare it
    was his plan
To be a bold policeman too, when he should be a
    man.
But midst all these — these splendid scenes of ele-
    gance and joy —
Our little Charlie ne'er forgot he was a Yankee boy,
And at their fêtes and gay parades in streets or
    Champs de Mars,
You'd see him marching 'neath our flag, the glorious
    stripes and stars;
And 'twas amusing very oft to see him marching there,
Beneath his country's banner with a martial step and
    air;
And when the Imperial Cortége rushed through
    rue de Rivoli,
The little Yankee boy was there, among the rest, to
    see;

And when the Empress rode away, with splendid
    coach and four,
Along that street as smoothly wrought as any palace
    floor,
With Helen at his side, he'd stand with an uncov-
    ered brow,
Where he was sure to catch her eye and sure to get
    a bow;
For, unlike England's Royal Queen, she deigns to cast
    her eye,
And bow to those who show respect when she is
    passing by;
And when the Prince Imperial dashed along the
    crowded way,
With cavalcade caparisoned in splendidest array,
Our Charlie dearly loved to see the little fellow
    ride,
With all those splendid mounted men escorting at his
    side;
For envy never touched his heart with e'en its
    faintest tints —
'Twould be as if a sovereign should be envious of a
    prince.

How can, think you, these pleasant scenes in faith-
    ful memory start,
And Charlie not relive again within a parent's
    heart?

O! when I'd seen the gray old world of which I'd
    read and dreamed,
And memory had daguerreotypes of how its wonders
    seemed,
I felt that I'd a double world instead of only this,
From which to draw the viands for my feast of
    earthly bliss;
But since our Charlie left our arms and we were
    whelmed in grief,
And he and Europe, side by side, are found on
    memory's leaf,
The retrospects of foreign lands and foreign travel wear
A hallowed charm, a chastened hue, because our boy
    is there;
And 'tis for this we fondly hope that travel with its
    lore
May now appear a holier thing than it appeared
    before.

THE VOYAGE.

'Twas eighteen hundred fifty-eight, July the seventh,
    at four,
With luggage placed on board the boat, we left Man-
    hattan's shore;

The little steamer took us on from Jersey's crowded
　　slip,
With many a friend who wished to see us safe on
　　board the ship,
And wafted off our little group as gayly as a dream,
To where the Persia, gallant ship, was riding in the
　　stream;
And hands were grasped and kisses given by fond
　　Affection's lips,
And warm adieus from friend to friend exchanged
　　between the ships;
And when the little steamer turned and darted
　　toward the shore,
White handkerchiefs were waved from both till we
　　could see no more.

Good-by, good-by, dear friends, good-by; dear native
　　land, adieu,
O! shall we e'er alive and well come back again to
　　you?

'Twas thus we thought, perhaps, we said, as we pre-
　　pared to go,
And gather in our little flock within our home
　　below;
And ere we'd oped our drawing-room and gathered by
　　ourselves,

And placed the children in their berths, (the children
    called them shelves,)
Old night had gathered round the ship and hemmed
    the prospect so,
We saw but moon and stars above and ship and sea
    below ;
And then commending all to God upon the bended
    knee,
We spent the night in gentle sleep, the first we spent
    at sea.
And day and night for days and days, without a mo-
    ment's rest,
The gallant Persia ploughed the way upon the ocean's
    crest,
Without a storm or boisterous wind, a single hour or
    day,
Until within the Mersey moored, the ship at anchor
    lay.

Who does not know how anxiously when people are
    at sea,
They make the most of incidents to break monotony,
And how invention does her best to call up some-
    thing new,
To see or hear or meditate or think about or do;
And such were all, or almost all, occurring day by
    day,

That caused a ripple o'er the face of dull *ennui* to
    play :
An iceberg of enormous size one evening hove in
    sight,
And some few whales came up to spout far distant to
    the right,
And one poor fellow, on the way to his affianced
    bride,
Deceased and then was solemnly committed to the
    tide, —
And, saving these few incidents, the actors in the
    play
All improvised the incidents they had to cheer the
    way.
But what with incidents we made and those we found
    supplied,
And voyage made so very brief by prosperous wind
    and tide,
It was a very pleasant trip, which, till life's sun shall
    set,
We shall delight to think about and never can
    forget ;
But ah ! to me there's something more than what
    these scenes impart,
That memory gathers from it all and shrines within
    my heart.

A little boy in sailor's dress and scarcely three years
    old,
Whose thick red flannel coat and pants kept out the
    piercing cold, —
For e'en July upon the land may very scorching be,
And still be cold as Greenland where we're far away
    at sea ;
But cold, the bitterest sort, that comes from biting
    frosts and snows,
Could scarcely get a nip at him within those flannel
    clothes ;
And while the other boys and girls, and men and
    women too,
Were shivering with the bitter cold and almost frozen
    through,
He, merry as the merriest lark that ever chirped a
    lay,
Was never cold, but warm enough, through all the
    livelong day ;
And so well known and loved by all was that mild,
    merry child,
He carried pleasure where he went and sunshine
    where he smiled ;
And ere he'd been a week at sea, so well he played
    his part,
He'd gained respect of all on board and every sailor's
    heart ;

So that when disembarking from this gallantest of
    ships,
A "Good-by, Charlie," gayly leaped from every
    sailor's lips.

Now always as these pleasant scenes before my vision
    lie,
All heard again by memory's ear and seen by mem-
    ory's eye,
I see within the tissued scenes before my eyes un-
    rolled,
Whate'er supplied the silver threads, 'twas Charlie
    formed the gold.

THE RETURN.

Two years had passed and we'd each day been seeing
    something new,
And home, sweet home, with all its charms, came up
    to memory's view;
That gallant ship, the Arago, and gallant Captain
    Lynes,[1]
Were soon to come and bear us where the sun of
    freedom shines.

[1] Captain Lynes perished by falling from the banks at Niagara in the
summer of 1862.

Ah! gallant Captain,— so alike the kindly friend to
    all,
Not cringing to the rich and great and crabbed to
    the small;
Whoever ever sailed with thee but when he had to
    part,
He bore away, where'er he went, thine image in his
    heart?
Old Ocean might not spread thy couch beneath his
    yesty waves,
But old Niagara gave thee one of his sublimest
    graves.

Farewell, Old Man, thou'lt live and live on yonder
    fadeless shore,
When dread Niagara, with his waves, shall cease to
    rage and roar,
And all that ever sailed with thee across old Ocean's
    main
Will love to meet and talk with thee and rove with
    thee again.

The Arago, that gallant ship, the English channel
    ploughs,
She's shot from Havre on her way and stops for us
    at Cowes,

And all on board the little boat, we, from Southamp-
        ton glide,
And soon are near the Arago and lying at her side
The portal opes, the steps let down, and, joyous and
        elate,
We gayly leave the little ship and get on board the
        great.

For home, — for home, — how sweet the thought, for
        those who've been to roam,
That they're at last on board the ship that's soon to
        bear them home ;
And if the steamer stems the tide as she has done
        before,
They soon shall be safe home again upon their native
        shore.

But one day out and boisterous gales began, in furious
        spite,
To roar and rave and lash the sea unceasing day and
        night ;
The seething ocean boiled and heaved, and, like a
        dancing cork,
The staggering steamer pitched and rolled until we
        hailed New York ;
And scarce one day and scarce one hour and scarce
        one minute e'en,

The battling wind-god ceased to add new terrors to
    the scene.
Through Switzerlands on Switzerlands, midst moun-
    tains capped with snow,
And through impervious passes oft the steamer
    seemed to go;
And how that steamer passed those gulfs and moun-
    tains capped with snows,
And shot among those jutting rocks, alas! God only
    knows;
But she did stem the mountain waves, and yawning
    chasms spanned,
Until, all safe, we'd set our feet upon our native
    land;
And not one friend who'd said adieu, when we went
    off to roam,
But still was there alive and well to bid us welcome
    home.

These scenes still live as fresh as when we saw and
    heard and felt,
And never can the vision fade or in oblivion melt;
And never shall we cease to see until life's curtain
    fall,
The little one who hallowed it and sanctified it all,
And spun the little golden threads that bound it to
    the heart,

Too sweet and strong to burden or be ever rent
    apart ;
For all throughout those weary weeks within that
    rocking ship,
And through that lagging, weary, long, disgusting,
    filthy trip, —
When all declared, 'pon honor, if they ever got
    ashore,
They'd never leave their homes again to tempt old
    Ocean more, —
Our little Charlie, midst the gloom, was like a ray
    of light,
He gayly sported through the day and sweetly slept
    at night ;
And every staggering sea-sick soul, whom nothing
    else could cheer,
Imbibed a sunbeam of delight whenever he was
    near.

Dear little bud of innocence, too sweet and pure to
    bloom,
And waste thy fragrance in the fields this side the
    silent tomb,
Why shouldst thou not have been so gay, so uncon-
    cerned and free,
When guilt had never dropped a stain or spoke a
    word to thee ?

Yes, blessed boy, we'll ne'er forget, until our dying
    day,
Whose little face amidst that scene could chase the
    gloom away.

DOUBTS.

WHEN Love and Friendship find the ties of Love
    and Friendship riven,
We try to think, and we *may* think, our dear ones
    are in Heaven,
But doubts, like motes in Faith's clear eye, obscure
    its upward stare,
Until, at last, it cannot see the loved and lost are
    there ;
And then we cry, O! can it be, that our lost friends
    to-day
Are not among God's conscious ones, but dead, un-
    conscious clay ?
And then the clouds begin to flit o'er Faith's un-
    clouded sky,
And every star is wrapped in gloom to her bewildered
    eye ;
And then the picture grows so dim and almost fades
    from view, —
The future meeting with our friends that chastened
    fancy drew ;

And then we try to wipe the mote from Faith's
  bewildered eye,
That she may see with clearer gaze the vision in the
  sky ;
And then we go with chastened heart to Heaven's
  unerring tome,
For light that shows as plain as day that there's a
  life to come ;
And although He who cannot lie has made the truth
  so plain,
That, though man dies and turns to dust, yet he shall
  live again,
A fear will sometimes mar our joy, a doubt will
  shake our faith,
And human nature weak and frail hope's brightest
  visions scathe ;
And then we fly to any source that added light will
  give,
To make more sure the glorious truth that our
  departed live.
We catch at that important fact that wheresoe'er we
  roam,
We find the faith, however gained, that there's a life
  to come ;
And surely God would ne'er have given, His whole
  creation through,
A faith or instinct in the mind to prove at last
  untrue, —

That points us to a glorious world surpassing bright
    and fair,
To prove a mirage to our faith on our arrival there.

And then we to our altar go and leave our offering
    there,
And try to mount to God's abode upon the wings of
    prayer;
And never do we go in vain, — we ask and we
    receive,
The light comes down and then, O! then, 'tis easy
    to believe.

And then we sit and meditate and bring the prod-
    ucts home,
And group them till the picture is a very life to
    come;
Our loved and lost, alive and well, and happier than
    before,
Are loving, roving, triumphing, where they will die
    no more;
And then we sigh, if spirits e'er from Paradise may
    roam,
And visit this poor earth again they used to call
    "sweet home,"
O! that the dear ones would come down and for a
    moment rest,

And plant pure thoughts and pleasant hopes within
    the throbbing breast!
And then we feel an inward peace, a sweet and holy
    calm,
As if upon our wounded heart an Angel dropped a
    balm ;
No impure feeling, wish, or thought, could in ou.
    hearts be found,
Because a heavenly visitant had made it hallowed
    ground ;
And O ! the odor of that scene, — it was not driven
    away,
But floated sweetly in our hearts for many and many
    a day.

Ah ! no one knows but he who tries what heavenly
    fruitage springs
From sitting down to meditate on high and holy
    things ;
And every moment wisely spent will some new treas-
    ure ope,
To strengthen faith, to brighten joy, and cheer the
    heart of hope.

And every day and every hour we find some little
    gem,
To set within and sweetly deck Faith's beauteous
    diadem ;

And though revealed in Heaven's own tome for mor-
    tals to receive,
And all are left without excuse who dare to disbe-
    lieve, —
It aids the most undoubting faith when there is that
    will show,
'Tis backed and aided by a truth we understand and
    know.

'Tis God's command to all the world to keep His
    Sabbath-day,
And every one who loves his Lord will cheerfully
    obey ;
But when he finds that man and beast have natures
    suited best,
Where one in seven, no more, no less, is made a day
    of rest,
The good will feel an added thrill of reverence for
    the day,
And with devouter, gladder hearts, the sweet com-
    mand obey.

And so from all the gleams of light that meet us as
    we go,
And all the truths already learned and all we come
    to know,
And all the aid and all the light analogy supplies,

And all imagination gets from earth and sea and
    skies, —
And most of all and best of all, the noon-day sun-
    shine there,
That gathers round the human soul that seeks the
    · place of prayer, —
From all these sources we can draw, and never need
    to fail
Of giving Faith's pure eye a power to look beyond
    the veil;
And seeing Paradise so plain, no doubts or fears could
    scathe,
And we've fruition almost here instead of wavering
    faith.

O! when our dear ones flee away to be with us no
    more,
And all the rites that we can pay to sacred dust
    are o'er,
And we return subdued and sad to our once cheer-
    ful home, —
But now the saddest, gloomiest spot beneath the
    starry dome, —
There's nothing but the Christian's hope can shed a
    ray of light,
There's nothing else but trust in God can make us
    feel 'tis right;

And hope and trust and every help the mourner can
    employ
Can scarcely give the wounded heart a genuine feast
    of joy;
And time must shed its healing balm in gentle dew-
    drops down,
Before the sorrow change to joy or cross become a
    crown.

'Tis sweet that there's so many a source to which
    we've power to go,
For that which takes full many a pang away from
    want and woe;
And if to every furnished source we heartily re-
    pair,
And pick up every little thing to weave to gladness
    there,
We all should gain, whoe'er we be, the greatest or
    the least,
The crumbs of comfort quite enough to make a royal
    feast,
And home itself would beam with bliss, although one
    tie is riven,
That God should take its little one to be with Him
    in Heaven.

THE PRAYER.

O Thou who didst the fiat speak and out of chaos
    sprung
This beauteous earth, so nicely poised and in mid-
    ether hung,
And at whose word the breath of life through inert
    matter ran,
And waked its atoms into life all marshalled into
    man, —
To Thee we come, before Thee bow, and towards
    Thee lift the soul,
For Thou who mad'st the Universe canst all its parts
    control.
With two petitions we have come, they're all we
    bring to-day, —
Grant us, O Lord, a listening ear, and hear us while
    we pray :
O ! give us power to fathom what Thy providences
    teach,
And grace to study what they mean and practice
    what they preach,
That when we take the cup of joy or feel the chas-
    tening rod,
We may be drawn with purer joy and warmer love
    to God, —

Then though our eyes are daily wet, such ties were
    rent in twain,
The smile shall glitter 'mongst the tears to think of
    Charlie's gain.

WHAT IS A SPIRIT?

WHAT is a spirit? sighs the soul that finds dear
    friends are riven,
And tries to look beyond the vail and see them safe
    in Heaven;
But O! from wit's profoundest depth and fancy's loft-
    iest height,
No answer comes to tell it what or shed a ray of
    light.

There's many a Plato who has tried, since time its
    course began,
To give a definition which should tell us what is
    man;
But never has a sage or seer, although he did his
    best,
Succeeded yet in giving one that stood the final test.
To tell exactly what is man, we must define the
    whole, —
Not only what the body is, but also what the soul;

22

And though we feel we know so well the bodies that
    we wear,
I think we understand as well the spirits that we
    bear.
Life is a mystery to ourselves e'en in our earthly
    home,
There is no greater mystery in the spirit's life to
    come;
If spirits here not only live, but vitalize dead clay,
And bear it round where'er they list until their
    dying day,
Is it more strange that they can live without that
    weary load,
When wafted upon new-born wings to their divine
    abode?
But although what we then shall be may now be
    dark and dim,
No matter if, when we awake, we wake to be like
    Him.
But still we puzzle o'er the thought how spirits, when
    above,
Appear and act and talk and think and see and live
    and move;
My humble Muse presumes to think that in their
    higher sphere
They are and act exactly as they were and acted
    here,

The difference being but this, methinks : a spirit here,
    though pure,
Must fight its way and win the day or never be
    secure, —
But there, where nothing gross or vile can ever-
    more annoy,
Whate'er they do or think or feel are elements of
    joy ;
The house it lives in here below claims many a
    thought and care,
Sometimes it needs a new costume, sometimes it
    needs repair, —
But *there*, no house demands its care, and in its high
    employ
There's nothing that can block its way to truth and
    love and joy.

Were not existence everywhere mysterious through
    and through,
'Twould seem far less how spirits live than soul and
    body do ;
The spirit is the vital thing, the body inert clay,
Which that must vitalize or this can never live a
    day,
And half the wonder seems to cease, when, from the
    body free,
The vital spirit lives in its own immortality.

O ! when we ope the pearly gate, on golden hinges
     hung,
And enter into Paradise and join the happy throng,
I do not think that higher life within that home of
     bliss
Will seem to us so new or strange or different from
     this, —
The spirit there will feel the same as in its earthly
     lot,
'Twill feel that its surroundings change, but that itself
     does not ;
And when it moves or looks or learns or acts, —
     whichever one, —
Volition sends the fiat out and lo ! the work is done.
And if that spirit while on earth were thrilled with
     Christian love,
It finds the things that cheered it here are cheering
     it above ;
When Paysons and when Judsons mount to yonder
     world of bliss,
They find their happiness the same as they enjoyed
     in this ;
And Heaven's employs as well as joys are just the
     same as they
Had been pursuing in this world for many and many
     a day.

HOW DOES A SPIRIT LOOK?

How shall we in the spirit land, when made im-
    mortal, look?
It is not writ on Nature's page nor in God's errless
    book ;
But I've no doubt, to spirits' eyes, our spirits will
    appear,
The very same that we appeared to eyes that saw
    us here ;
And, therefore, those who knew us here will recog-
    nize us there,
For just the lineaments we wore when upon earth,
    we'll wear,
And if we've doubts of some we knew or sometimes
    wholly err,
It is because they seemed below not what they really
    were, —
But in that clear and piercing light to clear and
    piercing eyes,
To seem and be are synonymes where no distinction
    lies ;
But as, on earth, resemblances full oft the vision
    strike,
That show the wearer one we knew or one exceed-
    ing like,

We watch his motions, features, airs, and tones and
    accents long
Before we're fully satisfied that we are right or
    wrong, —
So in the spirit land, methinks, the happy beings
    know,
Full often at a single glance the ones they knew
    below;
But oftener far a single glance suffices not to prove,
That 'tis or is not one they knew whom they behold
    above, —
And so they have to look and watch again, again,
    again,
Before the truth like sunlight breaks and makes the
    matter plain.
Sometimes they see earth's poorest ones on highest
    seats above,
And earth's élite on humbler seats at Heaven's pure
    feast of love;
And thousands there they often find whom they had
    never thought
Of seeing there among the blest in that delightful
    spot;
And thousands they expected there are sought, but
    never found,
Among the pure and lofty ones within that hallowed
    ground.

The deathless spirit here below with all its sins for-
      given,
Is just the same as it will be when safe arrived in
      Heaven;
Whate'er it likes, whate'er dislikes of earthly moral
      fare,
'Twill like or dislike, just as here, those very viands
      there, —
For earthly bliss and heavenly bliss must one in
      essence be,
They're not diverse at all in kind, but only in
      degree.

O! yes, methinks, this world of ours and that which
      is to come,
Are only different rooms within our Heavenly
      Father's home;
In this there are unnumbered foes assaulting every
      day,
And he that would securely live must watch as well
      as pray;
In that there never lurks a foe to injure or annoy,
But work is play, and watching rest, and prayer is
      praise and joy;
In this, among the vile and gross, the spirit, though
      a saint's,

Like some rich gem, a casket needs, to keep it from
    attaints ;
In that, the casket's thrown away, for one might
    look in vain
For anything within that realm to mangle, scar, or
    stain.

LIFE NEVER ENDS.

'Tis sweet to think that life begun can never, never
    end,
Surpassing sweet, if we but make the One who gave,
    our friend.
When we have passed our lives below and we are
    done with time,
And we are borne from earth, our home, within a
    foreign clime,
It is not on a stranger land that we are rudely
    thrown,
Where people, language, customs, laws, are novel
    and unknown, —
Where life, by violence, turned awry, must in new
    channels flow,
And every sweet pursuit must cease that we began
    below ;
But on a bright and balmy land, a sweet and sunny
    shore,

Which we had read and thought about and visited
before, —
Whose language we had studied here, whose customs
we had learned,
And whose pursuits and feasts of bliss we had by
faith discerned,
And all its bright inhabitants we long had learned
to know,
For some we'd heard and read about and some we
knew below;
Some were our neighbors, kindred, friends, our children, husbands, wives,
And now we meet to part no more, but live immortal lives.
O! when we mount, at God's command, above yon
starry dome,
And enter into Paradise, we all shall feel at home;
The friends that knew shall know us there and welcome us above,
And those we knew not, knit to us in bonds of
warmest love, —
And long as long eternity through endless years
extends,
We shall be swelling every hour the number of our
friends.

THE CHRISTIAN'S PATMOS.

THE hearty Christian, while he lives on earth's dim
    homestead even,
Finds many a Patmos where he goes and gazes into
    Heaven,
And if, with those inspirings fired, the Heavenly
    spirit gives,
'Twill be the faithful portraiture that in the bosom
    lives,
And when he enters Paradise and walks the sweet
    parterre,
He'll find the essence of it all upon his canvas —
    there.

The artist on the landscape looks until his bosom
    fires,
And with its inspiration full, he to his home retires,
And in his cluttered studio, among his works of
    taste,
That landscape on his canvas lives, all true to
    Nature traced.
Not every ruin, hill, and tower, and shrub, and flower,
    and tree,
That we upon the landscape saw, we on the canvas
    see ;

And yet so *like* the landscape and its portraiture
    appear
That he who'd ever seen the first would recognize it
    here.
So, when the contemplative soul, that thrills with
    heavenly love,
Looks from his Patmos here below to Paradise
    above,
He takes upon his heart of hearts daguerreotypes of
    Heaven,
And breathes its spirit fresh and warm within the
    portrait given, —
And when he mounts to Paradise and walks its
    flowery shore,
A single glance attests the fact, — he's seen the place
    before ;
And thus the pure in heart may have, wherever
    they may go,
E'en while within this vale of tears, a genuine
    Heaven below ;
For he who seeks the truth to know, and seeks it at
    the fount,
Will, like the Hebrew, always find the pattern on
    the mount,
And only when he does not ask, or when he asks
    amiss,
Does he e'er fail to get the true apocalypse of bliss ;

And all we need to reach the skies, howe'er abstruse,
    is given,
If, when exhausting all our powers, we ask for light
    from Heaven.

THE PURE IN HEART LIVE ON THE VERY CONFINES OF HEAVEN.

O! 'TIS a sweet, transporting thought, that to the
    pure in heart,
This earth of ours and yonder Heaven are but an
    inch apart,
And we can live so near the line betwixt that world
    and this,
That we can breathe the balmy air and pluck the
    fruits of bliss,
And if our thoughts and joys and theirs harmoniously
    combine,
Can talk with those we loved below but just across
    the line, —
Nay, more than that, can cross the line, our loved
    and lost to meet,
And rove with them and talk with them along the
    golden street.

O! if we never meet again our sainted little boy,

Until, in our immortal robes, we're in his home of
    joy,
'Twill not be that, by stern decree, we're rudely
    kept apart,
But that our bosoms do not throb in harmony with
    his heart.

UPON WHAT MISSIONS DO SPIRITS VISIT EARTH? AND HOW DO THEY DISCHARGE THEM?

When spirits leave their homes of joy and to dim
    earth return,
It must be on a mission of no trivial concern,
And we in fancy try to find, surveying one by one,
Not only what the mission is, but also how 'tis
    done.
The senses — those mysterious ducts, through which,
    with ceaseless flow,
Comes all the knowledge that we get of anything
    below —
Must grapple matter and extract, like Hybla's bees,
    whate'er
We choose to make, while here below, the deathless
    spirit's fare;
And whether gross or vulgar food upon its table
    lies,

Depends upon the soul for which the senses bring
    supplies;
And when the spirit mounts above, unfettered, pure,
    and free,
And has put on its spotless robes of immortality,
The breath of odors is not lost, the charms of beauty
    dimmed,
Nor music's voice is silent where the song of love is
    hymned,
Nor touch expires where contact is a source of bliss
    and love,
Nor pure gustation quits the feast at which they sit
    above;
And so although the senses die, their pure ethereal
    parts
Still live, the deathless ministers of gladness to their
    hearts;
And when the spirits roam the sky, they're never
    once remiss,
But ceaselessly are bringing them fresh thrills of
    heavenly bliss;
And when they come to visit earth, these ministers
    of love
Come down and serve the spirits here as sweetly as
    above;
And though rude matter fill the world, they never
    fly to this,

For one sweet dew-drop of delight to swell their
cup of bliss.

The bee sometimes to poisonous plants on merry
pinions flies,
And bears its nectared sweetness home upon its yellow thighs,
And when it seeks the loveliest flower, 'tis not its
grace attracts,
But 'tis the unseen nectar that it buries in its wax:
So, when the spirit comes below among material
things,
And flits around from spot to spot upon its airy
wings,
'Tis not gross matter, howe'er pure, that lures it to
the earth,
But that pure something all unseen that constitutes
its worth.

We have to do far coarser work than blessed spirits do,
We see the bodies of our friends, but not their spirits
too,
While they in turn behold our souls as open as the
day,
Undimmed by e'en a shadow from their rude unconscious clay;
And when our dear ones visit us, their spirit-eyes
behold

Not these frail frames, but that bright gem that these
    frail frames enfold ;
And that we do not see them on their visits from
    the skies,
Is that we do not cultivate the spirit's keener eyes;
O ! if we did, how oft our hearts in ecstasy would
    greet
Our living ones, our happy ones, that we should daily
    meet !
We know that truth has richest lore that mind un-
    helped can learn,
But richer yet, that grace must help or mind can
    ne'er discern.

If these are facts, how sweet the thought, when dear
    ones are no more,
Their presence may be palpable and pleasant as
    before, —
Nay, more, if, in our heart of hearts, the grace of
    God o'erflow,
We can hold sweeter converse now than when with
    us below.

O ! thou sweet girl, my first-born child, so early
    summoned home,
With all the pure in Paradise in fadeless bliss to
    roam, —

And thou, companion of my youth, who, when thy
  work was done,
Didst fly with joy to that same Heaven to join the
  little one, —
And thou, dear little blue-eyed boy, too pure and
  sweet and good
To spend e'en six short fleeting years this side the
  swelling flood, —
Ye are not dead, ye are not lost, ye are not absent
  even,
If I'm but living high enough and near enough to
  Heaven.

O! yes, kind Heaven is always kind e'en when it
  seems severe,
A blessing quivers in a sigh and glistens in a tear,
And, to the one who'll take the boon, a blessing
  trickles down,
Not only from our Father's smile, but also from his
  frown.
Our blessings are immortal, if we choose to make
  them so,
They're ours, not only while we hold, but when we
  let them go;
A friend in Heaven, if we are wise, will far excel
  in worth,
E'en while sojourning here below, a thousand friends
  on earth.

O! may we then, whate'er befall, look trustingly
    above,
And feel whate'er our Father does He always does
    in love,
And say with filial confidence that He on yonder
    throne
Has snatched our dear ones from our breasts to nestle
    in His own!

WORCESTER.

DEAR Worcester, city of the vale, the good old Bay
    State's heart,
If there's a spot most dear to me, of all on earth,
    thou art;
The most of all the structure built by study, toil, and
    care,
That constitutes my humble life is genuine Worcester
    ware;
The dear companion of my youth here kindled first
    my hearth,
Which, though so humble, was to us the brightest
    spot on earth;
And when her vigil ceased, and lo! the vestal took
    her flight,

Her sweet successor came along and kept the fires
    as bright.

'Twas there our little ones came down alighting from
    above,
And filled "sweet home" to running o'er with
    sweetest earthly love.

Thence flew to Heaven our little one, the first that
    God had given,
So sweet! she scarce could be more sweet when safe
    at home in Heaven;
And then the black-eyed mother rose to join her in
    the skies,
As ripe for bliss as one could be, this side of Para-
    dise;
And last flew up on cherub wings our little blue-eyed
    boy,
The Benjamin of home, sweet home, to realms of
    fadeless joy;
And now they're sleeping side by side, within you
    green retreat,
Which Worcester skill and Worcester taste have
    made so pure and sweet;
And now whene'er I think about my dear domestic
    flock,
On which I'd built my happiness as on a solid rock,

But three are left, the other three, from my fond
    bosom riven,
Are sleeping in yon verdant vale and praising God
    in Heaven;
And now whene'er on Fancy's wing among my flock
    I roam,
The three bright spots to which I fly, are Worcester,
    Heaven, and home;
And when we all bid earth adieu, and dust returns
    to dust,
And we're all sleeping side by side, as soon or late
    we must;
And when we gather, if we may, in mansions in the
    skies,
And rove among the pleasant scenes that checker
    Paradise;
If spirits may a blessing drop on some sweet spot
    below,
Replete with dear mementoes of events that thrilled
    them so,
I'm sure we never should forget a blessing to impart,
The best that we could find in Heaven to Massa-
    chusetts' heart.

DEATH.

O DEATH! we sometimes call thee wretch, knave,
 demon, monster, fiend,
And every loathsome epithet from Hatred's kingdom
 gleaned,
Because thou tak'st these garments off our wearied
 spirits bear,
That they may wear the glorious robes immortal
 beings wear;
But when, from Jordan's farther bank, we look across
 the tide,
And see the monster that we left upon the other
 side,
He'll seem a Seraph snatching us from sorrow and
 disease,
To seek the realms where bliss and health are borne
 on every breeze.
The Surgeon seems a heartless wretch who flourishes
 his knife,
So like a stoic 'mong the threads that form the web
 of life ;
But when, from every throb of pain, the skilful surgeon wakes,
Full many a throb of rosy health and merry vigor
 breaks ;

The stoic melts to tenderness and sunshine lights his
    brow,
And that same surgeon has become a lovely being
    now.

O Death! whate'er thou really art, thou seem'st a
    fiend or friend,
As vice or virtue sees thee o'er its restless pillow
    bend:
The grace of God within the heart robs death of
    many a sting,
And thou dost seem above its bed an angel on the
    wing;
But guilt implants unnumbered stings and barbs the
    stings beside,
And makes thee seem a wretch indeed, the deepest,
    darkest dyed;
And bad and good in character, at every depth and
    height,
See death at different angles and in different rays of
    light.
And so the veteran archer seems, no matter how
    demeaned,
To be of every grade between the angel and the
    fiend;
While at that height, that lofty height, by spotless
    Enoch trod,

The archer never throws a dart, the summons 's served
  by God.

When these frail frames are racked and torn by
  anguish and disease,
And skill has no more power to help and earth no
  more to please,
It does not prove the being fiend, who clips its
  earthly ties,
And lets the deathless spirit free to float to Paradise, —
Nor when, in buoyant health and strength, he calls
  the spirit home,
To wing its way to Heaven before disease and anguish come.

Death's charged with many a cruelty he never ought
  to bear,
And clothed with many a ghastly look he does not
  really wear.
The anguish gushing from disease ne'er issues from
  his sting,
And sickness is the dreadful curse *our crimes* and
  follies bring.
He ne'er employs Disease to work with its exhausting
  pangs,
But takes the victim oft away from his envenomed
  fangs,

And often calls immortals home with all an angel's
     care,
Before disease has touched their frames or sent its
     venom there;
And when age, tottering on its way, has almost
     reached the tomb,
How kindly Death comes bending o'er and takes the
     old man home!

O! when the sick man writhes upon his bed of
     agony,
And friendship, round him, feels his pangs almost as
     much as he, —
When Death steps in, O! what a change within that
     room appears! —
The suffering's gone, — the groans are hushed, and
     nought is left but tears,
And every crystal, leaping out, lets in the heart
     relief,
And carries out, from feeling's fount, a globule of
     its grief.

O Death! when stripped of everything that is not
     really thine,
Thyself and mission both appear enchanting and
     divine,
And none but they, with moral eyes, abnormal or
     obtuse,

Would call thee monster, or would load thy mission
    with abuse;
Thou dost not seem as thou wast wont in days and
    years whilom,
Ere thou didst come and visit me three times within
    my home, —
For though I felt that dearest ties were at those
    visits riven,
I knew the dear ones thou didst take were taken up
    to Heaven;
And whensoe'er I think of thee, I think of those I
    love,
Not mouldering in the silent tomb, but crowned and
    throned above;
For though the tear-drop wet the eye and sorrow
    thrill the heart,
To think how very sweet the ties that thou didst
    rend apart;
The triumph of my sainted ones, thrilled by that
    touch of thine,
Makes thee appear angelic and thy mission all divine.

O! let us then give Death his due, nor charge upon
    his head
The ghastly train of loathsome ills that gird the sick
    man's bed;
He comes to break the thread of life now grown a
    weary bond,

To throw it over Jordan's stream to knit to life
    beyond;
He comes to cut the soul adrift from all its earthly
    ills,
That it may float away, away among the heavenly
    hills;
He comes to its dim prison of clay and sets the spirit
    free,
To breathe the air and rove the fields of immor-
    tality;
And if, as Nurses take their wards what time they
    deem the best,
E'en in the midst of sport and play, to seek a bed of
    rest,
He comes to us in perfect health and kindly bids us
    come,
While full of hope and full of joy, to our eternal
    home;
We, like those wards, may think it hard, but like
    them, at the test,
Find that the hour the deed was done was e'en for
    us the best.

O Death! I do not pray thee haste, nor linger on
    thy way,
Nor dare, alas! prescribe for thee the fitting hour or
    day;

My chief concern shall only be, whene'er thou call'st
    me home,
To be prepared to say with joy, I come, O Death!
    I come.

THE GRANDMOTHERS.

Dear Charlie, could the memory fail, within your
    home above,
To recollect a single one you used on earth to love,
I'm sure 'tis not your dear Grandma who used to
    love you so,
She's lingering just on Jordan's brink and dearly longs
    to go ;
She loved you much, because she thought her Charlie
    was so smart,
And had a sweet and pure and kind and warm and
    loving heart ;
And when she felt that you must die, it pierced her
    bosom through,
And O ! she wished with all her heart, that she could
    die for you.
She'll soon be there, dear Charlie, soon, released from
    every care,
And then she'll seek for you the first of all the
    others there ;

For though there be full many a one she loved as
    well as you,
Who was as near and dear to her and full of prom-
    ise too,
I do not doubt, when she is gone and Jordan's stream
    is passed,
She'll look for you the first of all because you left
    her last.

Have you forgotten when you went, as you were
    wont to go,
To see your Grandma and to say, "Dear Grandma,
    how d'ye do?"
And when you saw her hands and face, you, in an
    undertone,
Said softly to the nursery-maid, "How wrinkled she
    has grown!"
And then you said as if you felt a little touch of
    shame,
No matter, Esther, for you know that Grandma's not
    to blame.
Then you went back and kissed her cheeks and
    looking in her eye,
You patted both her wrinkled hands, and gently said
    good-by,
And then as if a load were off too heavy to sustain,
Your fresh unburdened spirit rose on buoyant wing
    again,

And off you bounded through the streets, nor ceas'd
    until you'd come,
And given the magic of your heart to those you
    loved at home.

You'll not forget that dear Grandma, whose welcome
    was so sweet,
When we went out to visit her within her green
    retreat,
And although not so near the brink of Jordan's
    stream as she,
The dear Grandma who lived so near, you daily
    went to see;
She yet may cross the stream before the other leaves
    the brink,
And reunite, 'twixt you and her, the severed golden
    link;
She wept, dear boy, when first she heard that you
    and she must part,
And still your little image bears in her remembering
    heart;
She'll meet you soon, ah! very soon, on yonder
    fadeless shore,
To be reknit by ties so strong they'll never sunder
    more;
And when we all have passed the stream that you
    so early passed,

And meet with you and rove with you and talk with
    you at last,
O! then how kind the blow will seem that smote
    you in our bowers,
And O! how short the time will seem between your
    death and ours!
The woe that wrung our bleeding hearts when we
    were rent in twain
Will make the gladness more intense when we shall
    meet again.
There'll be no wrinkles on the hands of reverend
    age as now,
There'll be no furrows on the face that time has
    dared to plough;
There'll be no film to veil the eye nor bar to block
    the ear,
Nor any weak and tottering limbs as we behold
    them here;
But all that reach that happy place, whatever here
    they be,
Will waken with His likeness that is sweetly worn
    by thee.

But why do I attempt to teach my little Charlie,
    who
Knows more about the spirit land than all earth's
    sages do?

But God has told us in that world where joys eter-
    nal spring,
There'll be no blot or wrinkle there or any kindred
    thing;
And since we cannot hear thee tell how things
    celestial be,
It does our hearts good oftentimes to try to talk
    with thee.

OUR PHYSICIAN.

I LOVE not that physician, though an expert in his
    art,
Who only has a cultured head and not a feeling
    heart;
There's quite enough surrounds the sick to make the
    bosom sad,
Without a doctor's boorishness and sullenness to add.
When Friendship sees its dearest ones on beds of
    anguish lie,
And asks the surgeon every hour if they will live or
    die,
'Tis pleasant if a kindly word is spoken that reveals,
That, if he thinks we're acting weak, he has a heart
    that feels,
And such was ours, and such *is* ours, intensely
    trained and taught,

Not only in affliction's school, but in the school of
　　thought.
His three bright boys, the first a youth, and standing
　　just before
The well-known threshold that is passed on entering
　　manhood's door,
And two bright lads but just this side the pleasant
　　moment, when
They too should pass the boundary line betwixt them
　　and young men, —
All these at one fell swoop were plunged beneath
　　destruction's surge,
By that disease that, in our land, is childhood's
　　dreadest scourge ;
And now they're sleeping side by side, in slumber,
　　O ! how sweet !
Within three consecrated beds in Greenwood's green
　　retreat ;
And now, whene'er to childhood's bed he goes to
　　bring relief,
He lives these scenes all o'er again and feels anew
　　his grief ;
And when fond love bends o'er its child for weary
　　nights and days,
And asks a thousand silly things a thousand different
　　ways,
He bears with weakness, and if safe, he drops a
　　word to cheer,

But if he must, he tells the worst, but tells it with
    a tear.

Ah me! if human care and skill had had the power
    to save,
Our Charlie would not be to-day reposing in his grave;
That little spirit sweet and pure with earth's fond
    ties unriven
Would be not making Heaven his home, but making
    home a heaven.

Ah! Doctor, we have ne'er forgot how, in the sum-
    mer heat,
Although ill health required that you should seek
    some cool retreat,
You staid and staid and watched his health in every
    light and shade,
To see if aught within your power could comfort,
    cure, or aid;
And sometimes at the midnight hour, the time to
    solace cares,
We heard your feathery footfalls tap upon the cham-
    ber stairs,
And then you said that being awake, — you scarcely
    knew the cause, —
You'd step around the corner here and see how
    Charlie was.

Alas! we understood it all, and felt the proof it
    gave,
That we, erelong, must go and stand at little Char-
    lie's grave;
But yet your kindness, though it made our bleeding
    bosoms smart,
Will live forever and be shrined in our remembering
    heart;
And when your care and skill had failed and you
    could do no more,
And he had closed his mild blue eyes and sailed to
    yonder shore,
The last sweet token that you gave how much your
    heart was here,
We saw come quivering from your eye, — it was a
    crystal tear.

THE VOLUNTEER WATCHER.

THERE was an angel daily came with soft and care-
    ful tread,
And hovered round the cherub boy upon his restless
    bed,
And night and day, as sure as air to fill a vacuum
    stirs,

Whene'er the mother's vigil failed, the substitute was
    hers;
And though no ties of kith and kin attracted to our
    home,
The holier ties of sympathy compelled her heart to
    come, —
Scarce willing that another's hand should aid the
    little boy,
Because she thought a stranger face might vex him
    or annoy;
And sleep and rest were quite forgot or their demands
    denied,
While bending o'er his restless couch at little Char-
    lie's side.

Ah! Lady, there are hearts that keep these mem-
    ories fresh and new,
And warmly throb with heartiest prayers alike for
    yours and you, —
For could the kindest care secure what often it
    secures,
Our little one had sure been saved by such sweet
    care as yours;
And there's a pair of mild blue eyes now lighted up
    above,
That daily turn their gaze on you with all a cherub's
    love;

And there's a pure and spotless heart within the
　　realms of joy,
Among whose vital threads are wrought your kind-
　　ness to our boy.
Your sainted father knows it all, for, with celestial
　　art,
He reads your kindness written in our little Charlie's
　　heart,
And feels intenser thrills of bliss since he can see so
　　plain
His care to train your heart aright was not applied
　　in vain.

THE FUNERAL.

The sable hearse came rumbling o'er the pavements
　　to the door,
And carriages, with sober steeds, were standing there
　　before ;
And friends had gathered in the rooms with serious
　　mien and air,
As if they felt in all its force that death was really
　　there.
And then the pastor of the flock — within whose
　　warm embrace,
We'd found for many and many a day a sweet, warm
　　resting-place ;

And where, with faith as sweet and pure as burned
    in Abraham,
Among the flock our little boy had been a fairy
    lamb —
Took up the Book and opened it, and from its pages
    read
Sweet thoughts the spirit dropped for those who're
    mourning for the dead;
And then he lifted heart and voice to little Charlie's
    God,
To drop a blessing down on us while smarting 'neath
    the rod;
And then we took his body up, a precious, precious
    freight,
And carried it away to sleep within its native State.

'Twas where, within yon hallowed grove, in richest
    verdure dressed,
The wicked cease from troubling and the weary are
    at rest;
We stood with sympathizing friends beside our Char-
    lie's bier,
To take our last, fond, farewell look and shed the
    parting tear.
The youthful pastor once our own, kind, studious,
    and devout, —
Whom Charlie never once forgot and loved to talk
    about, —

Was there beside us with a heart almost as sad as
    ours,
That death had come and nipped a bud in our do-
    mestic bowers.
And then he calmly oped the Book that heavenly
    love had given,
That tells us of a future life for all the good in
    Heaven ;
And there beneath that open sky and on that verdant
    sod,
He lifted his petitions up commending us to God.
Our Charlie needed not his prayers, for lo! in fields
    above,
He'd lighted and was roving now where all is bliss
    and love.
Then towards that little sleeping boy the sympathetic
    drew,
And gazed upon his angel face and looked their last
    adieu,
And left him to the stricken ones who felt the
    keenest smart,
Because the ties of heart and home were rudely torn
    apart.
And as we bent above our boy with grief we could
    not hide,
And felt how very sweet 'twould be to slumber at
    his side,

The fleecy clouds above our heads, too thin for
    copious showers,
Looked down as if they pitied us and mingled tears
    with ours;
And then we gazed and then we wept, and till the
    scene was past,
We could not feel that farewell look would really be
    the last;
And then the dear heart-stricken one, within whose
    fond embrace
The little fellow, all through life, had found the
    sweetest place,
Put three pure lilies, white as snow upon a moun-
    tain's crest,
Within his little tiny hands that rested on his breast;
And then we left him sound asleep unruffled by a
    care,
With this fond hope that we some day should sleep
    beside him there.

THE CONCLUSION.

DEAR Charlie, I have done my task, nay, I'll not
    call it task,
'Twas a sweet duty from the first, my heart began
    to ask;

I could not bear to think a boy that such sweet
          promise gave,
Should die so young and then lie down forgotten in
          the grave ;
I could not bear that death should come and ruth-
          lessly destroy,
Nor leave behind, except at home, memorials of my
          boy.
Perhaps I should have done my task in other ways
          than song,
Perhaps I have not sung enough, perhaps I've sung
          too long;
But since but few will read the book, and few of
          these but those
Who've passed, alas! through kindred scenes and
          suffered kindred woes, —
With howe'er little skill and power I may have done
          my part,
They'll take, instead, the breathings of a chastened,
          sorrowing heart.
The critic may the volume read and ridicule my
          views,
The stoic may the pages scan and cauterize my
          Muse ;
But ridicule and cautery will reach no heart but
          mine,
They cannot alter or disturb a single pulse of thine;

Nor can they, with their powers combined, my pur-
    pose e'er destroy,
Of telling where my book may go about my darling
    boy.

A few more years, a few more days or minutes it
    may be,
Will waft us to the pearly gate to dwell in Heaven
    with thee;
And though I cannot even hope an offering poor as
    this
Will add a single thrill of joy to Charlie's cup of
    bliss,
I do not doubt that e'en in Heaven 'twill be a pleas-
    ant thought,
If I have kept thy pretty name from being quite
    forgot, —
Or caused thy sweetness like a flower's, when crushed
    in perfect blow,
To linger longer than it would within these bowers
    below.

THE END.

CAMBRIDGE: PRINTED BY H. O. HOUGHTON.